THE  ELIN

JANNIE IRELAND

Copyright © 2025 Jannie Ireland

The right of Jannie Ireland to be identified as the Author of the Work has been asserted by them in accordance with the Copyright, Designs and Patents Act 1988.

First published in 2025 by Bloodhound Books.

Apart from any use permitted under UK copyright law, this publication may only be reproduced, stored, or transmitted, in any form, or by any means, with prior permission in writing of the publisher or, in the case of reprographic production, in accordance with the terms of licences issued by the Copyright Licensing Agency.
All characters in this publication are fictitious and any resemblance to real persons, living or dead, is purely coincidental.

www.bloodhoundbooks.com

Print ISBN: 978-1-917449-8-23

For Graham and Sabrina

AUTHOR'S NOTE

The story goes that in 1284, a stranger came to Hamelin in Germany. This was at a time when the town suffered from an alarming rat infestation. The newcomer told the town council that he would get rid of the rats and he was promised a large sum of money if he succeeded. When he played his pipe, all the rats followed him to the Weser River and drowned. But when the piper returned to the town council, they refused to pay him the promised money.

The piper took his revenge. He played his pipe again and this time every child in Hamelin, followed him into the mountains and were never seen again.

That is the story of the Pied Piper of Hamelin. But this is not that story.

This story is about what happened afterwards – to THE CHILDREN OF HAMELIN.

1284

MIDSUMMER'S DAY

In the barn a child crouched behind a bale of straw, kept quiet and still, and waited to be found. *Wanted* to be found. It seemed a long time now since the seeker had begun his counting and the other children had ran off to hide. On this bright summer's day, she and her playmates didn't have to work, but could run about and play to their hearts' content.

Had they forgotten her? Should she come out? Earlier, shrill children's voices rang out as they were found and raced to touch home before the seeker. Now, she could hear them no longer. Had they all gone home? Other sounds too were absent. Those of parents building the Saint John's fires to be lit tonight, in celebration of the midsummer solstice. She was looking forward to that and so was her little sister.

Thinking of her sister, she got up from her hiding place. She shouldn't have left her sibling that long. She was only six. Ma would scold her, if she found out that the older girl had left her little sister to run off and hide by herself.

'You look after your sister. Don't let her out of your sight. The two of you are all I have left now.'

There had been more children in the family, older brothers

and sisters. All were taken by a terrible disease that swept through Hamelin a few years ago, killing adults and children alike, and leaving her crippled.

She and her sister should have been hiding here together, the child berated herself. Instead, she had let the little girl run off towards the oak-lined lane, where thick tree trunks provided enough cover to hide behind. She might still find her there, or perhaps the younger girl had returned home.

Once more her attention was drawn to the unusual silence surrounding the barn, as if every nearby creature held its breath. She limped towards the heavy barn door and slowly pushed it open.

There wasn't a soul outside.

Walking as fast as her shrivelled leg allowed, she hobbled back to where she and her sister had played with their friends.

On the quiet air, the sound of a wind instrument floated towards her from afar.

The lame child stopped and listened, spellbound for a moment, before she resumed her steps. In Harrow's Row, she halted, to take in the strangest sight.

In the open space between her home and those of her friends, where earlier they had played, a small group of grown-ups had gathered. Oddly, they neither moved nor spoke but stood frozen in mid-gesture and mid-sentence.

Where were her parents and where was her sister?

Out of the corner of her eye, she spotted movement. Harrow's Row led to Church Lane and it was there that something stirred. The music too seemed to come from there. Weaving around the adults, she limped towards Church Lane.

Along Church Lane she found both her parents. She went up to her mother and gently tugged on her arm. 'Ma?'

The mother didn't answer. Didn't even look at her. The

child tried again, this time shaking her mother's arm a little harder. 'Ma, what are you doing?'

When the mother didn't reply, the girl turned to see what her mother was so intently staring at. Only then did she discover her playmates who, together with many other children, followed the music.

Something wasn't right, the lame child sensed, as she watched the long line of children cheerfully skipping behind the music maker while all along Church Lane, adults stood and watched them passing by. Silently. Motionless. Just like her parents. Witnesses, turned to stone.

There was no time to reflect on it, though. She needed to find her sister. As she hobbled along the line of children, she finally discovered the little girl in their midst. The older girl pushed herself through the throng, until she ended up by her sibling's side. Taking the younger child by the hand she tried to pull her away, but her sister pulled free and slipped further into the crowd. By the time the older sibling caught up with her, they had left the town and were heading for the mountains.

Desperately, the lame child wondered what to do. Why didn't her sister listen to her? Why did she behave as if under a spell? The other children too looked bewitched. And why did she seem to be the only one who was not?

In her mind she heard her mother's voice.

'Look after your little sister. Don't lose sight of her. The two of you are all I have left.'

Then she knew what she must do.

ONE

1978

Katrin opened her eyes and peered into near darkness. She felt cold. Where was she? Not in the box bed she shared with her sister. She would have felt Trude's warmth, if she were.

As she became aware of the hard, uneven ground beneath her, she sat up. Her eyes, growing used to the dimness, identified bumpy, knobby stone walls and the dry mud ground covered in dead leaves, twigs, lichen and moss.

What was she doing here? Ma? She tried to call but the sound of the word wouldn't come out, as if her voice was rusty. Frightened she looked around.

Where cobwebs hung from the ceiling, a single spider tried to make itself scarce by climbing an invisible thread. An earthworm burrowed in the soil nearby and from up high something brushed past her, threatening to entangle itself in her hair, before it fluttered onward. A bird? No, a bat, more likely. There was a smell of rotting vegetation in the stale air.

What was that sound? Katrin held her breath to listen. Nearby was soft, regular breathing. Who else was here? An opening in the distance spilled a weak light to reveal countless other children lying asleep around her, like a crop of wheat mown down by Pa's scythe.

2011

Erika Kramer put the phone down and looked at her fiancé. 'That was the Koppenberg Klinik. They've invited me for an interview.'

'Yesss!' Peter punched the air. They hugged and grinned idiotically at each other.

'Everyone in our final year applied there. No one has heard back from them yet. I'm the first,' said Erika.

'And possibly the only one.'

When Erika looked sceptical, Peter added, 'Well, you did have top exam results.'

'It would be fabulous to work at the Koppenberg. Not only is it within cycling distance, the salary is higher than at other hospitals, and it would mean working for Claudia Wagner, something everyone who trains to be a psychiatric nurse dreams of.'

'Wagner, you say? Any relation to our mayor, Thomas Wagner?'

'They're married.'

'What's so special about her?'

'Doctor Wagner is a pioneer in her field, an innovator. She lectures at universities all over the world. The Koppenberg Klinik uses only the latest treatments and therapies.'

The couple, both in their early twenties, returned to the kitchen, where they'd been preparing dinner when the phone rang. Cooking was something both enjoyed and they often made their evening meals together, if Peter, a junior journalist, wasn't on an assignment.

Two days later found Erika trying different outfits for the interview that afternoon. She posed in front of the full-length mirror in the bedroom and sighed, unable to make a decision.

'I'm trying to go for the subdued stylish look,' she quipped, 'to fit in. An article I read about the Koppenberg Klinik described the hospital as *"a triumph of subdued elegance and style."* Although I actually can't quite remember if they were referring to the building or its leading psychiatrist.'

Peter, at the table near the window, turned around from the laptop he was working on.

'Take Donald.'

Named after Donald Duck, their ancient Citroën 2CV was just within the budget of a junior journalist and a student nurse.

'I was planning to. Cycling is not ideal in these clothes. I don't want to get there all sweaty, out of breath and covered in bicycle oil.'

As she steered the bright yellow car uphill, Erika caught her first sight of the Koppenberg Klinik, a white building gleaming through canopies of leafy tree branches in the afternoon sun. Soon, she arrived at its ornamental gate, where the guard checked her appointment before waving her through. Architects and interior designers had made every effort for the building to resemble more than a regular psychiatric hospital. The reception area was an attractive and welcoming space, wood panelled and decorated with large potted plants. Now and then the soothing sound of a water feature interrupted the hushed passages. On the way to her interview, Erika asked about the paintings and sketches displayed along the pastel-coloured corridors.

'All were created in art therapy. Doctor Wagner believes in art as part of the healing process, as well as a diet of organic food and connecting to nature,' the receptionist explained.

'Connecting to nature, how?'

'We have a large garden. Some patients like to garden.'

During her interview, Erika discovered more differences between the hospital where she had trained and the Koppenberg Klinik, with its holistic range of treatments.

Excited and exhilarated after returning home, she told Peter all about it.

'And how did the actual interview go? Any chance you'll get a job offer?' he coaxed her back to Earth.

'They'll let me know soon.'

Later, in bed before sleep, Erika's mind was still occupied with what she'd seen and heard that afternoon, as she snuggled up to Peter.

'What I like about the Koppenberg is how much thought has gone into the design of the building, the facilities, patient care… everything really. I was told they're all Doctor Wagner's ideas.'

Erika drifted off and barely caught Peter's half-muttered reaction.

'Much thought usually means much expense.'

1978

Katrin stared at the whiteness of her uneven legs, one unnaturally thin, the other as it should be, and hugged herself against the cold. How did she get here? Where was everyone? Her sister Trude and her parents, were they here too, amongst the others? Her eyes strained to recognise the sleepers but it was hard to distinguish their features. She wanted to get up and search for familiar faces, but the supine bodies left little space to walk around – that and the low ceiling.

She thought of her family, the land they worked on for the farmer and the small dwelling on the patch of land that was home, but she remembered nothing else.

The distant sound of church bells reached her ears and she crossed herself. Matins or Vespers? It had been midsummer and the Saint John's fires had been lit, that's why she was dressed in her summer clothes. After the celebration, is that when they had come to this cave – to explore, to play, to hide, or... what?

She was so focused on what she was trying to recall, at first she didn't notice when another child sat up and looked around.

A small voice called out. 'Mummy?'

Katrin didn't know what to say and the boy's voice called out again. 'Mummy?'

When there was no answer, he began to sob. Katrin tried to get on her feet but, forced to stay on her knees by the low ceiling, she crawled towards the boy.

'Don't cry,' she said. 'What's your name?'

He didn't answer, instead someone else replied for him. 'His name is Matti.'

In the dim light Katrin saw the outline of another child sitting up.

The little boy's sobs were quieting down. Katrin sat down

beside him on the rocky ground. He was no older than three or four.

'I'm Katrin,' she said. 'Don't worry, Matti. I'll get you out of here and then we go home. Where do you live?'

'I – I don't know,' he said and started to cry again. Katrin put an arm around him and heard stirring as more children sat up and started to call out.

'Anna?'

'I'm so cold. Why are we here?'

'Mechtild? Are you there? Mechtild?'

'Daddy?'

Katrin added her voice to theirs. 'Trude? Are you there?'

From the back of the cave came an answer. 'Katrin? Is that you?'

'Trude? Stay there. I'll come to you.'

Soon they were hugging each other close, relieved at having found each other.

'Why are we here and who are all these children?' Trude asked.

'I thought maybe you knew.' Trude shook her head. 'We have to get out of this place, or we'll freeze to death. We have to go home.' Katrin sounded more confident than she felt.

She called out to the others who were awake. 'Come on, let's wake everyone up.'

Together, they gently shook the sleepers and called out to them.

'Wake up! Wake up!'

No matter how hard they tried, those asleep would not wake, and in the end the ones who were awake gave up on their efforts.

'We can come back for them later,' said Trude. 'Let's go.'

Katrin took the lead, staying close to her sister. It was slow going as they crept forward. The ground was covered with sharp-edged loose rocks; they were barefoot. Occasionally, someone behind them cried out, after bumping their head on the low ceiling. Katrin would have slipped on a patch of wet rock, but steadied herself by holding on to the wall beside her.

The nearer they got to the opening, the better they could see. Katrin felt the wind on her face, as it forced its way into the cave. A few more steps and she stood upright in the opening. So bright was the light there, she put her hands in front of her face to cover her eyes.

Trude was the first to step out of the cave and into daylight, with Katrin, on her uneven legs, limping close behind her. As they stepped away from the cave, Katrin turned to survey the children behind them.

And for a moment the image of a long line of children who followed a tall, thin man emerged from her memory. A stranger, striding in a long coat, with its tails flapping behind him. Then the memory evaporated.

2011

Erika stepped off her bike, breathing hard, relieved she'd made it on time on her first day at the Koppenberg Klinik.

The shift started at eight. At ten to eight she entered and approached the reception desk.

'I'm Nurse Kramer. I've been told to ask for Senior Staff Nurse Martens.'

'Ah yes, take a seat. I'll let her know you're here.'

Erika didn't wait long. When Nurse Martens approached, Erika recognised her as the person who had interviewed her.

'Good morning and welcome to the Koppenberg. Let me take you to the staffroom to meet your colleagues.'

Conversations dwindled to silence as they entered and curious faces turned in Erika's direction. The newcomer was instructed to shadow a colleague on her first day, a giant with dreadlocks called Kwame. He showed her how to find her way around the building, introduced her to patients and brought her up to speed about their care plans.

Towards the end of the round, they found a young girl bleeding from cuts on her arms. When they entered her room, the girl tried to stem the blood soaking her bed sheet. A sharp piece of plastic broken off from a plant pot on the windowsill was lying nearby. She turned towards Kwame, her eyes thick and swollen.

'I'm sorry, I'm sorry, I've done it again,' she cried.

'Okay, Anya. Deep breaths. We're gonna sort this out. Breathe out for me.'

The crying stopped.

Kwame, his arm around Anya, pressed the sheet against the wounds. 'Let's have these wounds cleaned and treated, shall we?'

Together, the nurses supported the girl to a medical room.

'I'm such a loser. I tried so hard not to cut, but I didn't know what else to do,' said Anya, while Erika bandaged her wounds and Kwame updated Anya's file.

'You're not a failure, it's just a temporary blip. A setback, that's all,' Kwame reassured her.

Later, Erika got lost in the maze of passages and double doors. While she hesitated in front of one pair of doors, finding them locked, a nurse appeared from the other side.

'What are you doing here?' the nurse asked sharply.

'I was looking for the art therapy room, because a patient in there fainted. I was sure I had to go through these double doors.'

'Not these doors.' It sounded unfriendly.

'Can you tell me how to get there? I'm new here. I started today.'

She was given instructions.

'What's on the other side of these doors?' Erika asked.

The nurse scowled. 'None of your business. You'd best get on with your job.'

Erika finished her shift and raced home, all the way downhill, to the tiny flat she shared with Peter above Pizzeria Venezia in central Hamelin.

'How was it?' he said, looking up from his MacBook in their bedroom. He wrote for the *DeWeZet*, the local newspaper, but dreamt of writing for the nationals, the *Frankfurter Allgemeine* or *Der Spiegel*.

'Good. It was good, but exhausting. I'm hungry now. I was too excited and nervous to eat lunch. Is there anything to eat? I hoped you'd cook dinner.'

'I planned to take you out instead. We should celebrate your first day at work. Where would you like to go?'

'Actually, I don't feel like getting changed or going out. How about we get some pizzas and a bottle of red from downstairs?'

At dinner Erika was in high spirits, but afterwards, while putting plates in the dishwasher and clearing up the kitchen, she quieted down.

'You're looking very thoughtful,' said Peter. 'Come on, out with it.'

'I was just thinking of something that happened at work.'

Erika told him about the locked doors and the hostility of the nurse she had met when trying to enter.

Peter, slouching in his chair at the kitchen table,

straightened and his eyes showed interest. 'Do tell me when you find out what's behind those doors.'

Erika dumped her stack of files on the table and made herself a cup of tea. After three weeks in the Koppenberg Klinik, she felt settled. The staffroom was quiet at four o'clock in the afternoon, a good time to update some patients' reports.

She opened a file and took up her pen, when hurried footsteps in the corridor approached and the door was thrown open.

'Nurse?' a voice demanded. 'Can you come with me? I need assistance.'

Erika looked up and saw the nurse she had met after losing her way on her first day. Long greying hair was twisted into a tight bun. The corners of the woman's mouth drooped. The uniform she wore was too tight to hide her plump body.

Erika left her tea and her files and got up. As they hastened along the corridors, she tried to make conversation to overcome the awkward silence.

'I'm Erika Kramer. We met on my first day here. I don't know if you remember.'

'I do remember, Nurse Kramer. You can call me Nurse Bauer.'

They walked on.

Really? Nurse Bauer? While all the other nurses are on first-name terms? She really doesn't like me, Erika concluded.

They rounded a corner and found themselves in front of the same double doors where they had first bumped into each other. Nurse Bauer tapped some numbers into the security keypad, which unlocked them. Erika held her breath in anticipation.

She would finally be able to tell Peter what was behind those doors.

What she saw was unremarkable. It was just another wing in the klinik. Walls and ceiling were painted in washes of pastels, pink and peach creating a warm atmosphere. Floors, doors and furniture were made of wood. Patients' paintings, tapestries and other wall hangings were on display. She heard an arpeggio of sound and saw wind chimes in front of an open window.

A closer look showed some differences between the ward she was assigned to and this unit. There were bars in front of the windows and, though it was visiting time, she couldn't see any visitors. Come to think of it, where were the patients? Not in the coffee corner, the reading room with its magazine racks and bookshelves, or the television room they passed.

'Where are the patients?' Erika asked.

'In their rooms, either resting or asleep.'

Erika tried not to look surprised. Some of her patients needed a nap after lunch, however by three o'clock they were up and looking forward to visiting time from three thirty onwards. It was past four now.

Nurse Bauer halted in front of a door with "Medication Room" etched on a small, copper plate. She unlocked it and they entered. A table and chairs stood in the centre of a small, windowless room. Medicine chests with glass doors or drawers covered all four walls. The older nurse took a hypodermic needle and a glass vial from one of these, broke the vial and extracted the colourless fluid into the syringe.

'There's a patient who refuses to take her medication. We'll have to give it to her under restraint. I will hold her and you will give her the injection.'

Erika had needed to restrain a patient only once before. She'd found it an upsetting experience during her training. She wanted to be a psychiatric nurse to help people, not to hold them down. Reluctantly, she took the syringe and followed the older nurse.

Erika was surprised to find the patient's room locked. Although patients' rooms on her ward were under surveillance at night, they were never locked.

Nurse Bauer tapped in a code to unlock the door and entered. 'Katrin? We've come to give you your medication.'

The patient had her back turned towards them. She was kneeling on the bed, looking out of the barred window. She slowly turned and Erika saw a small woman with braided brown hair who looked to be in her mid-forties. Grey eyes took in Erika, coolly assessing her. Erika smiled reassuringly.

'Hello, Katrin. I'm Nurse Erika.'

TWO

1978

The plateau in front of the cave narrowed into a track embedded with stones. Katrin, with Trude by her side, felt small pebbles shifting underfoot as she hobbled downhill in the grey light of dawn. The freezing wind poked her with icy fingers and crept under her shift, lifted the hem and whipped up her hair. The cold chilled her fingers and the tip of her nose into numbness and seeped into her bare feet. Trude's lips showed a bluish tinge.

Behind Katrin, one of the youngest children whimpered. 'I'm freezing. It's so cold.'

'Let's walk as quickly as we can. Moving faster will warm us up,' a tall boy with thin, gangly limbs and a wheezy voice suggested.

Everyone walked more energetically then and Katrin, limping along, worried about not being able to keep up with them. The panting behind her grew louder. Puffs of breath appeared in the frigid air as more and more children overtook her and her sister. Ice crystals covered each blade of grass along the track and leafless trees were silhouetted starkly against the mountainous backdrop. If this is winter, Katrin thought, bracing herself against the wind, why am I not wearing my woollen gown and undergarments?

They'd nearly reached a bend in the track, when Trude slowed down and pointed upwards.

'D'you see that? Look at those funny clouds.'

Katrin looked up towards where white streaks were visible against the sky, strange straight-lined cloud formations.

'You don't think it's a sign, do you?' A girl with long, unruly hair, in front of Katrin and Trude, chipped in.

'A sign? A sign of what?' another girl responded.

'Dunno. A sign from God? My granny, before she died, used to say: if there's a mystery, it might be a sign from God. I've always wondered what they would look like, these signs.'

They looked up again. The straight white clouds were fading.

'When we're home, I'll ask my Pa about those clouds. He'll have seen them too,' said Katrin.

Stepping up their pace to catch up with the rest of the group, they marched onwards. By now a watery sun had dissolved most of the clouds. They rounded the bend and nearly bumped into those in front, who had stopped dead.

'What's wrong?' Katrin asked. When no one answered, she and Trude pushed through the hedge of bodies to the front.

An unfamiliar object lay beside the track, a few yards away from them. A shiny, metallic cylinder, bright red with white squiggly loops, and a small hole on one side. Trude, daring as always, stepped forward, crouched down and picked it up.

'It's as light as a baby bird,' she said. Then, after she'd looked inside the hole, 'It's empty.'

She turned it upside down and some drops of a brown liquid spilled onto the ground. Trude carefully placed it back and they resumed their walk, but not before Katrin saw the girl who had spoken up earlier mouth: another sign?

Katrin ignored it but felt uneasy. Her senses were sharpened and her heart was beating louder. During their descent they came upon two more unfamiliar objects or signs. The first was a small, thin rectangular piece of iron nailed to a tree and covered in shapes.

'What does it mean?' Trude asked Katrin.

Katrin stared at it and shrugged.

Soon afterwards they discovered a curious pattern of furrows on the ground, where it was muddy from a shower of rain. Katrin knew tracks: bird tracks, rabbit tracks, fox tracks. She could recognise those. But these tracks were different. They were a geometrically shaped pattern of lines. Katrin increasingly felt that everything looked the same and not the same. At the end of the track they came upon a wider path, smooth and straight and black with a white stripe in the centre.

They were still gawping at the wonder of this when up above they heard a loud noise, a buzzing or whirring, and they looked up. Something appeared high in the sky, large and bird-shaped. Far larger than any bird they'd ever seen, tracks of white smoke trailing behind it. They stared in disbelief as the giant bird flew overhead. And the noise! It was faint, but Katrin could tell it was coming from above them. It was coming from the bird.

Something is wrong, Katrin thought. Then it struck her.

'The bird. It's not flapping its wings.'

2011

Erika, on the pale-grey leather sofa, smiled politely as she chose a piece of cake from the selection on the coffee table in front of her. Far too nervous to eat anything at all, she thought it might be rude to refuse. 'I'll have the redcurrant tart, please.'

The elegant hand that placed the delicacy on the Meissen cake plate beside Erika's coffee cup showed pearly pink tapered nails and a ring with a large sapphire encircled by a row of tiny diamonds. Everything about Claudia Wagner was exquisite: her long, blonde hair pulled back and fastened into a chignon at the neck, her smart Jil Sander trouser suit and the rosewood desk behind which she had received Erika a little earlier.

At the start of Erika's shift that morning, her supervisor had approached her. 'The boss wants to see you for coffee and cake at four o'clock today.'

'Any idea why?' Erika asked. The older nurse shrugged. 'Sometimes she invites staff for no other reason than to get to know them.'

'What is she like, the boss?' asked Erika, as she looked at the schedule on the wall to see where she was assigned.

'You'll see.'

Erika thought of nothing else all day, with a slightly sick feeling in her stomach, the way she felt just before a dentist's appointment.

At four o'clock sharp she knocked on Doctor Wagner's door.

'Come in.' It was a low-pitched, well-modulated voice.

Erika knew, because she had googled her during her lunch break, that the woman who greeted her with a firm handshake and a smile was in her early sixties, but she looked younger. Clever make-up and a trim figure took care of that. Doctor Wagner motioned for her to take a place on the sofa.

'You don't mind me finishing this email, do you? I'll be with you in a moment.'

Though asked in a charming way, Erika had the impression it mattered very little whether she minded or not. She studied the silver-framed photos on the bookshelves near her, which were mostly family snaps: Claudia Wagner herself at various ages and a wedding photo of her with her husband Thomas Wagner, the mayor.

There was a knock on the door, and the secretary entered carrying a tray with a cafetière, cups and saucers. She placed it on the coffee table. Before she left, Claudia Wagner stopped her.

'Astrid, we're not to be disturbed. Incoming calls through you, please.'

That sounds ominous, thought Erika, as her employer crossed the room, sat down opposite her in a leather seat that matched the sofa, and lifted the cafetière.

'Coffee?'

'Yes, please.'

Doctor Wagner took a sip of her coffee. 'I've read your file and I'm very impressed. Excellent college results and your colleagues here speak highly of you. How do you find working here? Anything you would like to discuss? Any problems?'

Erika tried not to show surprise. She expected she was here to be reprimanded for something she'd done wrong.

'No – no problems at all. I like it here. I love my job.'

'Good. I'm glad to hear it. How would you feel about a somewhat more challenging assignment? A vacancy has become available in our secure unit. One of the nurses there is leaving us. Would you be willing to replace her?'

There was just the slightest moment of hesitation, as Erika considered the question. Would she get on as well with the staff in the secure unit as the colleagues she worked with at present? She sensed that refusing wasn't an option, though.

'I'd love to.' She hoped her voice sounded neutral enough.

'Excellent. You'll be an asset to the department, I'm sure. Now, these are our long-term patients, suffering from severe delusions. They cannot and never will be able to live independently in our society. Nurse Bauer will inform you about each individual patient. I believe you've met?'

'Yes, I briefly helped out with a patient when there was no one else available.'

'Super. Can I count on you to start tomorrow morning? Ask for Nurse Bauer at reception. She is the Senior Staff Nurse.'

Doctor Wagner got up and shook her hand, to indicate that the interview was at an end.

Erika stood up too.

'What kind of delusions do these patients suffer from?'

The psychiatrist frowned and seemed reluctant to answer at first.

When she spoke, she sounded grave. 'They're all convinced they're from the distant past and fell asleep in a mountain cave to wake up in the present time.'

'That's... extraordinary.'

'Yes. It is. Now, if you'll excuse me, I have another appointment waiting.'

Erika moved towards the door. As she made to leave, she turned. 'All? Did you say, all?'

'Yes. All.'

That night Erika had trouble sleeping. Too many thoughts skittered through her head, like monkeys bouncing restlessly from branch to branch. It was bad enough to have to work occasionally with Nurse Bauer. To do so every day would be a challenge. For some reason, the older nurse clearly disapproved of her. And what would the other nurses be like? There had been no time to ask anyone in her department, after her meeting with Doctor Wagner. The only colleague whose phone number she had in her contacts was Bettina, with whom she'd gone to a concert the previous Saturday night. Luckily, Bettina had picked up immediately when Erika tried her number earlier that evening.

'You poor thing! Nobody wants to work there. She's conned you into it,' was Bettina's reaction, after Erika told her what the meeting with Doctor Wagner had been about.

'Well, I couldn't refuse, could I? Not to her face. I didn't want to lose my job.'

After both were silent for a while, Erika continued. 'Anyway, what's so bad about it? Is it Bauer?'

'Well, yes. She's the supervisor from hell. Also, there's always a large turnover, lots of staff leaving and new nurses being recruited. Never a good sign. They're continually short of staff... There are rumours, too.'

'What kind of rumours?'

'Unresponsive patients. More illness than in any of the other departments. More deaths too, I've heard. But I don't know if it's true. It's all shrouded in secrecy.'

Erika remembered Katrin, the woman who refused to take her medication, whom she had injected in restraints. Was that what it would be like, working there? She hoped not.

'I'm going to miss you guys,' she said, miserably.

'Hey, it's Kwame's birthday next week. There's a party. Nigerian food and Nigerian music, you'll love it.'

'If I'm invited.'

'Of course you are. I'm inviting you now. You'll be able to catch up with everyone and tell us what it's really like in there.'

1978

'What does it mean?' Katrin asked one of the older children.

The children, after following the smooth, black trail for what seemed a long time, had stopped and gathered together in front of another rectangular metal plate attached to a pole.

A tall girl slowly traced the letters on it, one by one. Nobody else could read. 'H-A-M-E-L-I-N. It says Hamelin.' The subdued mood of the children, lifted a little. A few even showed a toothy grin and hopped on the spot a couple of times, excited that they really were approaching Hamelin: home. 'We should follow this road, it might lead us back to town,' said the tall girl.

No one contradicted her and they marched on, wearily and half-frozen. They'd barely walked another kilometre when far behind them a growling rent the air and a curious horseless carriage approached. Jumping out of the way, Katrin saw people sitting inside as it passed and one of them waved. It travelled at great speed, faster than any horse drawn carriage, and it was brightly coloured and made a lot of noise.

Over the next hill another terrifying encounter was waiting for them. These colossal beings did not make a noise but stood God-like. Towering skeletal giants dominated the landscape, in a long line of tall bodies, connected to each other by thin metal wires, an army of immovables.

'Angels,' whispered one of the children.

'Monsters,' another.

'Saints,' a third.

Transfixed, they stared in horror or in awe until one of them yelled, 'Run!'

Panic transformed the meek bunch of children into a stampeding horde. Everyone sprinted away, except Katrin, who couldn't run and Trude, who stayed beside her. When they finally caught up, Katrin recognised a familiar feature in the distance. There was no doubt about it.

'Look! It's the East Gate.'

For the first time since she had left the cave, she felt untroubled and excited.

'And the Haspelmath Tower,' Trude pointed out from beside her.

'I can see the steeple of the Nicolai church at Market Square,' another voice piped up.

With renewed energy they walked towards the East Gate. The closer they came, the more horseless carriages they noticed. At this early hour few people were about, and those were dressed in unfamiliar garments. Katrin was fascinated by the bright colours. Curiously, none of the grown-ups' heads were covered and women's hair was undone and hung loose over their shoulders. As Katrin and her companions approached the Gate, these people stopped and stared at them. She didn't know why. They were most likely foreigners from afar, such as she had heard about in stories.

As Katrin passed through the East Gate and entered East Street, another memory surfaced. The last time she saw her parents was here, at this very spot. She was certain of it. Other children's parents had been there too, watching and standing still. Not just still, but frozen like statues.

THREE
2011

'Nurse Bauer is attending a family funeral today. I'm Nurse Jaeger, standing in for her.'

Erika who had dreaded coming into work this morning, felt relieved. This motherly woman seemed friendly enough.

'I'm not sure I'm sufficiently qualified or experienced to work in this unit. I've only just started working here, mainly with outpatients.'

The end of Erika's sentence hung in the air between them, expectantly, as if she hoped Nurse Jaeger would say, "We can't have that. You'd better return to your previous department. We'll get someone else." Instead, Nurse Jaeger smiled.

'How familiar are you with delusional disorder? Have you had any experience with it during your training?'

'No. Not really. I've looked after patients suffering from eating disorders and schizophrenia during my year of work experience, as part of my training, but no one with delusional disorder.'

'It's a relatively rare mental illness. If you've looked after patients with schizophrenia, you'll find those with delusional disorder easier to care for. Their behaviour is less bizarre.

Patients seem to be functioning normally. But they go through periods of depression, even occasional aggression.'

'I would like to read their case files and treatment plans.'

'Of course. I'll make sure you get time to read those. This afternoon might be a good time. This morning you can accompany me on my patient round.'

'I'd like that. How many patients are there?'

'Twenty-eight at the moment.' Nurse Jaeger prepared the medicine trolley.

'Doctor Wagner told me they all suffer from the same delusion.'

'That's right. What we are dealing with here is shared delusional disorder. It's when symptoms of a delusional belief are transmitted from one individual to another.'

'Must be difficult for their families.'

'These patients have no family.' Nurse Jaeger sighed before she continued. 'Look, all I know is that they were found together, a group of homeless children, appearing out of nowhere and roaming the streets. They were filthy, inarticulate and most were illiterate. The authorities at the time suspected they'd been part of a commune or cult, or in hiding somewhere. Social services made enough of an effort to find their families. No one came forward. No one's ever been to visit them here, either.'

'How long have they been here?'

'I don't know precisely. They were here before me. Shall we get started? We can talk more after the patient round.'

On the way to their first patient, Nurse Jaeger quietly instructed Erika. 'Patients will try to convince you they do not belong here. They'll tell you they belong in another time or another country and were transported here. Do not argue or laugh at them. It'll upset them. Be supportive, okay?'

'Okay.'

'We'll be administering medication and taking patients to their physio sessions, or for a walk in the garden. With this fine weather, patients like to take a walk instead of a swimming session in the indoor swimming pool or spending time in the gym.'

Again, Erika was struck by how much this hospital reminded her of a spa hotel. She had never been to one, but had seen enough photos to spot the similarity.

'I thought these patients would have psychotherapy rather than physio. Do they have any physical problems, as well as mental?'

'Only those caused by a sedentary life. Also, they get depressed and movement releases serotonin, the happy hormone. And yes, they do have psychotherapy. Art therapy too and occupational therapy.'

Nurse Jaeger tapped the keypad to unlock their first patient's door. If this is a spa hotel then it is one with prison cells, Erika thought. Attractive-looking prison cells, she corrected herself, after entering the room.

There were bars in front of the large window, through which a lawn, chestnut trees with deep shadows, a duck pond and leafy lanes were visible. An assortment of plants in terracotta pots were lined up on the windowsill. This was a light, bright room and its walls were completely covered with drawings and paintings. Their subject matter ranged from the market square at the Nicolai church and people wearing what looked like medieval dress, to a cabin surrounded by fields of wheat and potatoes. Another sketch portrayed a family of medieval peasants eating around a table, much like van Gogh's *The Potato Eaters*. The artist had a remarkable talent, for these looked anything but the products of an amateur or hobbyist.

The patient, a woman, ate breakfast at the table and sat with her very straight back to them. When she turned, Erika recognised her as Katrin, the patient she had met when assisting Nurse Bauer.

'Morning, Katrin.' Nurse Jaeger placed the woman's medication beside her plate. 'This is Nurse Kramer. She'll be taking care of you and the other patients here.'

Katrin looked directly at Erika but did not respond or show any sign of recognition.

'We met a few weeks ago,' said Erika. 'I was with Nurse Bauer then.'

'We've come to take you for a walk in the garden,' said Nurse Jaeger. 'You'd like that, wouldn't you?' Erika winced at the nurse's tone of voice, as if she was addressing a child or a helpless old biddy.

'I would like to work in the garden.'

Erika, who had not heard the woman speak before, thought she sounded articulate and intelligent.

'We'll see. When you've finished your breakfast, take your medication. Nurse Kramer will stay with you while I go and see Martha next door.'

'Magda. Her name is Magda,' corrected Katrin. 'She had a bad night. I heard her crying. I wished I could've gone to comfort her. No one else did.'

'Yes, I heard. I'll talk to her about it.'

After Nurse Jaeger left, Katrin turned towards the remains of her breakfast and Erika sat on the only other chair in the room. It was quiet for a time while Erika studied the artwork pinned to the walls.

'Did you do these?'

No answer.

'They're very good. I wish I could show these to a friend of mine. He's an art dealer. He organises exhibitions. I think he might be interested when he sees these.'

'They're not for sale,' was the curt response. 'I need them to keep the memories alive.'

'There's always the possibility of making prints or art cards from them.'

Nurse Jaeger returned and after Katrin had taken her medicine they went to the garden, with Erika on one side of their patient and Nurse Jaeger on the other. It was then that Erika became aware of Katrin's leg.

As they stood admiring a border of fragrant lavender, geraniums and wild primroses, Katrin crouched down and raked her fingers through the soil.

'This needs water. There hasn't been enough rain. I need to do the gardening this afternoon.'

'Only if one of the nurses has time to spend with you, Katrin,' Nurse Jaeger told her.

'I could sit with Katrin in the garden while reading my files this afternoon. There are plenty of benches round here,' Erika offered.

'We don't read patient files in the presence of patients,' replied Nurse Jaeger, stiffly. 'It's inappropriate.' Then, using a friendlier tone, 'Katrin planted this border only last year and look at it now. Such an abundance of flowers, such gorgeous colours. She's a talented gardener, with green fingers, as the saying goes.'

'She's a gifted artist as well,' said Erika. 'Earlier, I told her – didn't I, Katrin? – that I have a friend Jan Mazur who owns an art gallery in Blomberger Street. I would love to show him Katrin's paintings and drawings. He might be interested in organising an exhibition of Katrin's work.'

She looked expectantly at Nurse Jaeger, hoping she would back her and convince Katrin that getting her work into the public eye might be a good thing.

To her surprise, Nurse Jaeger turned bright red, then took

her by the elbow, fingers pinching hard into Erika's flesh, and steered her away, out of Katrin's earshot.

'What do you think you're doing, putting such ideas into that poor woman's head?'

'I just thought...' said Erika, rubbing her painful upper arm.

'You just thought what? Raise her hopes? Make false promises?'

'No, no... I...'

'Hmm.' Nurse Jaeger scoffed. 'As if it's not difficult enough to keep that one calm and content. She's a troublemaker already.'

Erika, taken aback by the vehement outburst, now pulled herself together. 'My friend Jan Mazur just had a wonderful exhibition by a foot-and-mouth artist. It was very well received. Jan likes to help people with talent, who are different and who struggle in life. I thought it might cheer Katrin up. She looks so sad.'

'You know nothing about these patients yet, and you won't until you've worked here for a while. And even then, it's out of the question. It would upset the patient. Besides, Doctor Wagner would never give her permission.'

1978

Katrin's legs refused to keep putting one foot after the other. Exhaustion had taken hold of her, caused not only by the distance she had walked on her unequal legs, but also by the amount of new impressions along the way.

It had all seemed so simple after she woke up in the mountain cave: leave the cave and go home. Ma and Pa would be cross with her and Trude for staying out overnight. There might even be a beating with Ma's slipper, but she never stayed vexed for long. All would be well in the end.

But it had not been that easy. Katrin was frightened and overwhelmed by unfamiliar objects and never-seen-before landmarks on their walk.

Within these town walls, even more surprises lay in wait for them. The town seemed bigger and noisier and more populated than she remembered. Katrin tried to make sense of it all and not to blunder into people, who stared at them. Women frowned, looked her up and down, taking in her dirty feet and dishevelled dress. They wandered through unrecognised streets and alleys, turning corners at random. As the children searched for their homes, clustered in a doorway a couple of lads loitered, each with a small, white stick between two fingers or in their mouths. They sucked from it as smoke curled upwards and an acrid smell floated in the air.

As the youths passed by, they flung mocking phrases at the children, followed by hoots of laughter. The children turned the corner, arriving at Market Square, in front of the Nicolai church. Everyone was here on this market day.

Rows of stalls overflowing with produce, their awnings flapping in the wind, crowded the square. In the spaces between, a dense flow of people hustled, bustled and haggled over the price of the wares as vendors loudly and repeatedly called out to attract customers.

Katrin and her companions stood and watched from across the road. One of the older girls spoke up. This girl, whose name Katrin did not remember, was born with a harelip and the words that came out of her mouth were unclear. Usually, this girl remained silent. Until now.

'We'll cross the market. Perhaps we'll see someone we know. If not, we can all gather in the church. I will speak to Father Hillebrand. He'll know what to do.'

The children started to mingle with the waves of people moving between the stalls and so did Katrin, holding Trude by the hand so they wouldn't lose each other.

They wove through the crowd, trying to avoid bumping into people whose bulging bags swung into Katrin's hips and legs. Her nose tingled with the rich and unfamiliar aromas of spices and the earthy smell of flowers and plants. At one stall she spotted turnips, swedes and onions. Root vegetables for a hearty winter soup, of the kind Ma made. Where some carrots had spilled onto the muddy ground, she saw some of her companions furtively pick them up, wipe the mud off and put them in their mouths. They ate hungrily. Until that moment she'd had no appetite. But when the smell of freshly baked goods cut through all the other scents, she could taste the fresh bread in her mouth and she salivated.

Another stall sold apples and Katrin searched the ground where one or two had fallen from the crates and rolled away. She crouched down to snatch these and scampered away from the stalls and the milling throng of customers to find a quiet corner on the steps of the church. Sitting down, she bit greedily into one of the apples and gave the other to Trude.

When all the children had gathered, they entered the church. The space inside exuded calm and quietness. The air was tinctured with the scent of incense and burning candles. Safe from the din of the market, here they might rest awhile. Awed, Katrin looked up at the high arched windows with their stained-glass representations of saints, angels and apostles.

Following an impulse, Katrin knelt down on the tiled floor between the rows of pews, crossed herself and folded her hands in prayer. Others did the same. When she heard footsteps approaching, she looked up and saw a lady in a grey knee-length dress with a white collar coming towards them. A gold crucifix on a chain hung on her chest and a short veil covered her hair. The lady halted in front of them and spoke in a foreign tongue.

The girl with the harelip responded. 'We've come to see Father Hillebrand. He knows me. Tell him Gretl Jakob's daughter needs to speak to him.'

The woman looked confused for a moment. Then she gestured for them to sit and wait in the pews.

When she returned, alone, she carried a large willow basket filled with buttered bread rolls which she handed out. The hunger in their bellies made the children grab the food and greedily rip into it with their teeth. The woman urged them to take another roll each until the basket was empty.

When Katrin had finished eating, she wiped the butter drips from her chin with the back of her hand while, in front of her, Gretl turned towards the woman in grey and asked for Father Hillebrand again.

Before the woman had time to respond, the church door swung open and a group of men, all dressed the same – in green, wearing peaked caps – marched in. Most of the children were still eating, but now they stopped dead and looked up with large, frightened eyes.

The men spoke briefly with the woman, then approached the children and one of them asked a question. None of the boys and girls understood him and all kept quiet. The question was followed by something that sounded like an order and the men, big and strong, hauled the children to their feet and pushed them towards the church door. What little resistance there was amongst the children was easily dealt with. Most were too scared to disobey and walked away from the church, surrounded by the men in green.

Instead of going back to Market Square, they took the opposite direction through a narrow alley. Katrin fought back tears. Where were they going? What was going to happen to them? She felt powerless, like never before. Never? There had been that one time. Something similar had happened then. When Trude and the others were forced to walk against their will. They had followed a tune. Music had made them march onwards. And there it was, the tune, emerging from the depths of her memory. Her lips shaped themselves into a whistle.

Quietly at first, then increasing in volume, she whistled. Trude, nearest to her, heard it and joined in. Others too joined in and before long they were all whistling that old tune.

At that, the men in green who accompanied them stopped dead to become like pillars of salt, as Lot's wife did in the Bible. As did Pa and Ma and the other parents when their children walked away from Hamelin, following the music, Katrin now remembered, as she continued to whistle. Only when the children were around the corner did their whistling fade. But then male voices shouted behind them and they heard heavy boots, and for the second time that day one of the children called out, 'Run!'

Some bolted, some stayed together, others dispersed. Katrin hobbled a little faster, with Trude beside her.

A few seconds later Katrin heard a squeal, then a scream, followed by an ominous thud. Around the corner she stopped and recognised the diminutive body, lying crumpled in the street. It was one of her companions. Then a man with blood on his face stepped out of his carriage, staggered towards the boy and knelt down beside him.

FOUR

2011

Katrin was not the only patient who liked gardening, Erika discovered. Martin, a big guy, slow and gentle, who carried a considerable amount of weight, did as well. Contrary to Katrin, though, he seemed relatively happy with a ready smile for the nurses. Once, Erika witnessed something extraordinary in the garden: sparrows, starlings and finches came and sat on Martin's shoulders and head, completely at ease. Another time, Erika noticed that Martin filled his pockets with a small amount of gravel, tiny pieces of bark and dried leaves. Next, he did the same with a handful of potting soil, moss and some small plants. Back in his room she coaxed him to reveal what he needed the vegetation for. After some hesitation he pulled something from underneath his bed: a glass jar with a piece of gauze stretched over the top and held in place with a rubber band. The gauze, once a bandage, had tiny holes in it, to allow air in for the snail, whose home this was.

'I found this little fellow in the garden and thought he'd be good company,' Martin said. Erika didn't have the heart to tell anyone.

Later, on that sunny day in early Spring, she slipped away

from the Koppenberg Klinik in her lunchtime and cycled down to the bank of the Weser to meet Peter at one of the riverside cafés. He'd managed to get a table out on the crowded terrace, a popular spot. They ordered sea bass and dauphinoise potatoes.

'I hope it won't take too long,' Erika told the waitress. 'I have to be back at work by two.'

She was assured there would be enough time.

'How's work?' asked Peter. Erika told him about Martin and his pet snail, after which the waitress returned with their wine.

'I'm surprised Bauer let you out for lunch,' Peter said, taking a sip of Chablis.

'I had to suck up to her all morning,' Erika smiled. 'I brought a few blueberry muffins in, the ones I baked last night, to pacify her. She loves those. Plus, I cleaned up after one of her patients vomited. There's quite a bit of that going around at the moment. Patients vomiting. He wasn't the only one.'

'Food poisoning?'

'I don't think so, or we nurses would have been ill as well. We eat the same food. It's probably a virus.'

'If it's a virus, you nurses would have caught it.'

'Hmm. Their sickness began after we started them on a new medicine. I've been wondering if that has anything to do with it – a side effect, perhaps.'

'What's it called?' He picked up his mobile from the table. 'I'll google it, see what the side effects are.'

'It's called Periozadone. Not a name I'm familiar with.'

Erika moved her chair into the sun, closed her eyes and, like a sunflower, turned her face upwards. She exhaled and relaxed back in her chair, enjoying the first warmth of spring.

'Have you found anything yet?'

'Nope.' Peter tapped and scrolled on his phone. 'It's not on the lists of licensed medicines. I'm now going through lists of off-label and unlicensed medication.'

'As far as I know, clinical trial runs of unlicensed medicines can only be done after obtaining informed patient consent,' said Erika.

'Perhaps your patients gave their consent.'

Erika scoffed. 'Not bloody likely. They would have had to read and fill in forms riddled with medical jargon.'

Lunch arrived and they talked about holiday plans instead.

A week later, after more patients had been violently sick, Erika carefully broached the subject with Nurse Bauer, while they updated patient files in the staffroom.

'We've had many patients vomiting since we started them on the Periozadone. Do you think the vomiting might have something to do with the new medicine?'

Her supervisor looked up, eyebrows raised. 'It's prescribed by Doctor Wagner. She knows what she is doing.'

'I looked up Periozadone because I wanted to find out whether nausea and vomiting is a side effect. It's not on any list of licensed medicines.'

Nurse Bauer glared at Erika. 'So it's off-label. That is frequently the case with rare conditions like delusional disorder.'

'If it's off-label or unlicensed, does that mean our patients are taking part in a clinical trial?' Erika persisted.

The expression on her supervisor's face hardened. 'As I said: Doctor Wagner prescribed the medicine and she knows what she's doing. It's not our place to question her authority. I suggest you get on with your job instead.'

Erika couldn't let it go. 'Is Doctor Wagner aware of the medicine's possible effect on our patients?'

Nurse Bauer got up from her seat. 'That's enough. We don't

know if the vomiting is caused by the Periozadone. It could be anything. A bug that's going around, as is often the case in hospitals. Now, I'm late for my patient round. Have you finished with those files?'

'I have.' Erika held them out towards the older nurse. 'Here they are.'

While Nurse Bauer went to put them in their filing cabinet, Erika would liked to have said: I was taught to find out everything we could about the medicines we deal with. That is part of our job. Don't you agree? But she kept that thought to herself.

On her way out, Nurse Bauer muttered something to Nurse Jaeger in passing.

'We've got ourselves another Helga Dietz on our hands,' were the words Erika caught.

1978

Detective Inspector Klaus Lenau wasn't having a good day. His wife was helping out her mother in Hanover for a couple of days, taking the children with her. He had tried to iron his shirt that morning, but the iron had been too hot and burned a hole in it. His car wouldn't start because he'd left the lights on last night. He had to wait an hour to charge the battery.

When he finally arrived at work, they'd run out of coffee filters and no one was available to go to the supermarket. Everyone had gone to the market church, after a phone call about a group of waifs and strays sheltering in there.

Listless, he leafed through files of current cases on his desk and stared out of the window. In the distance he heard the siren of an ambulance, when Constable Engel came by with an excuse to discuss last night's football match on the television. West Germany versus the USSR, it was a friendly, which West Germany had won, one-nil.

They were still debating Beckenbauer's elegant style and leadership on the field, when the phone on Lenau's desk rang. It was his deputy Sergeant Stefan Brückner, phoning from the hospital. One of the urchins they'd picked up from the church, a young boy, had been hit by a car while trying to escape. He was badly wounded, but no longer in danger of losing his life.

'Find out who and where the parents are,' Lenau said. 'They need to be contacted. What about the other children?'

'They're all here, Chief.'

'Good. Do they know who the boy's parents are?'

'Maybe. But they don't speak German.'

'Then you'll need a translator. Can you find out what language they speak? Are they gypsy children?'

'Judging by the look of them I would say they are, Chief.'

'Okay. I might know someone who speaks their language. How big is the group?'

'I would say... between thirty and forty children.'

'That many? Okay, leave it with me. Tell everyone to stay there for now and I'll bring someone who can translate.'

'Will do.'

Lenau put the handset back in its cradle and looked at the constable. 'You remember that fellow who taught some of our boys wrestling? Wasn't he from the Romany community? What was his name again?'

'Marius.'

'Do we have his phone number?'

Less than an hour later, the detective inspector and the wrestling coach were on their way to the hospital in Lenau's silver BMW.

'Nice car,' Marius commented, when they stopped at a red light. 'What does it do, flat out?'

'Dunno. About 200 kilometres an hour, I reckon.'

The lights went green and Lenau accelerated. The powerful engine purred.

'Must've cost a tidy sum,' his passenger patted the seat.

The soft leather was of the finest quality.

'It wasn't cheap.'

The car swung smoothly to the right and entered the hospital driveway. Lenau parked the BMW next to an ambulance, near the hospital's main entrance. They got out, passed the ambulance, where paramedics lowered a patient in a wheelchair, and headed for the wide double doors. The receptionist looked up as Lenau and his translator approached.

'Your colleagues and the children are in the staff cafeteria, which has been cleared for you. It's in the basement. Take the elevator to your left and press the U button.'

'How's the boy doing, the one who ran into the path of a car?' Lenau asked.

'They're still operating on him. His condition is no longer critical, though.'

'And the driver?'

'Nasty bump. Hit his head on the windscreen. He's understandably upset about what happened. If you need to speak to him, he's in there.'

She pointed at a nearby waiting room. Lenau strode towards the area indicated, with Marius at his heels.

The air in the room they entered had an undertone of cleaning detergent. The once-white walls displayed cheap prints. The ceiling was covered with polystyrene squares and fluorescent tubes, one of which flickered, as if on its last leg.

The man with Sergeant Stefan Brückner looked miserable and, through the white bandage around his forehead, a faint red spot was visible.

'Chief,' said Brückner, 'I was just about to take Mr Weber to the station for a statement.'

'Mr Weber, I'm Detective Inspector Lenau. Can you tell me what happened?'

The man spoke with a high, plaintive voice. 'I didn't see the boy coming. He appeared suddenly out of a side street and crossed the road without looking left or right. He was running fast. I stepped on the brake immediately, but it was too late. By then I'd already hit him.'

Lenau nodded and signalled to Marius to follow him from the room.

As soon as they entered the basement and looked around, Lenau sensed there was something unsettling about these children. He wasn't surprised to find them quiet and subdued after what had happened to their friend, or intimidated by their environment. But there was something else about them, something unidentifiable. They weren't like any children he knew. Apart from his own two, he weekly coached a youth football team. Kids were sturdy. They just got on with life, whatever happened. This lot seemed... traumatised?

The constables with them, Becker, Schmidt, Ziegler and the others, had organised colouring books and puzzles for the children, but none of them were touching those. Instead, they sat deflated and mute on chairs or benches. Some seemed to pray with their eyes closed and their hands pressed together. He saw their lips moving. A religious bunch, hey? Lenau thought and pensively rubbed his chin.

'Tell them they have nothing to be afraid of. Their friend is going to get better and we only want to ask them a few questions,' Lenau told Marius, who did so. He was met with silence. He tried again and finally, one of the girls in the group spoke.

'She doesn't speak Romany,' Marius told Lenau.

'What *does* she speak, then?'

'I've no idea.'

'So, they're not from your community?'

'No.'

'Perhaps we should try French or English,' suggested Constable Schmidt, sitting nearby.

'I would have recognised those,' said Lenau.

'Danish, then?' Becker proposed.

'Nah,' Ziegler weighed in, 'my neighbours are Danes. They sound different.'

There was a Polish cleaning lady in the hospital, who spoke enough German to inform Lenau that the children spoke neither Polish nor Russian.

'Get social services here,' said Lenau. 'They might know how to talk to these children.'

2011

Who was Helga Dietz? Erika wondered. Two days after the disagreement with her supervisor, she sat on the garden bench outside the staffroom during her coffee break, when she was joined by another young nurse. Sylvia, from Berlin, had started to work in the secure unit of the Koppenberg Klinik just six months before Erika. Both were interested in cooking and baking, and had occasionally swapped recipes.

'Do you know a Helga Dietz?' Erika asked, after a few minutes of small talk.

'She was the nurse you replaced. Why do you ask?'

'I heard Bauer and Jaeger talking about me. Bauer said: "We've got ourselves another Helga Dietz." Any idea what she meant?'

'I'm not sure, but there was a lot of tension and arguments between Bauer and Helga. Helga stood up to Bauer. She wasn't a doormat and she didn't keep quiet if she disagreed with someone. Perhaps you should talk to Katrin.'

Erika was surprised. 'But Katrin is a patient.'

'That doesn't mean you can't talk to her. Helga got very close to Katrin, especially after her sister Trude died. Katrin was inconsolable and Helga was the one who helped her through.'

'What did Trude die of?'

Sylvia looked around as if to check no one was within earshot, before she leaned towards Erika. 'The official version at the time was that she had a critical heart condition that had gone unnoticed. I'm not sure that's the truth, though.'

'Why not?'

'Katrin didn't believe it and neither did Helga. Katrin would have known if there was something medically wrong with her sister. There would have been signs.'

'What did *Helga* think was the cause of Trude's death?'

'I don't know. I'd only just started here. But – you know Astrid, Doctor Wagner's secretary? She's a friend of mine and she told me Helga got fired after she went to talk to Doctor Wagner about Trude's death. There was a hell of an argument, apparently; both were shouting at each other.'

At that moment Nurse Bauer appeared in the doorway of the staffroom.

'If you've finished your *kaffee-klatsch*, there are patients to see. Nurse Kramer, the patient in room eight refuses to eat.

Nurse Sturm, the patient in room nineteen is in distress and says he'll only talk to you.'

Both nurses got up and went indoors, but not before Erika had quietly asked Sylvia if she had Helga Dietz's phone number.

'I haven't. But I'll ask Astrid.'

Helga Dietz lived at Emmern Street, at number nine. Erika had tried to phone her, but there was no reply. On impulse, instead of cycling home after her shift, Erika decided to pay her predecessor a visit. The house had several doorbells, indicating that it was divided into flats. She pushed the only bell that had no name next to it and waited. There was no response, and Erika was about to get back on her bike, when she heard the rattle of a sash window being raised above her and a woman's voice called down:

'Can I help you?'

Erika looked up. 'I came to see Helga Dietz.'

'She left about three months ago.'

'Do you know where she went? Did she leave an address?'

The woman shook her head. 'No. Rumour has it, she was going back to Brunswick, where her family lives.'

1978

After Lenau dismissed his translator, two tired-looking social workers finally turned up in the early afternoon.

Their first reaction on seeing the children was indignation.

'Has no one thought of giving these children a bath and clean clothes? Look at them, they're filthy and they smell like a pack of pole cats. Have they been fed and given something to drink?'

Half a dozen tongue-tied policemen shuffled their feet and shifted their weight.

'We're trying to find out their names and where they're from, so we can contact the parents of the boy who was hit by a car. They don't speak German and they're not willing to talk,' Lenau explained.

'If I was cold and hungry and in an unfamiliar environment, I don't think I'd have much to say for myself either,' the younger and prettier of the two social workers, the one who had introduced herself as Christa Sachs, snapped at him.

Lenau frowned. 'What do you suggest?'

'Come back tomorrow. We'll sort them out. This is a hospital. They have plenty of baths and food here. Beds can be improvised for the night and clothes can be found via a charity we know.'

'We can't just leave and expect you to look after them. These children are dangerous and will try to run away as soon as we've turned our backs.'

Lenau told her what had happened earlier, and the clutch of constables around him nodded.

'They whistled? And that makes them dangerous?' was the social worker's reaction.

'I know how it sounds,' said Schmidt, 'and I'd find it hard to believe too, if I heard this from someone else. But I was there and I'll tell you: as soon as they started whistling, I couldn't move a limb. First there was only one little girl, then all the others joined in and that was when I felt paralysed. My feet wouldn't move and I couldn't even blink. It was the strangest thing.'

Lenau saw the woman taking in the bedraggled little heaps in flimsy clothes, eyes red from weeping, hugging themselves and each other. He knew what she was thinking. How can these lost souls be dangerous?

'I have a meeting to go to,' he told the social workers, 'but I will leave my men with you. Before I go, I'll speak to the hospital's administrator and ask for their cooperation and support in bathing and feeding them. I will also suggest keeping them here overnight and putting temporary beds in this basement. The room needs to be kept locked overnight, though, and my men will guard them.'

Lenau returned to the hospital the next morning, where he found the flock of vagrant children at breakfast in the basement. How different they looked now, with clean faces and clean hair.

Those who chatted quietly but excitedly amongst themselves as they ate even had a little colour in their cheeks. They no longer wore their otherworldly clothes. Those had been replaced by warm and decent looking clothes from the charity. But the biggest surprise Lenau found was the women sitting amongst the children.

'What are the women doing here?' he asked Becker, who had stayed the night.

'Word must have got out,' Becker answered, 'that here was a large group of parentless children. Foundlings, so to say. The women came and brought breakfast. Some are off-duty nurses and some are cleaning staff.'

'There's something you need to see, Chief,' said Wernz, another constable who had guarded the children overnight.

He took Lenau to one of the women in a nurse's uniform, who chatted quietly to the children.

'This is Nurse Domin. She has something to show you.'

The nurse shook Lenau's hand and lifted a stack of papers from the seat beside her.

'Last night, when I came to see the children, I asked them where they were from. Their answer was steadfast: Hamelin. Then I suggested they draw a picture of the place and this is what they drew.'

She showed Lenau the first drawing, that of a mountain range. The second drawing depicted a mountain with a gaping hole. A cave, he presumed. He looked at the third one: mountains with a cave in the centre of the drawing. He went through all the drawings. They all showed mountains and a cave. He felt a rising excitement. Now they were getting somewhere. The children belonged to a sect who lived in a cave in the mountains. They might find the boy's parents yet.

'How do you manage to understand and talk to the children?' he asked. 'I couldn't make head nor tail of what they were saying, yesterday. They spoke some incomprehensible dialect.'

'I'm from East Friesland,' Nurse Domin smiled. 'The regional dialect we speak there uses similar words. It's some sort of medieval German, which I studied for a year at university, before I gave up. Nursing suited me better.'

'Can you ask them something for me?' said Lenau. 'Ask if any of the children could take us to that mountain cave. Ask them how far away it is and how long it took them to get here.'

She nodded and exchanged words and gestures with the children.

'They walked from sun-up to midday,' she said.

So, not that far by car, Lenau thought. Half an hour, at most.

'We need one or two children to come in the car with me. We'll need you too, to translate,' he said.

She told him her shift was about to start, but that she would ask her supervisor's permission.

Two of the children were prepared to show them the way to the mountain cave. One of them was called Trude and the other one Katrin. Sisters, apparently.

FIVE

2011

Peter Hahn parked his vintage NSU Fox motorbike behind the office of the *DeWeZet*, the local newspaper in East Street, and took off his helmet. The small city bike was much better than a car for getting around quickly.

With his laptop under his arm, he entered the building via the back entrance, taking the steps two at a time, pausing to pick up a Nespresso from the machine before arriving at his desk. After Ilse Schwarz, his editor, he was usually the first to arrive. It was seven thirty when he unzipped and took off his leather jacket to hang it over the back of his chair.

Peter checked his emails first and responded to the urgent ones. Then he had a quick scour of social media, to keep updated. On Instagram he'd been sent photos of rats, part of a project he had initiated a few weeks ago under the heading, "*Are Rats Returning to Hamelin?*"

The idea had come to him when he and Erika were having dinner outside the pizzeria below their apartment. She'd nearly choked on a sip of wine, then pointed to a spot across the road. 'I just saw a rat. It came out of the alley there and disappeared in the crack of that wall.' Afterwards, they had joked about rats in Hamelin and the legend of the Pied Piper.

A few days later he returned home one evening and, knowing that Erika had gone out with friends, popped into a snack bar and ordered a curry sausage and sweet potato fries. Waiting for his takeaway, he saw a movement outside on the pavement, amongst bits of sausage and fries, spilling from an overflowing bin. He was sure it was a rat. It was still there, nibbling, when he dug his phone out of his pocket and took some photos.

The next day he went to his editor and suggested he'd do a daily feature about rats in Hamelin.

'It's nothing special, though,' his editor had objected. 'There are rats in every city, skulking around eating places after dark.'

'I know that,' Peter said, 'but this is *Hamelin*. That could give it an edge. It's just a bit of fun. We could ask readers and our followers on social media to send us photos of rats they spot in town.'

Because nothing much newsworthy was happening at that time, Peter had got his way and now they published a daily photo of a rat, accompanied by Peter's witty comments.

Erika wasn't the only one who'd found her idealistic ideas, fostered at nursing college, had little to do with the reality of her job. Peter, who wanted most of all to be an investigative journalist, had discovered this too.

After studying journalism at university, he initially felt lucky to get a job at the *DeWeZet*. But a year is a long time to write about local amateur dramatic productions, minor sporting events, baking competitions, dog grooming award ceremonies and the yearly carnival. He was still a dogsbody, a year on, a general assignments reporter.

'What do I need to do to become an investigative journalist?' he'd asked Axel Voight, a correspondent at Reuters, whom he admired and, in a moment of frustration with the job, had contacted out of the blue for advice.

'Don't expect to be writing front-page stories, or even having your name on any stories at first. It's all about getting to know people and the system. Work on projects in your own time, then submit the finished article. Don't wait for the editor to give you assignments. In journalism, it's all about taking the initiative. *That's* how you become an investigative journalist.'

1978

Katrin held on tight to her seat in the back of Lenau's BMW as it left the town via the East Gate, following the sisters' directions. They drove slowly, so they could direct the driver.

'Where is your horse?' Trude had asked through the interpreter, before they set off.

Nurse Domin had asked the man called Inspector Lenau and they had both laughed.

'In here,' the inspector had said, knocking on the front part of the carriage, and to their great surprise he lifted up the cover and invited them to look inside. No trace of a horse there, but some rusty iron boxes and coloured line twisting and connecting one part to another. It smelled unfamiliar.

Katrin recognised the stretch of black pathway they were on, gently rising and falling between pastures and trees in every shade of green against the backdrop of a mountain range. This was where they had walked the previous day.

'Look for the mountain path we were on before we got to this road,' she told Trude.

Katrin stared at the wheel in Lenau's hands and the tiny lights that twinkled in the front of the carriage. But most of the time she stared in wonder through the clear panel beside her. She had noticed these in the place of healing where they had slept that night. You could see the world outside right through these panels. They were thin but strong and kept the cold out.

Though hot air blew around her head and down at her feet, it was cold.

There were the giant metal creatures, still standing, rooted in the landscape. Trude pointed at one.

'Pylons,' said Nurse Domin in the front of the car, who sometimes talked like Trude and Katrin, using the same words.

Katrin tasted the word on her tongue and whispered it to herself. A strange word for a strange, motionless creature.

Her reverie was interrupted when Trude sat up straight, pointed and called out loudly, 'There! That's the path. Look! Can you see it? That's where we came down from the mountain.'

Nurse Domin translated her exclamations for the inspector, who turned the carriage around on the nearly empty road and drove back to where Trude had indicated. The carriage turned slowly into the track and followed it as far as it could. When it narrowed to the point that it became impossible to drive, they stopped and all four of them got out.

They continued on foot. Katrin and Trude led the way. None of them spoke. They needed their breath, for the climb was much harder than the descent had been the previous day. At last, they reached the plateau in front of the cave, from which the children had spilled forth.

Trude and Katrin walked purposefully towards the mouth of the cave. Where the opening had been, now they found only rock. The entrance to the sleepers was closed.

SIX

2011

On Erika's birthday, her twenty-second, she treated each of her patients to a chocolate brownie she had baked the previous evening. She entered Martin's room first and found him sitting on his bed, large tears sliding down his cheeks.

'What's wrong?'

When he didn't answer she placed the largest brownie she could find for him on the table. He loved cake, especially chocolate brownies.

'Karlchen has gone,' he sniffled.

Martin had named his pet snail Karlchen. Ever since Erika knew of Martin's secret she'd smuggled pieces of apple, pear or cucumber into his room.

He wiped his tears with the tissue she handed him, blew his nose and showed her the empty jam jar. It looked as if someone, a cleaner perhaps, had thrown the content away. She promised they'd go and find another snail in the garden soon.

During the rest of her round, after receiving birthday wishes and compliments on her home baking, Erika asked patients when their birthdays were.

Everyone's answer was the same.

'The twenty-first of December. On Midwinter Day.'

Mystified, Erika mentioned it to her supervisor on her return to the nurses' station.

'It's the day they were found. We don't know their birthdays. Neither do we know their exact ages. Social services estimated their age at the time and it stuck,' Nurse Bauer explained, while her eyes remained fixed on the screen in front of her and her hands tapped rapidly on the keyboard.

'I imagine we'll celebrate that day in a big way,' said Erika. 'If you need someone to organise a party, I'd love to have a go.'

'I bet you would.'

The sarcasm caught Erika unawares and it stung. After nearly two months at the closed unit, she should have been used to it. Don't let her get to you, she told herself. Don't give her the satisfaction.

Until that moment she'd felt light-hearted, looking forward to celebrating her birthday after the morning's shift. Peter had managed to get tickets for a performance of *Wicked*, the musical, including dinner afterwards and a night in a hotel in Dortmund, an hour and a half's drive from Hamelin. She had the following morning off.

Erika loved musicals. When Peter showed her the tickets that morning at breakfast, pretending at first that he'd forgotten to get her anything for her birthday, he nearly lost his balance as she jumped up and hugged him exuberantly.

Katrin too wished Erika a happy birthday, when the young nurse came to collect her later that morning. They went to the garden to pull out the weeds between flowerbeds.

'So when is *your* birthday, then?' Erika asked Katrin as they worked, although she already knew the answer.

'The twenty-first of December.'

'That's odd, because all the other patients gave the same answer.'

'Yes. It's everyone's birthday.'

Unexpectedly, Katrin, who had hardly said anything until now, spoke quietly as she went on gardening. 'It was Trude's birthday too. One year, they let us spend that day together, as a special treat. We talked and talked in our own language. The nurse who supervised us didn't like that at all. She told us to stop it and said it was impolite to speak a foreign language in the presence of someone who couldn't understand. We just laughed and continued anyway, so then she threatened to end our get-together. That's when we gave in. We still laughed though, afterwards. She was fearless and funny, my sister Trude.'

'What language did you and Trude speak that day?' Erika asked with interest.

Katrin shrugged. 'I don't know what you'd call it. We called it our first language. They told us it was some old dialect and that we should learn to speak proper German. We did, but I never forgot my first language and neither did Trude. I don't know about the others. I don't see or speak to them.'

'You don't? Not even on your birthday?'

Katrin shook her head. 'No, on the day before our birthday, the twentieth, we make birthday cards for each other. They are delivered by the nurses the next morning. We do get treats. Cook makes our favourite dinner and one of the nurses comes in to sing "Happy Birthday" and brings in our very own mini birthday cake and a small present. Usually a book.'

'Sounds nice.'

Katrin turned to face Erika and the look she gave her said it all. These birthdays were not "nice". They were desperately lonely affairs. The one exception had been the birthday she had spent with her sister. And that experience would now never be repeated.

A few days later, Erika assisted Nurse Jaeger taking stock of their medicine cabinets: checking which drugs needed reordering, which had passed their use-by date and should be sent back to their suppliers, as well as counting needles, bandages and other medical supplies.

Nurse Jaeger, who suggested Erika call her Beate when Nurse Bauer wasn't around, asked about the theatre trip to Dortmund, which prompted Erika to give her a detailed account. Beate remarked she was glad Erika had enjoyed herself. After all, it was her birthday. Personally, she preferred opera.

'Have you ever been to the Bayreuth Festival?' Erika looked for a cloth and some detergent to clean the now empty medicine cabinet in front of her.

'I try to go every year, usually with a friend. Stephanie and I have been at least eight times. Last year we couldn't go because my mother was ill and needed looking after. She had no one else, so it was down to me.' She added hastily, 'Not that I minded.'

Erika began to warm to Nurse Beate. Until today they'd hardly exchanged more than a few words at a time.

'Is she better now, your mother?' Erika wiped the shelves and restocked the cabinet with boxes of medicines and needles.

'She died last summer. Cancer got her in the end.'

'I'm sorry. You must miss her.'

Nurse Jaeger gave a little nod and smiled. They watched as a nurse walked past their window in deep conversation with a male patient.

'Beate, may I ask you something that's been on my mind since I started working here?' Erika sensed she should tread carefully.

'Go on.'

'I wondered why our patients here don't spend any time

together. They're mostly on their own in their rooms, behind locked doors. And if they're not in their rooms, they are with a nurse doing activities or therapy, or they walk in the garden. But there doesn't appear to be any communal time. I suggested I'd organise a little party on their birthday, the twenty-first of December, but Nurse Bauer would have none of it. Why is that?'

'Because when they are together, these patients are dangerous. They need to be kept separate, at all costs.'

The answer startled Erika.

'Dangerous?' she echoed. 'How? They all come across as innocent, childlike, almost. Capable of tantrums, maybe. But *dangerous?* I would describe these patients as absent-minded daydreamers. Lost in their own thoughts. I can't imagine any of them becoming aggressive.'

'That's because you only see them one at a time. You've never seen them together.'

'Have *you?*'

Beate admitted she had not.

'But Doctor Wagner has and she strictly ordered us to keep the patients on this wing separated. Or for no more than two or three patients at any time to be together.'

Erika reflected on that for a moment. 'Still, it's unusual, don't you think? During my training I spent part of my work-placement year on a wing with patients suffering from schizophrenia and other serious psychoses. They were never kept apart from each other or locked up. Nurse Bauer herself told me the patients here suffer from delusional disorder and therefore are easier to deal with than schizophrenics.'

'They are. Only, not when they're together.'

'I'd love to know why.'

'I can't answer that for you. But I can tell you this: be careful. Nurse Bauer doesn't like it when you ask too many questions and neither does Doctor Wagner. You wouldn't be the first to lose your job because of being too nosy.'

'Is that why Helga Dietz lost hers?'

'How do you know about Helga Dietz?' Beate didn't wait for an answer. 'Yes, that's why she was fired. Putting her nose where it didn't belong. So, you should watch it and be careful if you want to keep your job.'

Later, Erika managed to take a small container from her locker and carry it to Martin's room unnoticed. The previous day, they had searched all over the garden for another snail to keep the big man company, but had found none. On her way home, Erika had popped into the pet shop and bought one.

'I did some research,' she told Martin, 'and apparently snails need calcium to stay healthy. As soon as I can, I'll bring you some eggshells from the kitchen. That should do the trick.'

For the first time in days Martin looked happy again.

1978

In the end, Katrin had to be prised away from the rock face. She hung on, with her fingers buried deep in the cracks, and called out to the sleeping children inside the cave.

'Can you hear me? We're here! We did not forget you! Call out, call loud, so we can hear you!'

After the silence that followed, Nurse Domin spoke, 'Could it have been another mountain with a cave from which you walked to Hamelin?'

Trude shook her head. 'No, it was here. This was the place we came from.'

When Lenau suggested they go back, Katrin refused. Clinging with all her strength to that part of the mountain she'd been hugging, she hollered when the inspector pulled her away by her shoulders.

In the car, with Lenau driving back at full speed, hot tears spilled down Katrin's cheeks. Even Trude, who put an arm around her, could not comfort her. Katrin blamed herself for walking away from those who had still been asleep. She should have woken them up. This was all her fault. Besides, nothing made sense anymore. Everything seemed different in the world they'd woken up in.

Even though they could speak to Nurse Domin, what was there to tell, other than they were from another Hamelin and that their parents were farmhands who worked the land? Katrin did not remember what happened immediately before they woke in the cave and neither did the others.

What she did remember was Ma's wide smile and how it revealed the gaps between her teeth. Ma's patience when, during the long winter evenings, she had taught Katrin and Trude to spin yarn with a spindle. She remembered Pa grabbing her by her hands, swinging her round and round until she screamed with excitement, and riding on his strong shoulders as he walked home after a long day's work. Where were they now? Would she see her parents again? What was going to happen to her, Trude and the others? They'd been told by these strangers not to worry, that they were safe and would be looked after, that the boy struck down by a fast carriage would heal, but Pa had always told them not to trust strangers.

2011

As summer nudged towards early autumn, Erika and Peter took a week off for a holiday in the Black Forest. Both liked to hike and they looked forward to going for long walks from the modest guest house they had booked.

'Do we pass Brunswick on the way?' Erika had asked Peter.

'Near enough.'

'There's someone I'd like to visit. Her name is Helga Dietz. She's the nurse I replaced. It's customary to have a briefing with your predecessor in our profession, to be updated on patients' care plans. I never had that briefing, because Helga Dietz was fired on the spot. She'd asked too many questions, which senior staff didn't like. I too have questions. I don't have her address but there can't be too many Helga Dietz's in Brunswick.'

Peter googled it. 'Nineteen.'

'Oh.' Erika felt put off for a moment.

Peter was less easily defeated. 'Let's try private nursing agencies. She might not have found another job in a hospital again, but agency work is another option.'

'You're right.' Erika beamed. 'That's what I would have done in her situation.'

At the fourth agency, when Erika asked to speak to Nurse Dietz, she struck lucky.

'Just a moment. I'll see if she's still here,' was the reply.

Moments later, Erika arranged with Helga Dietz to meet in the café of the Museum of Modern Art.

1978

Detective Inspector Lenau and Commissioner Braun did not usually socialise with one another. They weren't friends and they belonged to different strata in society. Their education and social statuses were as different as their incomes. Braun's holidays were spent on the Bahamas or in Florida. Lenau took his family to Italy or Spain, or, if he felt very adventurous, to Greece. At work, they kept their exchanges to police matters.

Then there was the little matter of their ages. Lenau had been born after the war, in 1947, whereas Braun was born in 1923. Once, he overheard Braun sighing to someone of his own age, 'but we lost the war.'

Lenau had nearly said, 'Yes, and thank God we did.'

But he kept that thought to himself. And, like most Germans, he dealt with the inheritance of the war in the only way he could: by working hard to restore the country and hoping that time would heal the scars.

The day after Lenau took the two girls to the mountain, he was told to join Braun in his office. From behind his desk, Braun asked about the newly-arrived children.

Lenau gave him a quick update. 'We've not located any parents yet. Social services will try to find foster families. Thirty-five is a lot of children, though. They doubt they will find that many families. They say the old orphanage might have to be reinstated.'

Braun wrinkled his nose in disgust. 'It's a dilapidated old building, unfit for purpose, I should think.'

'My thoughts precisely, sir.'

'Anyway,' Braun said, 'at yesterday's council meeting, everyone was extremely interested in the appearance of the children in our town. I couldn't tell them much, but you could. I'm organising a little dinner party this Friday evening. Seven thirty at my house. I'd like to invite you and Mrs Lenau, if you can make it.'

Unable to find a ready excuse to turn the invitation down, Lenau accepted.

Mrs Gisela Lenau was delighted with the invitation. As soon as her husband mentioned the dinner party, she organised a babysitter for their two young children, made appointments with the hairdresser and the beautician, and set an afternoon aside to shop for a new outfit.

'How formal is it? I don't want to be under- or overdressed.'

When Lenau shrugged, she gave him a disapproving look.

'Oh, never mind. I'll phone Renate. She'll know what to wear.'

Renate had been Gisela's best friend since they were at school together. Lenau doubted his wife really needed advice on a dress, but suspected she rather liked to show off the invitation.

On the evening of the dinner party, it was raining heavily when the Lenaus arrived at the Commissioner's house in a residential part of Hamelin. They found a row of expensive cars parked close to the house. Lenau parked the silver BMW as near as he could. If nothing else, at least his car matched those belonging to the other guests.

'We do have an umbrella in the car, don't we?' Gisela asked.

'In the dashboard compartment.'

She rummaged for a few seconds. 'No, it's not here.'

Lenau looked behind their seats, then, in response to his wife's withering looks, got out to check in the boot. On his return, realising they had no means of keeping dry, they sat in silent gloom while rainwater poured down the windows.

'We'll be late if we wait any longer,' Lenau said finally. 'Let's make a dash for it. It's not that far.'

'My hair will be ruined and so will my new shoes.' Gisela's words sounded like splintered ice.

'No, they won't, because you will hold my coat over your head.'

They still arrived at the Brauns' front door half drenched, their wet clothes clinging perversely to their bodies.

'You poor souls! Let's get you dry before you meet everyone,' Mrs Braun exclaimed.

Having dried out in the reception room, the Lenaus were introduced to Hamelin's finest. Lenau recognised Thomas Wagner, the town council's treasurer. Wagner, bronzed, tall and handsome, was already tipped as a political star with a glittering career around the corner. With his charisma and natural charm, he was expected to rise to the level of national politics.

Commissioner Braun appeared. 'I see you two haven't been offered a cocktail yet. You must think me a bad host. Come with me and I'll show you what we have on offer.'

He led the couple towards a bar crammed with bottles, ice buckets, maraschino cherries and lemon slices. Gisela decided on a Tequila Sunrise, whereas Lenau opted for the Cuba Libre.

When they rejoined the other guests, Lenau was struck by the tall woman next to Wagner. Her blonde hair was loosely pinned into a knot at the nape of her neck and she wore pearls and matching earrings to decorate a simple black velvet dress. Classic features gave her an aristocratic appearance.

'Who is that?' Lenau blurted, before he could check himself.

'That,' said Braun, with a smile of amusement, 'is Claudia Wagner, Thomas's better half and a distinguished psychiatrist.'

After dinner, conversation quickly turned towards the mysterious appearance of the thirty-odd unaccompanied children in Hamelin. Lenau answered questions patiently, telling them as little as he could get away with. After the questions came the speculations. Were these runaway children from an orphanage, perhaps? Or foreign children on a school trip who'd had a bus accident?

Claudia Wagner had said nothing so far. But now, her pale blue eyes held Lenau's.

'Have the children been vaccinated?'

To his embarrassment, Lenau felt himself blushing like a schoolgirl.

'They've had some medical tests,' he stammered. 'I don't know if vaccinations were amongst those.'

'If not, they could catch all kinds of infectious diseases,' Claudia explained. 'The sooner they have their immunisations, the better.'

Why they had been brought to this passage, Katrin didn't know. Neither did the other children. White walls were scraped in places and deeply scored with white scars. Above every door, Katrin noticed a large sign with white letters she was unable to read. Men and women in white passed by, moving with purpose, their soft white shoes making hardly any sound at all.

In this white, white world the children were lined up outside an open door. Just after the first of her companions went into the room, Katrin heard the child burst into tears, then cry out in pain. The row of children stirred uneasily. More children entered the room. More sobs. More screams. Fear rose in those waiting in the passage. A woman in a white apron and cap emerged from the room and spoke in shushing tones. Then it was Katrin's turn.

She entered the room, which was brightly lit. A man in a white coat sat on a stool, holding a small instrument, from which something like a bee's sting protruded, but made of metal. The child in front of Katrin, one arm bared, whimpered in fright.

Katrin shrank backwards until she touched a wall. She felt faint, as if there wasn't enough oxygen in the room. Time slowed and just like before, in her mind a tune surfaced and filled her until it shaped her lips into a whistle. Quiet and haltingly to begin with, it grew in volume as Trude and the others, who had remained in the passage, joined Katrin's whistling. Their whistling had a dramatic effect on the adults. The sharp instrument in White-coat's hand halted. He sat motionless, not even blinking behind his black-rimmed eyeglasses. White-apron too stood frozen on the spot, a fluffy white cotton ball between her thumb and index finger.

Katrin beckoned the other girl in the room to follow her back into the passage, where the others too followed Katrin who turned, walked and whistled through the corridors, the reception area and out of the building. Those who could have stopped them, who would have prevented them from walking away, were immobile. Outside, even the carriages stopped and every townsperson stood motionless. On the trees, not a single leaf stirred.

As if from somewhere far away, Katrin observed herself and the others as they whistled and marched onwards, trance-like. Where she was taking them, she knew not yet, but they had to get away. Away from the white walls. From strangers, from being trapped inside, the clamour and the clattering. The noise. *Especially* the noise. Suddenly, she knew where to go. Out of the city with its screeching, honking, beeping and squealing sounds, to the tranquillity, the quiet and the comfort of the land.

SEVEN

2011

Peter and Erika turned off the motorway and entered Brunswick. Already, leaves in tree-lined boulevards were turning red, orange and yellow. They arrived at their destination just after the appointed time of ten o'clock.

The museum was situated along a wide avenue bordered by elegant neo-classical mansions. Getting there had been easy with the satnav. Parking was much harder and it took a while to find a spot, a few streets away from the museum. Pale sunlight filtered through beech trees as they walked hand in hand, Peter's long strides accompanied Erika's rapid steps. Grimy grey concrete dominated the façade of the rectangular building, interrupted by large windows and high-rise columns; the latter supported the extensive canopied roof. To counteract the functionality of the building's cardboard box-like design, huge plant pots were strategically placed at equal distances along the façade and colourful posters of present and future exhibitions were displayed behind glass entry doors and some windows. Plenty of natural light illuminated the spacious entrance hall, where Peter bought his ticket for the photography exhibition.

The coffee shop was on the ground floor, to the right of the entrance; to the left was the museum shop with the usual cards, books and merchandise. Erika watched Peter ascend the broad, sweeping staircase to the first floor, then gave the coffee shop door a push and went in.

It was relatively empty. A few customers sat by the floor-to-ceiling window, along the length of the outside wall. Erika caught snatches of a murmured conversation, a spoon clinking against the side of a cup and the jazzy notes of a saxophone as she walked towards a woman with shoulder length fair hair, wearing a red coat and sitting by herself. "I'm wearing a red coat," Helga had told Erika on the phone.

'Helga Dietz?'

The woman looked up from her mobile phone. She was in her mid-thirties, perhaps, unsmiling, earnest, with a little too much make-up on, curious eyes and a dry, firm handshake. The half-empty cup of cappuccino in front of her had a smear of red lipstick at the rim.

Before sitting down, Erika went to get herself a coffee. Carefully balancing her cup, she threaded her way back past empty tables and chairs. It's a shame there is no one sitting here to appreciate the fresh freesias on the tables, she thought fleetingly.

An awkward silence fell after Erika sat back down. Either Helga too was searching for the right words, or she was waiting for Erika to speak.

Erika broke the silence. 'How's the job at the agency? Is it better or worse than working at the Koppenberg?'

Both, according to Helga. Worse because the salary wasn't as good. Better because she liked being back in her hometown and she ran the agency together with other nurses. She liked working freelance rather than being an employee.

'I get that,' Erika said. 'Perhaps I'll do the same after I have a couple more years of experience. Already, I don't like being told to keep my head down and keep shtum instead of asking questions.'

'What kind of questions?'

'Why the doors of our unit have to be locked. Why patients are treated like prisoners. Why they never get to spend time together. And why they are given medicines that are not on any list, neither amongst the licensed medicines, nor the un-licensed or off-label ones.'

'How long have you been working in the secure unit?'

'About two months.'

'Well done. It took me longer than that to ask the same questions. Neither Bauer nor Doctor Wagner would answer them. When I threatened to report them to the *Gemeinsamer Bundesausschuss*, Wagner said I had no evidence of anything untoward going on. She added she knew everyone personally on the board and would make sure I would never get a job within the healthcare profession again.'

'What did you do, then?'

'I love my job. I can't imagine being anything else but a nurse. So, I suggested I'd leave and wouldn't pursue the matter if she gave me a positive reference. She did and that's how I got this job.'

'I understand,' said Erika. Then, after a pause, 'One of the nurses told me you didn't believe Katrin's sister Trude died of an undetected heart condition.'

Something in Helga shifted, almost imperceptibly. Where before there had been an openness in her eyes and facial expression, Erika now perceived a more guarded look and a certain stiffness in the woman sitting opposite her.

'Who told you that?'

'Does it matter? Did you think it was the medication? Are those patients undergoing medical trials? I'm asking because over the summer we've had a lot of sick patients with blinding headaches, dizzy spells and disorientation, nausea and frequent vomiting.'

Helga sighed. 'Look. It's true, I was suspicious about the way Trude died. It was so unexpected. She had been perfectly healthy that day, and a few hours later, she was dead. Heart failure, they told everyone. But Doctor Wagner was right when she said I had no evidence that Trude's death was caused by her medication. I'm not a doctor or a pathologist. I didn't attend the post-mortem.'

'*Was* there a post-mortem examination?'

'I don't know. If there was one, I'm sure it was conducted by one of Doctor Wagner's friends.' Erika noted the deliberate cynicism in Helga's voice.

They sat in silence for a while. Erika drank the last of her black coffee, which had gone cold and tasted bitter. She wondered if it was too soon to leave. The meeting had turned out not to be as helpful as she had hoped, and she and Peter still had a long drive ahead of them.

'How is Katrin?' Helga asked, with some hesitation.

'She's doing okay. It's hard to say, though. She doesn't talk much, does she?'

'She didn't talk at all after Trude died. Or eat. I thought she might kill herself, either by starvation or otherwise. It was heartbreaking. I didn't think she'd get over her sister's death.'

'I was told you spent a lot of time with her.'

'Yes, she was put on suicide watch and was supervised twenty-four-seven. Mostly by me. When she started to talk again, she talked about Trude. How she and Trude had lived on the outskirts of Hamelin with their family in an earlier life. How they'd loved springtime and seeing newborn lambs frolicking about on the land.'

'An earlier life?'

'I know how it sounds. But the way she told me all this was

so realistic, so detailed; it was hard to believe she had made it all up.'

'So you think the reason patients like Katrin are in the Koppenberg is not that they are delusional, but that they vividly remember a past life and confuse it with their present life?'

'God, no. I never thought that. I probably shouldn't have told you. It's just that you seemed really interested to know what happened, and I thought... but you should really talk to Katrin yourself if you want answers.'

'I'll do that.'

Erika was about to get up and leave when Helga took something from her shoulder bag. It was a folded piece of card.

'What is it?' Erika asked.

'Trude wasn't the only one who died an unexplained death at the Koppenberg over the years. On that card you'll find the names of the others. I'm not suggesting their deaths weren't natural. But you never know. Someday it might be of use.'

1978

'What do you mean, gone? Slow down, man. I can hardly understand what you're saying.' Lenau, on one end of the phone line, was irritated by the urgency of the voice at the other end. Constable Becker took a deep breath and began again.

'So where are they now?' Lenau asked, after Becker finished his report.

'By the time we could move again they had left through the East Gate. No point going after them, they would have immobilised us again. But Brückner remembered the telescope in the lookout post at the top of the Haspelmath Tower. That's where he went and he is keeping in contact with me via a walkie-talkie.'

'Good work,' said Lenau, realising his men had done the best they could in the circumstances. 'Keep me informed.'

'Will do.'

After Lenau put the phone back in its cradle, his hand automatically reached for a biro. The pad in front of him was covered in doodles. Some people need to go for a walk to think. With him it was doodling. Aimlessly doodling patterns on a piece of paper. It had always been that way, for as long as he could remember. He needed to think of a way to take the children back to Hamelin. God knows what could happen to them if he didn't.

A little later, he was on his way to the shooting range.

'Look who's come to call. If it isn't Inspector Klaus Lenau.' The jovial voice, greeting Lenau in the long, low building behind the barracks at a local army base, belonged to Sergeant Oscar Stahr. The shooting instructor was a rotund shortish man with cropped hair and a shiny round face.

Lenau grinned. '*Salve*, Oscar. How are you?'

'Better for seeing you here. It's been a while.'

'I know. A practice session is long overdue. I just don't often have the time. Actually, I've come to ask you something. The ear defenders we use when shooting, would you lend me a few?'

The other man thought for a moment. 'It depends how many you need.'

'About ten.'

'Ten! That many? What do you need them for?'

'It's a long story and I need them urgently.'

'It's a big ask. There's always a shortage of ear defenders. I can lend you six and you could stuff weapon cleaning wads wrapped around a 38-shell in your ears. That's what we do here. It does the trick. You won't be able to hear anything.'

'Just what we need. I owe you one, Oscar.'

They agreed to have a beer together soon. Then Lenau put the ear defenders in the boot of his BMW and drove towards the Haspelmath Tower.

'Are you all right, Chief?' Stefan Brückner asked when Lenau appeared, panting, in the lookout post at the top of the tower, after running all the way up the stairs a short while later.

'Just give me a moment. Can you still see the children?'

'You should be able to see them for yourself.' Brückner showed him how to use the telescope.

When Lenau scanned the area through the lens, he saw a line of small figures slowly moving along the main road out of Hamelin.

'Right,' said Lenau, 'now we know where they are, you can come down with me. I need men and vans to get there before we lose sight of them.'

'What about–'

'The whistling? I might have a solution for that. Come on, let's go.'

As the children walked towards them, Lenau and his men stood side by side across the road. Waiting. All wore ear defenders. The children halted. Hesitated. Then, as they eyed each other warily, the girl called Katrin shaped her lips into a whistle. Others followed her example, but Lenau didn't hear a sound. Neither did his men. Not one of them froze. Calmly, they walked towards the children, grabbed hold of them and led them towards the waiting vans. Some of the older children tried to escape, but they too were rounded up and taken back to Hamelin.

On the following Thursday morning, Lenau was told Commissioner Braun wanted to see him in his office.

'Ah, Lenau. Sit down, we have a matter of importance to discuss.' Lenau took the seat opposite his superior, underwhelmed by the pomposity of "a matter of importance". 'What's happening with the children since their return to hospital?'

Lenau was surprised at his superior's concern about the children. 'They're still at the hospital. My men are keeping an eye on the situation. They're wearing ear defenders, just in case. The children are being well looked after and have started to learn German. It's amazing how quickly they are picking it up.'

Braun cleared his throat. 'I was asking because during a special council meeting last night it was decided to move the children into the old orphanage, so they can–'

Lenau interrupted. 'The old orphanage? The same one you yourself called "a crumbling old building, unfit for purpose", if I remember correctly?'

'If you let me finish, you'll see why it's the best solution for now. The only solution, in fact. They can't stay in the hospital basement forever. Neither are there enough families to adopt or care for them, according to social services.'

'Not in Hamelin perhaps, but surely if we contacted social services throughout Lower-Saxony, or even the whole of the *Bundesrepublik*–'

'If these were normal children, yes. But they aren't, are they? There is something truly disturbing about them. You know that as well as I do. That's why we don't want to send them to families all over the country.'

'They seem to have had some traumatic experience,' Lenau admitted, 'but surely with some form of therapy...'

'Precisely. If you hadn't constantly interrupted me, I would have told you that we're already onto it. The children have been assessed by Doctor Wagner. You remember her? She was at our little dinner party.'

Lenau nodded, to avoid interrupting Braun again.

'Well, she concluded that the children suffer from something called shared delusional disorder. They told her that they lived here in Hamelin at another time, when a travelling musician came to town and took them to the mountains. According to them, they fell asleep in a cave and woke up just before they appeared in our city about ten days ago.'

Lenau was for once too stunned to react.

'You can see how delusional that is,' Braun continued, 'thinking they are the lost children from a fairy tale akin to the old Pied Piper story. But something good came out of the meeting last night. Doctor Wagner offered to take charge of the children and the council approved her proposal for a new psychiatric clinic at the Koppenberg. It'll take no longer than a year to build, I was told. In the meantime, the old orphanage will house the children. I believe it's being cleaned and furnished today, so they can move in tomorrow or the day after.'

Having visited the old orphanage as part of his job, Lenau couldn't help but feel sorry for the little strays.

'Was there anything else?' Braun asked after he had started to shuffle through the papers on his desk.

Lenau still hadn't moved. 'No, sir.'

'Then that'll be all, inspector.'

EIGHT

2011

On their second day in the Black Forest, Peter and Erika set out on an eighteen kilometre hike from the little village of Schluchsee, along the lake of the same name. After a short stretch, they crossed the railway bridge, which separated Lake Schluchsee from a smaller lake. Heading past a boat rental place, they climbed a natural path to the scenic Amalienruhe area. As they continued along the shoreline, small groups of other hikers in sturdy boots, carrying small rucksacks, called brief greetings as they passed. Following the trail along quiet wooded tracks and lakeside paths they arrived at the Unterlingenhof restaurant with its sunny lawns, children's play areas and farm animals.

The restaurant itself looked like an upscaled version of a Swiss cuckoo clock. It was busy and hard to find available seats outdoors amongst other hikers, who were enjoying the sun, fresh mountain air and a spectacular view over the lake. The walk had made the couple hungry, so they squeezed onto an available table and ordered soup, bread and a selection of cheeses and sliced Black Forest ham.

'When we're back in Hamelin we should try to find out

more about your patients,' said Peter, taking small sips of his hot chocolate in an effort not to burn his throat.

'We?' Erika blew on hers to cool the scalding liquid.

'Yes. I've been thinking a lot about what Helga Dietz told you and the things we discussed earlier. All those unexplained questions. Why lock those patients up? Why keep them separated? Why give them unlisted medication? Were all those deaths caused by the medication, or not? But the first question that springs to mind is: who are these people? How long have they been there, and what should we make of what Katrin told Helga about her previous life on a farm, in another era?'

'That could be the delusion speaking.'

'Is that what you believe?'

'I don't know what to believe.'

Both were momentarily distracted by the arrival of a family, with a gaggle of young children, chasing each other with wide grinning faces until, with great shouts and whoops of joy, they discovered the children's play area and farm animals and ran off in that direction.

Once they'd gone, Peter continued their conversation.

'What do you make of Helga's theory that they all remember and confuse a past life with their present one?'

'Really, I've no idea.'

'But don't you want to know? Don't you want to find the answers to all those questions you have?'

'I do. But I wouldn't know where to start. More importantly, I don't want to lose my job. Which I might, if they catch me sniffing around the place. Look what happened to Helga. Already, they think I ask too many questions.'

'That's why it should be me who does the "sniffing around", as you call it. Not at the klinik, but on the internet and in the archives of the *DeWeZet* to start with. Although, perhaps you should talk to Katrin. See what you can find out from her.'

'I've been instructed not to believe any of the stories patients are telling us, because they're part of their mental illness.'

'The question is, in whose interest is it that you don't believe this patient? Just keep an open mind. That's all.'

They finished their lunch and resumed their hike, circling the bay at the widest point of the Black Forest lake. Trudging back past the hut belonging to the local fishing club, they arrived at the jetty for the ferry, the *MS Schluchsee*. They had decided to cover the last stretch of the journey by boat. Standing at the railing, while a fine spray settled on her face, Erika gazed at the trees on the bank trailing leafy branches in the water, the sun sparkling on gently lapping waves and small dinghies cruising in the far distance.

'We should do this more often,' she said.

Peter agreed.

By the time they left the ferry and headed towards their guest house, the sun was going down. Soon it would be dark.

1978

Katrin lay on a thin mattress, acutely aware of the springs of her iron bed. In an attempt to find a more comfortable position, she turned onto her other side. The bed made a terrible creaking sound. She tried to think of the good things that had happened today, to take her mind off the bad ones. The warm hug one of the nurses in the hospital had given her before their departure. The wooden cross on the wall with the familiar figure of Lord Jesus in the long room where they'd eaten their evening meal: long, doughy, slippery threads with tomato sauce and meatballs. Her new nightdress with its pattern of tiny daisies on a pale blue background was another good thing. Never had she worn anything that felt so soft against her skin.

After that she ran out of good things and simply relived what had happened that day, once they had left the hospital. After a short drive, the coach had passed through a gate, followed a driveway and stopped in front of a large, grey-brick building. Some of the windows were gaping holes. Katrin stared up at them.

'Don't worry. That part of the building won't be used during your stay,' said Nurse Domin, who, along with the social workers, was in charge of the children.

Everyone trooped towards the arched gate and the small, narrow door within. Through this door they stepped into a courtyard, a dismal place where no sunlight reached, its walls slimy, green and strangled by ivy. Splatters of bird poo covered a wrought-iron table and chairs. The ornamental lantern, near a partially disintegrated staircase along one outside wall, had smashed panes.

A door opened from within and moments later they stood in a brightly lit hallway where they were received by three stern-looking women in brown dresses and short brown veils. The one who had been introduced to them as Sister Cordula took them upstairs to a large room with cracked windows, where a row of beds lined the wall. The walls were bare and the floor was mud-coloured linoleum. In the hospital they had each been given a bundle of clothes, which were stored here in a large chest with many drawers, one for each child. A corner of the ceiling by Katrin's bed was damp and a metal bucket had been placed underneath it.

She looked around, searching for Trude, who was nowhere to be seen. Katrin panicked and dived towards the door, but before she could reach it, Sister Cordula grabbed her by her upper arm and spoke sharply. Nurse Domin approached and asked Katrin what was wrong.

'My sister. She's not here.' The nun's fingers clamped down harder into Katrin's flesh.

The women exchanged a few words. It seemed to Katrin that Nurse Domin was trying to put her case to the nun, but it made no difference.

'Trude is assigned to another dormitory, not far from here. It's the room next to yours,' Nurse Domin told Katrin.

'Why can't I sleep in the same room?'

'They've separated you into age groups. You're with the older girls, Trude is with the younger ones.'

Sister Cordula had clapped her hands then and told the children to go downstairs. Dry-eyed, but feeling as if a heavy stone had lodged in her chest, Katrin had done as she was told.

Now, Katrin shifted in her new bed. She had never slept without her sibling. Even in the hospital, Trude had slept beside her.

At the other end of the room, the door quietly opened. Katrin didn't turn around to look, to avoid the creaking of her bedsprings. Someone tiptoed through the dormitory, stopping at each bed. Katrin thought it might be Sister Cordula come to check if they were asleep. She closed her eyes, assuming deep regular breaths. Then her blankets were lifted.

'Budge up.'

Katrin rolled onto her other side and faced her sister.

'I couldn't sleep,' Trude whispered.

'Me neither.'

Not much later, arms and legs entwined, both were fast asleep.

2011

After their return from the Black Forest, on her first morning back at work, Erika found Katrin still asleep at nine thirty, during her rounds. She briefly thought about waking her up, then decided to leave it. Perhaps Katrin had had a bad night's sleep and needed this. Busy with other patients, other tasks, she didn't think of it again until quarter to twelve, when she went back.

The shape in the bed hadn't moved. Something was clearly wrong. Perhaps Katrin was ill. Erika gently shook the woman's shoulder. 'Katrin? It's Nurse Erika. Wake up, it's nearly midday. If you snooze the day away, you won't be able to sleep tonight.'

It was a while before a groggy Katrin responded. She sat up and looked at Erika as if she'd never seen her before. Erika gave her a glass of water, then sat on the edge of her patient's bed.

'Do you need my help to have a shower and get dressed? You look a bit peaky. How are you feeling?'

In truth, Erika thought Katrin looked dreadful. Her face was pale and puffy, as if she hadn't been in the fresh air for a long time.

'I can have a shower and get dressed by myself.'

'Okay, you do that, while I get you your breakfast and some strong coffee.'

When Erika returned, she found Katrin still in her pyjamas sitting on her bed, staring, with a vacant look on her face. Erika wheeled the trolley towards the table and put out the breakfast rolls and a pot of coffee.

'Perhaps you should have some breakfast before you shower.' Erika watched as Katrin slowly and unsteadily stood and crossed the room. I have to get some food in her, before I give her her medication, Erika thought. But what if Helga Dietz had been right? If the medication itself had turned her into this zombie, then giving her the medicine would make it worse. Katrin took a long time over the coffee and jam roll, while Erika struggled to decide whether she should give Katrin the medicine or not.

Afterwards, Erika cleared breakfast away, leaving the cocktail of pills on the table. Another glance at Katrin did it. Erika took the pills into the en suite bathroom and flushed them down the toilet. She re-entered the room as if nothing had happened. As if what she had just done could not cost her her job. She told Katrin she'd be back soon, as she wheeled the trolley from the room. But not until they'd exchanged a brief look of understanding.

1978

A pale April sun shone through narrow, grimy windows at the orphanage, where children's heads were bent over their notebooks and pencils. The only sounds in the classroom were the scratching of chalk on blackboard, sentences scrawled in Sister Magdalena's large hand and the tramping of Sister Antonia's boots as she marched along the rows of wooden benches, halting here and there to correct a child's writing.

Bending over her notebook, Katrin's cheeks were flushed from the effort to copy the words on the blackboard as neatly as she could, then a voice lashed out from behind the teacher's desk. 'Right hand, Katrin!'

And just like that, another memory flashed through Katrin's mind. Her mother punishing her for using her left hand to eat her porridge, or stir the cooking pot, or fling a handful of grains to their chickens. Sometimes, Ma would bind her left hand behind her back so she couldn't use it.

'But why, Ma? Why?' she remembered having sobbed.

'Because left-handed children are devil's spawn. Use your right hand.'

She guiltily took her pencil in her right hand and struggled on.

It was nearly four o'clock. Sister Magdalena took a large leather-bound book from her desk. Printed on the front, in golden letters were the words *German Folk and Fairy Tales*. Once the nun had settled back in her chair, she opened the weighty tome and searched for a story. At the end of the school day, this was the children's reward for good behaviour and being diligent pupils. This was Katrin's favourite part of the day.

'Today,' Sister Magdalena announced, 'I will read you a story about our town. It's called *The Pied Piper of Hamelin*. It's a tale of revenge and mystery.'

She began, but halfway through the story something unexpected happened. It started with looks. Children's heads turned towards each other, exchanging startled glances, followed by a restlessness and a wave of whispers, until Sister Magdalena shut the book with a loud bang and looked disapprovingly over the edge of her spectacles.

'I don't think you deserve to hear a story today,' she said. The effect was complete silence. After a short break, the nun opened the book again, searching for the page.

'One more disruption and we'll have no more stories. Is that clear?'

'Yes, sister,' muttered the chorus of children.

'Good. Arms crossed, eyes straight ahead. Not a whisper.'

The story was read to the end in total silence.

Katrin put her hand up.

'Yes, Katrin?'

'Sister, no rats went and drowned themselves in the river when the stranger came to town.'

Sister Magdalena looked too stunned to have an answer ready. Instead, she addressed another girl who had put up her hand. 'Yes, Inga?'

'Sister, our parents weren't in church when we followed the stranger out of the town. They watched us walking by, but they couldn't–'

'Sister, the man didn't wear yellow and red, like it said in the story. He wore many other colours too–'

'Sister, it wasn't a lame boy who couldn't keep up. It was a lame girl and she could keep up. It was our Katrin,' Trude spoke up.

'Sister–'

'Enough!' Sister Magdalena, usually a model of composure, furiously threw the book down. In the silence that followed, she fumed. 'No more stories. You're behaving like a horde of vandals. You need to be taught some discipline. Tomorrow, Saturday, you will scrub every floor and clean every window in this place. Do you hear me?'

'Yes, sister,' the chorus murmured meekly.

'Class dismissed.'

The children had now been in the orphanage just over four months. During that time, they had grown accustomed to the daily routine and learnt modern German within the first few weeks.

Days were long and busy. Woken up at six thirty, they were expected to be down for breakfast at seven. At seven thirty, those who had kitchen duty would clear tables and wash up. Lessons started at eight and lasted until four in the afternoon. After a half-hour tea break, supervised by nuns, Katrin and the others cleaned bathrooms, bedrooms and common rooms, as well as peeling potatoes, washing and scrubbing vegetables and setting tables for dinner. Evenings were reserved for homework and Bible studies, unless Doctor Wagner, who visited some weeknights, called to have a one-to-one chat. Bedtime was at eight for the youngest, half past eight for the others. By that time most of the children were too tired to wonder why they were here instead of being with their parents in their own homes.

Gradually, memories of their former lives had returned. The youngest would wake at night and cry for their mothers. Katrin and Trude weren't amongst them. In Katrin's bed, they whispered in their native language about life before waking up in the mountain. Katrin told her sister to keep the memories alive, to remember the faces of their parents, the names of their neighbours, the stories Father told, the songs Mother had taught them, the games they had played and the ways they had celebrated the seasons by bringing home the fruits of nature: windfall apples and plums in autumn, nuts in winter, beetroot and carrots in spring, cherries and berries in summer.

'We can't just forget all that. Or deny that other life ever existed. That's what she wants. She thinks we made it all up.'

'She?' Trude asked.

'That doctor. She didn't believe me when I told her about the time before we left the mountain. She smiles a lot and speaks as if she's your friend, but I don't trust her.' Katrin lay wide-eyed beside her sister, thinking. After a while, she whispered the question that burned foremost on her lips.

'Trude – d'you think we'll ever get back home?'

There was no answer. Trude was fast asleep.

NINE

2011

A few days after flushing Katrin's medication, Erika heard loud voices arguing in Katrin's room. The door was ajar. She found Katrin half undressed and looking defiant, with a trainee nurse called Steffi. Items of clothing were scattered all over the floor.

'What's going on?'

'I brought Katrin some new clothes to try on,' Steffi explained. 'Hers need replacing, they're faded and frayed.'

'New?' Katrin's voice was steeped in scorn. She turned towards Erika. 'Do these look new to you?'

Erika didn't answer immediately, but bent forward to give Steffi a hand in gathering the offending garments from the floor and folding them into a neat pile.

She tried to placate Katrin. 'They're not that bad. They're a lot newer than what you're wearing at the moment. The klinik might not have the means to dress you all in new clothes. I'm sure they're doing the best they can.'

'It's not so much that they're second-hand,' said Katrin. 'It's the kind of clothes. Look at them and tell me what they say to you.'

Erika saw baggy jogging bottoms, jeans with elasticated

waists, sweatshirts and hoodies. They said comfortable like pyjamas for the patient, easy to wash and dry for staff.

When Erika didn't answer straight away, Katrin went on.

'Look at those washed-out colours: grey, navy, faded black, pale blue. It tells me I'm not there. I'm invisible. Not worthy of colourful clothes. And as for the shapes, these could be for men or women, they're genderless. Do these clothes say feminine to you? No. There's not a skirt or dress amongst them.'

Erika agreed but kept that to herself. 'Would you like me to have a word with Nurse Bauer? Perhaps we could find you something else to wear,' she offered.

'Don't bother. That woman hates me. She thinks I'm a troublemaker and she'll probably say that what's good enough for the others is good enough for me. I've often asked if I could have different clothes, but she has always conveniently ignored it.'

'For now, we'll take these away,' said Erika. She lifted the bundle of clothes and put them on the trolley, then instructed Steffi to wheel the trolley from the room.

'I'll come back later, after I've spoken to Nurse Bauer.' With a last glance at Katrin scowling in her underwear, Erika closed the door behind her.

A couple of hours later Erika was back in Katrin's room, trying not to look pleased with herself. For the moment she put off sharing her good news and instead pointed at the weighty tome in Katrin's lap.

'What are you reading?'
'*Buddenbrooks* by Thomas Mann.'
'Any good?'
'Better than most of the books here. All they have are dreary romances and a few classics.'

'What sort of books would you like to read?'

'Not fiction. I'd love to read about the real world, and I'd love to read about time travel.'

'Time travel *is* fiction. It's not part of the real world.'

'Isn't it?'

Words, thrown down like a gauntlet, were accompanied by a hard and lengthy stare. Ever since I've reduced her medication, thought Erika, she has grown more awake. More rebellious, too. Had it been a good idea or not? Only time would tell.

'I came to bring you the good news. Nurse Bauer has agreed to let you have more colourful, feminine clothes.'

Instantly, Katrin's expression brightened and she sounded as excited as a teenager. 'How did you work that miracle?'

'I offered to go and scour the second-hand clothes shops myself, in my own time. She said that as long as I stayed within budget, it would be okay.'

What she didn't tell Katrin was that it had taken much persuading.

'We already have to spend more on Katrin than on other patients,' was Bauer's first reaction. 'She needs a pair of new orthopaedic shoes every few years because of her leg. Have you any idea how much those cost?'

Katrin sounded more than grateful. 'You'd do that for me?'

'It's no problem. I like browsing the shops.'

For one fleeting moment a shadow passed over Katrin's face. 'I wish I could come with you.'

Erika inwardly cursed her own tactlessness. 'Tell me about the kind of skirts or dresses I should be looking for,' she said, to cheer Katrin up.

1978

Katrin woke in pitch-black darkness and became aware of Trude standing beside her bed.

'I've had an accident. Can I sleep in your bed?' the younger of the sisters whispered.

'What accident?' muttered Katrin, barely awake.

When her sister didn't answer, the nature of Trude's "accident" dawned on her and she got up, crept from the room into Trude's, and lifted her sister's bedcover to survey the damage, wet and smelly.

'We should hide the bottom sheet,' she told Trude, who had followed her. They didn't know what had happened to a little boy who'd wet his bed the week before, but had heard his sobs and seen his tear-streaked face. Together, they stripped the sheet from the bed and rolled it into a tight bundle.

'Where to?' Trude whispered.

Katrin indicated to follow her. She had an idea. On the landing of their floor was a deep airing cupboard. The warmth of the boiler might dry the soaked sheet. Tomorrow, she would find an opportunity to transfer the dried sheet to the laundry room. Trude held the cupboard door open as Katrin stuffed the sheet as far behind the boiler as she could. They spent the rest of the night in Katrin's bed, asleep.

All did not go to plan. One of the nuns caught a whiff of something unpleasant when she opened the airing cupboard the next day and discovered the offending sheet. At teatime, after classes had finished, Sister Cordula entered the common room and called Trude away. They must have discovered who the bed with the missing sheet belonged to. At the other end of the room, Katrin got up slowly and stared after her sister, who was heard to whimper like a wounded animal.

'Sit down, Katrin,' Sister Antonia, who was in charge of their teatime break said curtly.

Katrin ignored her.

The nun approached. 'I said: sit down.' She tried to push Katrin down onto her seat.

Katrin stayed upright, not so much aware of the nun as of the fireball of fury in her chest, seeking a way out. And out it came in a way she neither consciously chose nor could control.

When the other children heard her whistling, they automatically joined in, while Sister Antonia froze.

Katrin tried not to think of her sore, dry throat, or the near impossibility of swallowing. She attempted to ignore the yearning in her hollow stomach, too. But it was no good. Visions of tall glasses filled to the brim with cool, refreshing water and chunks of freshly baked bread thickly spread with creamy butter filled her mind. She had no idea how long she had been here. Her head hurt and fear of being forgotten and left locked in this coal cellar gnawed at her. Earlier, she had heard a scuttling near the pile of coal she sat on, which had shocked her into jumping up and peering petrified into the darkness, looking for vermin.

Their walk-out from the orphanage had failed miserably when all doors and gates proved to be locked. As the main culprit, Katrin was taken to the coal cellar, "to ask God for forgiveness and reflect on your sins". Sister Cordula had called her a "wicked, wicked girl" as she had roughly pushed her inside and locked the door behind her, hours ago.

Hours or days? She had fallen asleep here on this coal heap, exhausted from crying and banging on the door and calling out. Just above her head was an iron grate providing some daylight and as the hours passed Katrin noticed how daylight made way for the darkness of night and how at last the light returned.

A flicker of hope emerged when she became aware of voices through the grate above. She scrambled up and began to climb the coal heap, to call for help through the grate. This was anything but easy as the neatly stacked coals shifted and rolled away with every move she made. When she lost her balance a few times, the coal dust made her dress filthy. Another reason for the nuns to punish her.

After arriving on top of the heap she brought her face close to the grate and took a deep breath to call out. But thirst had made her throat too dry to utter a cry. What pitiable sound emerged was too feeble to reach the two people standing in the garden near the grate. She recognised the social worker, Miss Sachs, but Katrin had never seen the man. Miss Sachs and the man were smoking cigarettes while in deep conversation. She tried repeatedly to attract their attention, but was unsuccessful.

'I don't know what to do,' Katrin heard the woman say. 'Mother Superior was adamant. The nuns don't want to look after these children much longer. They're scared after yesterday's incident. They think the children are possessed. Dangerous even.'

'If they are dangerous, they should not be placed in families or kept at an orphanage,' the man replied. 'This time, luckily doors and gates were locked. God knows what they'd do if they were left to roam the streets.'

'We can't keep them locked away forever, Thomas.'

'Perhaps it's for the best. Until we find out what's wrong with them. There's no doubt there's *something* wrong. Normal children don't proclaim they're born in the thirteenth century and were spirited away by a pipe-playing stranger, to resurface in the twentieth century. Not even those with a lot of imagination.'

'Where could they go? The nuns want to get rid of them sooner rather than later.'

'I can think of a perfect solution. But the children would have to stay here a little longer.'

'How much longer?'

'A year, perhaps.'

'A year?!'

'Possibly less.'

Christa Sachs dropped her cigarette butt on the ground and stamped on it. 'Well, aren't you going to tell me?'

'The council has finally given the go-ahead to build a new psychiatric hospital, something Claudia has wanted for years. Her conclusion, after assessing these children, is that they belong in such an institution. At least until they have been treated and cured.'

The social worker was about to speak, but the man, Thomas, put his hand on her mouth. Then he bent forward and kissed her, while Katrin watched through the grate. The kiss seemed to go on forever. Finally, they untangled.

'Now have I convinced you that this is the best solution?' said the man.

'Is that why you kissed me? So I'll put my signature on a document that will transfer the children from the care of social services into the care of mental health services or, in other words, your wife?'

'Of course not. You know how I feel about you. Come here and I'll show you again.'

More kissing. Katrin had seen and heard enough, though much about the adult conversation remained unclear to her. As she descended from the coal heap, there was the sound of a key being turned in the lock. The door opened.

'If you behave yourself, you can come out now,' a voice called out.

2011

The Tuesday after the clothes incident was Erika's day off and after breakfast she went out on her mission. Her budget of thirty euros wasn't much, but as she approached the slightly run-down end of town where the charity shops nestled together, she felt confident and optimistic. Easy-peasy, she thought. An hour or two, max. Then I'll treat myself to coffee and a freshly-baked pastry at Mensing's.

Erika had not exaggerated when she told Katrin she liked browsing the shops, especially vintage shops. Before she and Peter moved into their flat, they'd lived in separate student accommodation and hardly owned a scrap of furniture. Neither had much money to spend. What Erika did have was an eye for textures, patterns and quirky details, and the ability to envisage the potential in a bargain. Her style wasn't so much modern minimalist as carefree bohemian.

Two hours later, and the result of her combing through all the dresses and skirts in every shop she visited was meagre. She had asked to put one dress on hold in one of the shops, but it was neither floaty nor brightly patterned. She sighed, ready to give up, then approached the sales assistant behind the cash desk counter.

'I was hoping to find a dress or a skirt for a friend. Something colourful, with a wide skirt and a floral pattern perhaps. I've been everywhere, but I haven't found anything yet.'

'Have you tried H&M?'

'I'm on a really low budget, second-hand shops only.'

'Okay, well, how about the "First Friday of the Month jumble sale"? You can pick up some gorgeous garments there for very little. I've often done so myself. It's amazing what people throw out that's still nearly new. It's this Friday if you're interested. The earlier you go, the better.'

The shop assistant gave her the address: St Johannis Church near Ohrberg Park.

Erika swapped her Friday morning shift with a colleague and arrived at work on Saturday morning carrying two bags bulging with clothes. As soon as her work permitted, she took these to Katrin, whom she found kneeling in front of her bed, her folded hands lightly resting on the cover, her lips moving without making a sound.

'Oh. I'm sorry,' Erika said, feeling awkward having disturbed her patient at prayer. 'Shall I come back later?'

'No need. I've finished.' Katrin straightened and, turning towards Erika, noticed the bags. 'Are those for me?'

'I hope you like my choices. Why don't you try them on?'

'May I?' Katrin took the bags from Erika and emptied the contents onto her bed. A rich green top spilled out, followed by a full-length skirt with a delicate floral pattern, an ethnic dress and a stripy, hand-knitted cardigan. Erika had never seen Katrin so delighted, as she hugged the fabrics against her chest.

For the next half-hour, Erika felt an increasing glow of satisfaction as she watched a beaming Katrin emerge from her bathroom, each time modelling a new outfit, every one a perfect fit. It didn't matter to Erika that she'd had to dip into her own pocket; Katrin's smiles were ample repayment.

Katrin studied the handcrafted cardigan. 'I would love to knit something like this. Or a jumper. I think I could, it can't be that hard.'

'I'm not sure you'd be allowed to handle knitting needles.

They're quite sharp,' Erika sounded regretful as Katrin's expression hardened.

'What do they think I'd do with them?' she said bitterly. 'Kill myself? Attack one of the nurses? Gouge someone's eye out?' They both knew that was precisely what "they" would think she'd do. 'Now that it's getting too cold to do any work in the garden, I get bored. I don't always feel like reading, drawing, painting or watching television, which is how I spend my days at the moment. It would be good to do something else, something with my hands.'

Erika didn't reply, but the pencils on the table had given her an idea.

Erika waited for the right moment to approach Nurse Bauer with her request. The moment arrived when, both having finished their shifts at the same time, Erika offered to drive the senior nurse home. It was getting dark outside on a rainy November afternoon.

Nurse Bauer had complained that she would get drenched on her walk to the bus stop. Even her sturdy umbrella would not prevent her getting soaked. She was happy to accept Erika's offer, smiling, even.

Erika took that as her cue. 'My niece, at her school, is learning to knit with these chunky wooden knitting needles, specially designed for young children. They're round at the top, not sharp at all. If Katrin is allowed to handle pencils, she should be able to use these wooden knitting needles too, without causing any accidents.'

'If we gave Katrin these needles, we would have to give them to everyone,' Nurse Bauer replied. 'Then we would have to give them wool as well. Who'd pay for all that? At every staff meeting I'm told to keep costs down.'

Erika wasn't put off that easily.

'Katrin is the only patient who has asked to learn to knit. That doesn't mean the others want to. In my family, we're always knitting or crocheting. It won't be hard to find a pair of those needles and some wool – if not amongst my stuff, then at my sister's or parents' place.'

'And who would take the time to teach her? You, I suppose.' She didn't wait for Erika's answer, but went on. 'In your own time then. You can't neglect your work for one patient.'

They drove on without further conversation, both aware that Erika needed to concentrate on steering them safely through the rain. On arrival at Nurse Bauer's address, she thanked Erika for the lift. 'You seem very fond of Katrin. First the clothes, now the knitting needles. Whatever will you do next to make her happy?'

The remark stung and left Erika feeling alternately hot and cold. Had she been too obviously singling out Katrin? She made a mental note to spend equal time with other patients, smiled and shrugged. 'I feel sorry for her, she's lost her sister. They were close, I was told.'

'Yes, that was unfortunate. But most of our patients have no siblings. They just get on with it.'

If "getting on with it" means sleepwalking through the day, drugged to the gills, instead of living, then I suppose they do get on with it, Erika thought.

'Enjoy your evening,' she said aloud.

'You too. I'll see you in the morning.'

"*If you want answers, talk to Katrin,*" Helga Dietz had told Erika. "*Get as much information out of her as you can: names, dates, places,*" Peter had said.

With that in mind, the next day Erika went to Katrin's room as soon as her morning shift ended. When Erika, seated at the table, put a pair of wooden knitting needles and various balls of wool in front of her, Katrin's face lit up as she sat down beside her.

'I know you'd like to knit a cardigan or a jumper, but how about a scarf to start with? You cast on a row of stitches, you keep going until it's the length you want, then you cast off. Today I'll teach you the two basic stitches.'

Katrin picked a colour and Erika showed her how to cast on.

'Not too tight, and not too loose either.'

It didn't take long for Katrin to get the hang of it.

'How long have you been here?' Erika asked lightly when her patient had established a confident rhythm.

'Nearly thirty-one years,' Katrin kept her eyes on her knitting.

'And where did you live before you came to the Koppenberg?'

'In the old orphanage. It was more than just old, though.' A grimace of disgust.

'What do you mean?'

'Some of the building had collapsed. We stayed in the only part that was not too dangerous. When we were in the hospital, they didn't know what to do with us, so that's why we stayed at the orphanage until the Koppenberg Klinik was built. It was supposed to be only for a year, but it was nearly two.'

Until now, Erika had only spoken with Katrin to exchange practicalities. She was surprised how articulate the woman was.

'Who looked after you while you were there?'

'Sister Cordula, Sister Magdalena, Sister Antonia and some other sisters whose names I can't remember.'

'Sisters? Were they nuns?'

'Yes, nuns, very strict ones. Those of us who were too slow, spoke up or wet the bed at night were severely punished.'

Erika sensed talking about that time brought back painful memories, so instead of pursuing the matter she reverted to the scarf in the making. 'That's coming along nicely. Which colour would you like to try next?'

Before going home, Erika took her mobile phone from her locker and, making sure no one was within hearing distance, tapped Peter's work number. He responded after what seemed an eternity.

'I found out where Katrin and the others stayed before they were taken to the Koppenberg. It's a place she called the old orphanage. I've never heard of it. You?'

'Vaguely. I doubt it still exists.'

'Katrin told me parts of the building had collapsed. It was probably demolished after the children left. You might be able to find articles or photos, though. How are you getting on?'

'Not at all, is the simple answer. I dug up some old editions of the *DeWeZet* from the years before the Koppenberg Klinik was built, but I haven't found anything yet about the appearance of a large group of unaccompanied children.'

'That's odd. You'd have thought that would've made the front page in a town like Hamelin where nothing ever happens. Did you do a Google search?'

'Of course, and I discovered the city's archives are also online, so there's no need for me to go there in person. But I haven't finished with the *DeWeZet* editions of the late seventies yet. It's time-consuming and so is going through the city archives.'

'I could ask Katrin for more information, but too many questions at one time might upset her. Any idea what I should ask her next?'

'Names of people she remembers from the time before the Koppenberg Klinik would be helpful.'

When Erika returned the next day, Katrin triumphantly held up her knitting, to show the colours and the length.

'It's finished.'

'Great.' Erika smiled, cleared breakfast away and put a couple of much-thumbed knitting magazines on the table. 'I'll come back this afternoon and show you how to cast off. Meantime, you could go through these, to see if you can find your next project.'

Just after three o'clock, Erika's shift finished and Katrin showed her the pattern of a jumper she had chosen.

'It's only straight pieces, like the scarf, and when you sew them together it's a jumper. I'd like to try that next.'

'Good choice.' Erika showed her how to cast off, and while their hands were busy, she resumed her questioning. 'Yesterday you mentioned you were in a hospital before you were taken to the orphanage. How did you get there?'

'One of the boys got hit by a car. He was badly injured. When they took him to the hospital we went along too.'

'Who took him there?'

'I think it was the police, but I can't remember exactly.'

'Do you remember which hospital it was?'

'No. Why do you need to know?'

Erika considered for a moment what to tell Katrin and what to keep quiet about, and decided to be straight with her.

'It's unusual for patients to stay as long in a psychiatric clinic as you and the others here in this unit have. Perhaps if I knew a little more about your life before the Koppenberg, I could understand it better. There's very little information in your files.'

'What do you want to know?'

'The name of that hospital, for instance, plus the name of the order the sisters in the orphanage belonged to, and any other names. Who decided you should be taken to the orphanage? Was it Doctor Wagner?'

'I don't know. My memories of that time are vague. I was only eight and most of the time I didn't understand what was going on.'

Erika was about to leave, when Katrin called her back.

'Wait. I might have something.' Kneeling at the foot of her bed she reached underneath it and pulled out a cardboard shoebox, which she placed on the table. When the lid was removed Erika saw it was filled with birthday cards, papers, a notebook and a photo. It's a memory box, she thought while Katrin rummaged, then held up a piece of paper with the sketch of a woman's head. It was a child's drawing, nothing like Katrin's current artwork. Underneath it, in pencil, was the name of the sitter.

Nurse Domin.

TEN

On a Saturday morning in October, Peter, alone in their apartment after Erika left for work, sat at his desk in their bedroom and tried to find an online map of Hamelin from the seventies, showing where the orphanage Erika had mentioned was situated.

The sound of a key being turned in the front door interrupted his search. Coming out of the bedroom he found Berndt, Erika's father, wiping his shoes on the doormat.

Peter liked Erika's father. When he and Erika had first rented the flat, they'd loved it for the central location, but it had been badly neglected. Berndt had worked tirelessly along with the couple to strip layers of peeling wallpaper and remove the mouldy carpeting. When a near-perfect wooden floor underneath was discovered, he had helped Peter to restore it, while Erika, who expected to spend her working life in a white sterile interior, had painted the bathroom walls turquoise, the kitchen a lemony yellow, the living room burnt orange and the bedroom a contrasting pale pink and dark green.

'Erika not at home?' Berndt asked after exchanging greetings.

'She's at work until three today. Have you come to see her?'

'I promised her I'd have a look at your boiler. She said the water wasn't getting hot enough.'

Now Peter noticed the toolbox Berndt carried.

'Yeah, the shower only gets lukewarm and so does the kitchen tap. I'm useless with boilers, but I could make you a coffee while you're at it.'

Berndt put his toolbox on the kitchen table and opened it. 'What about the radiators? Are they hot enough?'

'Yeah, no problem there.'

'Hmm. Could be a faulty diverter valve. Let's see, shall we?'

As Peter switched on the coffee machine, Berndt started to remove the boiler cover. It didn't take him long to confirm that the diverter valve needed replacing.

'It's a common problem with old boilers like these.' Berndt seated himself at the kitchen table, his large hands lifting the steaming coffee mug Peter put in front of him.

'How much will it cost?'

'They're expensive, but I can order one via my company. That'll be cheaper. I'll let you know how much and when I can fit it.'

'Thanks.'

They drank their coffees in companionable silence.

'You've lived in Hamelin more than thirty years, haven't you?' Peter asked.

'All my life. Why?'

'Have you ever come across an old orphanage?'

'Certainly. It was actually *called* "The Old Orphanage". Bit of a haunted house, that was.'

'Oh, yeah?'

'Me and my mates, we went there a few times out of curiosity, to check the place out. It'd been deserted and neglected for years. I don't know why they didn't demolish it sooner. It was a monstrosity, ugly as sin.'

'When was it demolished?'

'Let me think... sometime in the eighties, perhaps.'

'Where exactly was it?'

'Next to the cemetery along Blomberg Street. That made it even spookier at night. One time, Hans, one of our gang, told us about a rumour the building was visited by ghosts at night. He dared us to go with him after midnight and keep watch.'

'And did you?' Peter leant forward. This was an unexpected side to Erika's dad, whom he would have described as a practical and down-to-earth kind of man.

'Oh yes, and so did Gert and Uzo. The four of us agreed to meet in front of Hans' house, an hour after midnight, and to bring our bikes because it was too far to walk. Waiting until after midnight seemed an eternity, but sneaking out wasn't hard. It was during the summer holidays and we were bored stiff, with not much to do. When I got to Hans' place, Uzo was already there. The three of us waited for Gert but he never turned up. Perhaps his parents caught him. In the end we went without him. We left our bikes at the gate and climbed over the fence.'

On the table, Peter's mobile pinged. He ignored it. 'How old were you then?'

'I would have been twelve and so was Uzo. Hans was older, thirteen or fourteen. He was always thinking up adventures and expeditions for us.'

'Did you get inside the building?'

'Yes. The doors were locked but some of the windows were broken and it didn't take long to get in via one of those. We had to be careful though, so as not to get cut by the remaining glass shards in the window frame. It was dark and hard to see where we were going.'

'Didn't you take torches?'

'We did but there's only so much you can see by torchlight. If we hadn't already been there during daylight hours it would have been even harder to find our way around.'

'Weren't you scared?'

'Petrified – and so was Uzo. As we went through the house, I heard him breathing behind me, loud and very fast. When Hans clattered into something, Uzo was the one who screamed. Hans laughed and said he shouldn't be such a baby, but I couldn't blame him for crying out.'

'What about the ghosts? Did you see any?'

'Of course not. I don't believe in ghosts. Not now. Not then.'

'So why did you–'

Berndt chuckled. 'Like I said, we were bored. We longed for adventure.'

Peter felt a sense of anti-climax because he'd believed Berndt had been working up to something. 'So that was it? You spent the night there and nothing happened?'

'That's what I would have said at the time. Because I had no words to describe what I felt while I was in that place, that hulk of a building. I couldn't express it then, neither could I forget. But it stayed with me for a long time, though I tried hard not to think of it.'

'Could you describe it now?' Peter's palms tingled and he itched to make notes. So there was more to the story.

Berndt thought for a moment. 'You know how a room can have a certain atmosphere, right? I hadn't been aware of it during our daytime excursions to that place, but that night I sensed those rooms were filled with an atmosphere of unfathomable sadness. As if everyone who had ever been in those rooms had left their sadness behind. It was almost tangible, like an unseen presence. Sorrow, loss, suffering, it was there, in those rooms. In every room. That's why, later, I was glad when they demolished the place. I knew it hadn't been a happy home for those who stayed there. Quite the opposite.' Abruptly, he changed tack. 'But, what's your interest in the place? Why are you asking me?'

Peter thought it best not to say too much about Erika's patients and their stay in the orphanage. 'Just doing some research for an article.'

Berndt finished his coffee and lifted his toolbox from the table. 'Right, I better leave you to it then. I'm off to the fishmongers. We're having *matjes* herring tonight.'

Peter walked Erika's dad to the front door. 'By the way, do you know who owned the orphanage?'

'The church, I expect. You might be able to look that up on your computer.'

He was right. After a little digging Peter discovered the orphanage had belonged to a convent. The Sisters of Mercy. Mercy, he scoffed, remembering what his prospective father-in-law had told him about the atmosphere in the building.

The convent still existed. They even had a website. He rang their phone number and made an appointment to go and see their administrator the following Monday afternoon.

Peter expected the convent to be a medieval-looking building in a quiet area, bordered by herb gardens, with birdsong and demure choral chanting the only sounds in a tranquil oasis.

Nothing could be further from the truth. In fact, the convent, an unattractive house most likely built in the eighties, was situated smack bang in the middle of town and squeezed between a homeless shelter and a women's refuge. The noise of passing traffic was deafening.

He parked his motorbike and rang the bell. A young nun

with black, curly hair and a dusky complexion let him in and took him to the administrator's office via a narrow passage, cluttered with bicycles and baby buggies. The walls on both sides were covered with noticeboards.

'It must be difficult for you to find peace and quiet to pray with all that noise on your doorstep,' Peter commented.

An amused smile appeared on the sister's face. 'Is that what you think we do all day?'

'Well—'

'You might have noticed the women's refuge and homeless shelter? They are part of the convent. Nowadays it's less about praying, fasting and churchgoing, and more about helping the vulnerable in our city.'

They arrived at the administrator's office and the sister knocked on the door, opened it, and stuck her head around the corner.

'Sister Benedicta? Your two o'clock appointment has arrived.'

A quiet voice answered. 'Thank you, sister. Show him in, please.'

The office was small and impersonal, with just enough room for a massive desk, a printer and a filing cabinet. A slim wooden crucifix with a bronze figure of Christ adorned the wall Peter faced, but there were no plants, photographs or personal knickknacks.

Sister Benedicta, wedged behind the desk, got up, offered Peter a limp handshake and invited him to take the seat opposite. Brittle is the word to describe her, Peter thought, all nerves and no blood. Like a dandelion after its bloom, blow and she might float away. Her eyes darted restlessly behind gold-rimmed spectacles, but most of the time she avoided looking directly at him. Instead, she busied herself with some papers, which she repeatedly picked up and put in a different place, or the same place, on the scrupulously organised desk.

'How may I help?' Her thin, colourless lips hardly moved when she spoke.

On the phone, Peter had already told her he was a journalist, writing for the *DeWeZet*, and asked if he might interview her for an article. She'd reluctantly agreed.

'The article is about children in care,' he explained. 'I've interviewed social workers and now I'd like to hear your view on the matter.' That was a lie, but it made his story more believable. 'Your convent owned the former orphanage, didn't it?'

'Yes, but that was a long time ago. The orphanage doesn't exist anymore. Such children are now looked after by social services.'

'I know, but I'll be writing about children in care throughout the years, not just in the present day. When exactly was the orphanage demolished?'

'In 1980.'

'My source told me that until 1979, a group of young children lived there and were cared for by your order.'

'I'm afraid your source is mistaken. The orphanage had been deserted since the early seventies until it was finally torn down in 1980.'

'Could you have a quick look in your files for me? Perhaps–'

'Certainly.' She went through the motions of typing and clicking on the desktop computer while Peter, who could not see the screen, waited.

'No. There's nothing here about a group of young children in the orphanage in the late seventies,' the nun concluded with a polite smile.

Peter went through a few more questions to give the impression he really was writing about children in care throughout the decades.

'Does the name Domin mean anything to you?' he asked, finally. 'I'm looking for a Nurse Domin.'

Sister Benedicta shook her head. 'The name doesn't ring a bell. But if she was a nurse, why don't you ask in the hospital?'

'That's exactly where I'm going next,' said Peter – and getting up, he thanked her for her time and left.

The hospital reception area was busy. When it was finally Peter's turn to speak to one of the receptionists, he asked for Nurse Domin.

'I can't just call her to come to reception,' was the answer. 'For all I know she might be assisting at an operation. The best thing to do would be to contact Human Resources. They might be able to help you, or let her know that you wish to speak to her.'

'Okay. So, where do I find the HR Department?'

'You'll have to make an appointment with them first, either by phone or email.'

She wrote down the phone number and email address on a small card and he made his way to the exit. He descended the steps towards the car park where his motorbike was parked, when he heard a voice behind him call out.

'Excuse me.'

He turned and saw a matronly nurse, in her fifties perhaps, approach him.

'I heard you asking about a Nurse Domin,' she said when she was close. 'Is it a Paula Domin you are looking for?'

'I think so, having searched on LinkedIn. I contacted someone by that name, but didn't get a reply. I work for the *DeWeZet*. I wanted to ask her if she remembers a group of children residing at the old orphanage in the late 1970s. Her name came up during an investigation.'

'Paula died about eight years ago. Cancer.'

'Oh. I'm so sorry. You were friends?'

'We were close friends.' She wrapped herself tighter in her cardigan.

Without a coat it was cold outside. Peter noticed she was shivering.

'I've got to go back inside now, but my shift finishes in about an hour,' she said. 'We could meet for a coffee if you like. She did tell me about the time she spent with children in the orphanage. I don't think she'd mind me telling you what I know.'

They agreed on a place to meet.

'I'm Regina, by the way, Regina Montag.'

'Peter Hahn.'

They shook hands and parted.

Mensing's was warm and smelled delicious. It was a popular bakery and coffee shop. Customers were crowding in front of the counter, deciding what to have from the assortment of freshly baked goods on display. Peter was lucky to find an empty table. He sat down with his coffee and *streuselkuchen*, and scrolled through the messages on his phone while keeping an eye on the door.

When Regina appeared, she dumped her bag on the chair opposite. 'Have you seen those almond croissants? I'm having one before they're gone.'

'What is it you would have asked Paula?' Regina asked on her return to the table.

Peter thought for a moment. 'First off, the owners of the orphanage deny there were children living there in the late seventies. However, one of those children, a woman now in her forties, says they did. Who is telling the truth?'

'The woman is. Paula often spoke to me about those children. She wondered what had become of them. You see, she had a special connection with them. For a time, she was the only one who understood their original language, before they learned to speak German.'

'Did she not know what happened to the children after they left the orphanage?'

'No, she didn't. As a matter of fact, the whole thing was quite strange. She'd been a welcome visitor, helping out with language problems to start with, keeping an eye on their health, answering their questions, reassuring them... and then one day she was told they no longer needed her. The children were leaving the orphanage after alternative living arrangements had been found for them. With foster families, Paula thought. She was happy for them, because the orphanage was such a depressing place. But she would have liked to have stayed in contact. That, however, wasn't possible, apparently.'

'Apart from speaking a foreign language, did Paula ever mention there was something odd about these children? Were they different from other children?'

Regina thought briefly before she replied. 'Well, confused, she used to say, scared and a bit other-worldly, but not naughty. No chance of that because those nuns were ever so strict.'

'There's another thing I would have asked Paula. Who was in charge of those children during their time in the orphanage, and who decided they were to be moved? Do you know? Did Paula tell you?'

'Yes. There were nuns who looked after the children day and night. Then social workers were involved and a psychiatrist. It was that woman, you know, the mayor's wife. What's her name?'

'Doctor Claudia Wagner, you mean?'

'That's it.'

'I'm hoping to find those social workers and ask them some questions too. It would be helpful to have a name. Did Paula mention any of the social workers' names, by any chance?'

Regina thought briefly. 'She did mention a Christine or a Christa,' she said hesitantly. 'I can't remember a surname.'

Peter thanked her for her help and left soon after that.

ELEVEN

On Saturday Erika's niece and nephew arrived, nine-year-old Suzi and eleven-year-old Jonas. Their parents were going to visit a trade show that day and Erika and Peter had offered to look after the children.

Ulrike, Erika's older sister, dropped them off. Before she left, she pulled Erika aside. 'Can we have a quick word?'

'Sure, I'll walk you back to the car.'

Erika put her coat on and they went outside.

'Can you do me a favour?' Ulrike began. 'They both brought their iPads. If possible, can you get them away from those screens? I tried to persuade them to leave them at home, but they created such a scene and we didn't have time for that this morning, we were in a rush.'

'No problem. I'll think of something to do that doesn't involve a screen.'

'That would be great, but I have to warn you: they're not the same since you saw them last.'

'What do you mean?'

'They've changed since getting those tablets for their birthday. We might have overindulged them a bit at first. They were so happy and spent hours playing those games, so we decided to limit it. The minute we took their tablets away, well, I'd never have expected the reaction. Screaming. Swearing. Refusing their food. It was scary. I discovered that they both played a game called Follow my Leader.'

'I know that game,' Erika said. 'We used to play it at school. One child is chosen as the leader and crosses the playground in a certain way, and all the others have to follow and copy.'

'Only this was online. It seemed harmless enough. But soon after that we received an email from the school inviting us to a special meeting, parents only. That evening we found out that we weren't the only parents with kids addicted to this particular game and subsequent worsening behaviour. There was a massive number of parents in that hall. Teachers too had found it harder and harder during lessons, with kids being rude, even violent. Children who had never been violent before. We discussed what we could do about it, such as limiting screen time, which we'd already done.'

They had arrived at the car.

'We'd better go,' Ulrike said. 'Good luck.'

Back inside, Erika found Peter and the children around the kitchen table, Jonas and Suzi glued to their iPads while Peter read the newspaper.

'Can you find out where that new roller-skating rink is that just opened?' Erika asked him.

The children protested, saying they'd rather stay home. Erika, determined to help her sister, insisted and ignored their long faces.

Traffic was slow and before long they were part of a traffic jam.

'Did you ask Katrin if she remembers a social worker called Christine or Christa?' Peter asked Erika.

'I did and she said she can't remember. They weren't in direct contact with social workers at the orphanage.'

'It's a long time ago, so I didn't think she would anyway.' Peter navigated through lanes of cars, bumper to bumper. 'I suppose it was worth a try. I'll make an appointment with social services on Monday morning. I'll tell them the same story I invented to get into the convent. That I'm writing an article about childcare in Hamelin and how it's changed over the years. You know, from orphanages to foster families, that kind of thing.'

They had arrived at the rink and stopped discussing the matter.

While the children were roller-skating, Erika and Peter sat watching them. She turned to him. 'This article you want to write, about what happened to Katrin and the others... it means a lot to you, doesn't it?'

'I hope it's my first step up towards investigative journalism, instead of being a dogsbody at a local newspaper.'

'I think it's more personal than that.'

Peter expected her to elaborate, but she just looked at him, steadily.

He got it. 'Oh.'

'Yes. Oh.'

She knew him well. There but for the grace of God... Was she right? *Was* this personal as well as professional? He too had been an orphan, after his mother, a single parent, died of a drug overdose. His dad had disappeared before he was born and no other family members ever made themselves known. He was alone in the world from age two. Several adoption attempts did not work out. His childhood and adolescence were spent moving from one foster family to the next, but he'd been comparatively lucky. Most families had made him feel welcome and wanted. In return, he'd done his best to adjust, help out with housework and do well at school. He was still in contact with some of the families.

At work on Monday morning, Peter made an appointment to speak to someone at the *sozialamt*, the social services. Later that morning, he received a phone call from Regina Montag.

'I've just remembered something Paula mentioned and I thought I should tell you. Remember I said she wasn't allowed to see the children anymore, just before they all left the orphanage?'

'Mm-hmm.'

'Well, Paula told me the refusal came as no surprise. You see, when she last visited the children, they'd changed. Until then, they were always responsive. They chatted, laughed, even joked with her. But now she found them apathetic. They didn't recognise her or seem conscious of their environment. Their eyes were open, but they weren't really aware of anything. She spoke to them and tried to coax them to reply but had to give up. Paula wondered whether they had been drugged. Concerned, she went to the nuns, but all she got out of them was that the children had become possessed.'

'Possessed?'

'They meant by the devil. Anyway, that was their excuse for not being able to handle them. They told Paula the children had become dangerous and would have escaped if the gates had not been locked. It was Doctor Wagner who calmed them down, apparently.'

'Did Paula know whether they were given any medicines and what they were?' asked Peter, as he scribbled notes on the pad in front of him.

'She didn't. They wouldn't tell her. She left the orphanage

upset and furious. She told me that if they had contacted her instead of Doctor Wagner, she could have calmed them down without any medication. Anyway, after that, the nuns refused to let Paula see the children.'

Peter thanked her and finished the call.

At the *sozialamt*, the name on the door was Mrs C Sachs. The C was intriguing. Peter wouldn't normally ask a personal question at the start of an interview, but needs must.

'Your first name wouldn't be Christine, or Christa, by any chance?'

The woman behind the desk looked up from her computer screen and frowned. 'It is Christa. Why do you ask?'

'I'm in search of a social worker called Christa, who might be able to tell me more about the now-demolished orphanage. Like I told your colleague over the phone, I'm writing an article for the *DeWeZet* about children in care over the years.'

'That must have been another Christa.'

'Really? You're about the right age and there can't have been that many social workers in those days. I did some research and the *sozialamt* was only a tiny department in the seventies.'

He had no idea about the size of the department at that time. It wasn't so much lying as bluffing, he told himself. He'd got the age right, though. She was in her early sixties, perhaps, and still good looking. She was one of those women who, he guessed, had grown more beautiful with age: symmetrical features, long chestnut hair twisted into a roll and skilfully applied make-up. Her style was classic and expensive: cream roll-neck top, mocha trousers and a tan suede blazer nonchalantly slung over the back of a chair. What was a woman like that doing in a place like this? She could have easily been in a more glamorous job, presenting on television or hosting events. Instead, she was here, anonymous in an anonymous building, sorting out other peoples' lives.

She held his gaze, steadily, coolly, before replying.

'If I *am* the Christa you're looking for, there's not much I can remember of the seventies or that orphanage.'

'But you did visit the orphanage in the late seventies?'

She shrugged. 'I might have. But memories of work in those days are a blur to me. There were more cases than we could handle.'

'The orphanage owners, the Sisters of Mercy, told me there were no children there in the late seventies. The place was simply waiting to be demolished. I have two sources though, who tell me a group of thirty-five children was living there and social services were involved.'

She sighed and changed tack. 'I can only vaguely remember it. It was an emergency situation. We did the best we could, but they were many and we simply couldn't find anything better at that time. Besides, they were considerably damaged and didn't speak German to begin with. There was no way they could've been placed with families.'

The hell she doesn't remember, Peter thought. 'What do you mean by: damaged?'

'There was something disturbing about those children. One day they just appeared and made their way into the town centre. No one knew where they came from, with hardly a stitch on their bodies and barefoot even though it was winter. We tried to find their families, but we were unsuccessful.'

'Wandering into town and not speaking German doesn't mean they were damaged or disturbed. Was there anything else?'

'I only heard about it. I didn't witness it myself. There was an incident while they were in the orphanage. One of the nuns told me the children had badly misbehaved and had tried to escape. But the doors were securely locked and they couldn't unlock them.'

'And then what happened?'

'The children stopped their misconduct and everything returned to normal. But the nuns were terrified afterwards, and convinced the children were devil's spawn. They refused to look after them any longer. Shortly after that I had a phone call from the nuns. The problem was taken care of and the children had been found another home.'

And that's where they still are, Peter thought, thirty-three years later. 'Do you know where they went and where they are now?'

'I'm afraid not. I gather the children were adopted, so it was no longer our concern.' She saw the expression on Peter's face. 'You have no idea how busy we were at the time. We were drowning in cases that needed our attention.'

Convenient, Peter thought. 'Do you know who adopted them?'

'No idea. Now, I've told you everything I know and I'm afraid I have a busy schedule. So, if you'll excuse me...'

That evening, Peter and Erika had friends over for dinner, who stayed late. It was nearly midnight by the time they went to bed and he found the opportunity to talk to Erika about his interview with Christa Sachs.

'I might try to speak to Claudia Wagner next,' he mused.

Instead of applauding his intentions, Erika sat bolt upright. 'No, no, you mustn't. My job's already difficult enough, with Bauer breathing down my neck all the time. If Wagner finds out there's a connection between you and me, she'll put two and two together and not only will I lose my job, she'll make sure I never find employment in this field again. I don't want you to interview her.'

Peter frowned. 'I thought we agreed I would do a little digging about Katrin and the others. You said yourself it's not normal to stay in a psychiatric hospital that long. Besides, there are the unexplained deaths. Don't you want to find out the truth?'

'Yes, but I thought you would do the digging online. Besides, you won't find out the truth from her. I asked her some innocent questions at our first meeting and she wouldn't answer them. Bauer shuts me down as well, every time I even so much as query something. I tell you, that place is like the DDR before the fall of the Wall: secrets, stonewalling, possibly even cover-ups.'

'If you don't tell her about us and I don't tell her, she wouldn't know, would she?'

'I think Bauer might have heard when I mentioned your name and what you do for a living to a colleague in the staffroom. I know Bauer, she'd tell Wagner.'

'You do realise this could be a breakthrough article for me, don't you? It might get me noticed by the national newspapers.'

'Oh, so your job is more important than mine? As you go up in the world, I find myself out of work.'

'You've often said you'd prefer to work for an agency. You're not happy at work, anyway.'

'You don't get it, do you? Look what happened to Helga Dietz. If Wagner finds out I've told you about these patients, I'm finished. They won't take me on at any nursing agency. That's how much influence she has.'

Peter tried to pull Erika into his arms, but instead of relaxing against him, she stiffened.

'What happened to you?' he said. 'Why this sudden change

of heart? It was you who started this, and who flushed half of Katrin's medicines down the toilet. You're already involved, you've already taken risks. So why not let me try to find out a bit more?'

'It's too risky.' Erika slipped from his arms. 'I need to get some sleep now. I have an early shift tomorrow. But just so we're clear: don't contact Wagner.' Erika switched off her bedside lamp and turned her back to him.

Frustrated, Peter did the same. Usually, he was a sound sleeper but negative thoughts, circulating in his head, prevented him from drifting off.

Hours later, he was still awake and went to the bathroom for a drink of water. Back in bed, he still couldn't find a good position to fall asleep in. He tried to relax, to concentrate on his breathing, to blank his mind, but nothing worked. At last, he plugged his earphones into his mobile, chose a boring radio programme to tune in to and finally fell asleep as pre-dawn light leaked into the sky.

At work the next day, he still wasn't his usual cheerful self, debating inwardly whether to try to get an interview with Doctor Wagner or not. In the end he decided against it, for Erika's sake. He didn't know how she would react if he went against her wishes and he didn't want to risk damaging their relationship. After that decision, he somehow felt better and went home intending to make up with her.

Reporting on an athletics competition at Hamelin University ten days later, Peter noticed a poster in one of the corridors. It announced a guest lecture by Doctor Claudia Wagner as part of the degree course in psychiatry.

A thought sprang to mind. As a former student, it wouldn't

be hard to attend. He didn't look any older than most of the students. After all, it had been less than two years since his graduation. He could slip in, attend the lecture and hopefully there would be some time for questions afterwards. He'd make sure to have his questions ready. Plus, he would not have to divulge his name. Erika couldn't have anything against it. But, just in case, he deemed it better not to tell her.

On the morning of the lecture, there was a problem. As Peter was about to leave, the editor asked him to write a piece on a local hero, a football star called Kurt Richter. She suggested he should arrange an interview and spend the rest of the morning reading up, so his questions would be well-informed. She thought she was doing Peter, a keen football fan, a favour. Peter searched frantically for an excuse but nothing came to mind, so he decided to be honest with her.

'I think I've discovered something really important to write about. I've been working on it for some time,' he confessed.

'What about?' his editor asked.

'I can't tell you yet, but the article should be ready in a few days' time. I planned to go somewhere this morning, to collect more information. Lenski would be delighted to do the Richter interview instead of me, I'm sure.'

Peter was right about that and his editor reluctantly let him go. Peter hurried out to his motorbike, since he was now late, and sped towards the university buildings.

TWELVE

After entering what he hoped was the right building, Peter followed the signs pointing towards the lecture hall, strode to a staircase and took the steps two at a time. The doors to the lecture hall were closed. He tiptoed inside, scanned the crowded hall for an empty seat and sat quietly. While his breathing slowed, he took a notepad and pen from his leather shoulder bag and placed them on the surface in front of him. On the pad were questions he meant to ask Claudia Wagner.

There was no need for him to pay attention to the lecture. Instead, he focused on the lecturer, fair-haired and tall for a woman, wearing an understated outfit offset by a pair of bold, chunky earrings. She must be popular to draw a crowd like this, he concluded, and confident as well. Not surprising, with such brains and charisma.

He'd often been in this lecture hall. Sometimes it was packed, like today, but often it wasn't. Usually there was a background of sound, people whispering, coughing, turning in their seats, rustling papers. Occasionally, there was complete silence, faces turned towards the speaker or taking notes. Today was such an occasion. Peter sensed how everyone in that hall was in awe of this woman.

When the lecture had finished, Doctor Wagner looked at her watch and said she could stay another fifteen minutes to answer questions. This was the moment Peter was waiting for. Because he was sitting at the back, she didn't see his raised hand and responded to those in front first. Finally, she pointed to him. 'The young man there in the back.'

He stood up and noticed how dry his mouth felt. 'You have twenty-five patients in a secure wing of the Koppenberg Klinik. All have been there for thirty-three years. They have no families. May I ask who is their legal guardian?'

Silence. As if every student realised this was an unexpected and challenging question. If Doctor Wagner was thrown at all, she didn't show it.

'In their case the klinik acts as guardian,' she said calmly. She turned towards someone else. 'And your question is?'

Peter, though, had no intention of giving up and spoke again. 'Is that ethical? If the klinik is their guardian, it means there is no one else to represent these patients. Someone outside the klinik, I mean. To decide perhaps that they no longer need to be kept inside.'

Doctor Wagner turned her attention back to Peter.

'Mr... what's your name?'

'Hahn.'

'Mr Hahn, are you a student here?'

'A former student. With an interest in psychiatry.'

'Mr Hahn, these poor patients you just mentioned have indeed been looked after by our staff in the klinik because they have nowhere else to go. They are unable to function in our society. That's how ill they are. They are a great danger to our society and to themselves. You are wrong as well about a lack of representation from outside. We have annual quality control. I hope that answers your questions. Now, my time is up. I have another engagement.'

As everyone got up to leave the lecture hall, Peter realised she was even more formidable than expected. She had answered his questions coolly and succinctly. One-nil to her, for now.

But this wasn't over yet, not by a long shot.

Although every bit of online digging and all his face-to-face interviews had thrown up more questions than answers, it was time for Peter to write his article. After work and an early dinner at home, he retired to the bedroom and opened his laptop. Erika would not be home from work until after eleven.

He read his notes and read them again. Still staring at a blank screen a good twenty minutes later, he got up to make himself a coffee. Just tell them the facts, he told himself. Give them the questions as well. Most people love mystery and secrets. Come on, think of a punchy title. Like *"Incarcerated for thirty-three years. Their crime? Mental illness."*

He approached the subject matter from an angle that showed the patients without agency from the moment they appeared in the town centre. They were never even given a chance, never taught life skills or how to cope with society. To be a voice for the voiceless was his aim. Once he started typing, the floodgates opened. He wrote down everything he knew, every detail that sprang to mind. So engrossed was he in putting words on the screen in front of him, that he didn't hear the front door open and Erika come in. Only when she entered the bedroom did he look up.

'That time already? How was work?'

'All right,' she said, but her drawn face showed otherwise. 'What are you up to?'

For a moment he thought about reading the drafted article to her, as he used to do, but then thought it wiser not to. It looked as if she'd had a hard shift, and because his article was concerned with her work, it would only make her feel worse. So he brushed the question aside with a "Just work", closed the laptop and suggested he'd make them some hot chocolate before bed.

Two days later, Peter took the finished article to his editor. At the end of the day, as he was about to go home, he was summoned to her office.

'We can't publish it,' she said, gesturing to the article on her desk.

'Why not?'

'You know very well why not. It's defamatory and damaging to the reputation of Doctor Wagner and the Koppenberg Klinik. We will be taken to court if we publish and the *DeWeZet* can't afford it. Doctor Wagner can afford to take us to court and I have no doubt she would.'

'What about free speech? What about getting to the truth? Doesn't that matter?'

'Oh, Peter,' sighed his editor.

She was a woman in her fifties, maternal towards young reporters like Peter. She was also unmarried and childless, a chain-smoker who tried to give up every Monday morning. 'Adolescent ideals. This is the grown-up world. Deal with it.'

The finality of her words told him there was no point in trying to persuade her any further. Disappointed, he went home. All that work, and for nothing. His first attempt at investigative journalism had just been torpedoed.

Later that evening Peter phoned Axel Voight, a successful reporter who'd had articles published in the national newspapers and magazines. They knew each other from university and Peter had asked Axel's advice before. Axel listened to Peter's account of his editor's refusal to publish the article and said, 'You can send the article to me if you like. I'll take a look at it, and if it's any good, I'll see what I can do.'

Peter emailed him the article straight away, not expecting anything would come of it.

Three days later, at two in the morning, Peter, a light sleeper, heard the "ping" of his mobile phone announcing a text message. It was from Axel.

> This stuff is dynamite. No wonder your editor didn't want to publish it. Die Tageszeitung is interested, though. You should contact them. Good luck.

The name, email address and phone number of the person to contact followed.

Die Tageszeitung, affectionately known as the *"taz"*, was one of the big national newspapers. Intelligent, leftist and edgy, it was a newspaper with a devil-may-care attitude. The kind of newspaper Peter could only dream of writing for.

Excited, he felt like going up on the roof and shouting about it, or somersaulting on the bed. He thought of waking Erika and telling her the good news, then decided it would be more of a surprise to see her reaction after it had been published.

But staying in bed and going back to sleep now was impossible. He felt too wound up. He got up, quietly left the bedroom and went to the kitchen, where he took a bottle of beer from the fridge.

Standing in front of the window, he drank slowly from the bottle. Not much to see other than buildings silhouetted against a light-polluted sky. He wondered how soon he could phone his contact at *Die Tageszeitung*.

The article appeared four days later, on page three in *Die Tageszeitung*. Peter couldn't stop smiling while he bought as many copies as he could lay his hands on.

Arriving at the *DeWeZet* earlier than usual, he placed a copy on each desk of his colleagues who had not yet arrived, folded open at page three. Then he knocked on his editor's office door.

'Peter? You're early.' She turned from her screen to face him.

'I want to show you something.' Peter gave her the newspaper and pointed at the article.

He held his breath, bracing for her reaction.

She cast a quick glance, before responding. 'I see you went to the *taz* and they published it. Congratulations.'

'I didn't think you'd mind. This way, any negative consequences won't affect the *DeWeZet*.'

She frowned. 'Don't be so sure. Your name is underneath the heading. If anyone at the Koppenberg Klinik reads this, all they have to do is find you on social media to discover you're currently employed by the *DeWeZet*.'

'But it's only me they would be coming after. You can always say you refused to publish the article.'

'Hmm. We'll see.' And with those words she returned to her screen.

His colleagues showed more enthusiasm and were generous with pats on the back and compliments.

'I suppose you have something to celebrate tonight?' said Horst, whose desk was nearest to his. In all the commotion of reactions, both negative and positive, Peter hadn't thought of it.

'I suppose I have,' he said with a grin.

With the remuneration for the article, he had sufficient means to take Erika out for a special meal. He decided it might be nice to invite her parents as well. From the beginning of his relationship with Erika, they had treated him like a son rather than a stranger and had always been generous towards him. Now that he had something to celebrate, it was time to return their generosity. Peter picked up his phone and tapped on Berndt's number. Erika's dad answered straight away.

'Hi, it's Peter here. I was wondering if you and Carla had anything planned for this evening?'

'I've booked us a table at Nobu's for eight and invited your parents to join us.'

Standing in the doorway of their small utility room, where Erika was sorting laundry before loading the washing machine, Peter pretended to be nonchalant.

Erika stopped separating colours from whites and turned to look at him.

'Are you out of your mind? That'll cost a fortune. We can't afford it.'

'Yes, we can. I've got something to celebrate.'

'What?'

'You'll have to wait until we're in the restaurant. Here, let me do that.' He gently pushed her away from the laundry basket. 'You go and get yourself ready. I'll finish this.'

On her way out, Erika turned around towards him. 'Are you sure? About the restaurant, I mean. It's one of the most expensive ones.'

'Yes, I'm sure.' Peter smiled.

They walked to the restaurant, since it wasn't far from their apartment. Erika's parents arrived as the young couple were about to enter. A waiter took them to their table and left them with menus, saying he would return to take their order.

'Have you tried Japanese food before?' Peter asked Berndt, who was studying the menu.

'I've eaten sushi, but this is a class above, by the looks of it.'

'It says here: "fusion cuisine, a blend of traditional Japanese dishes with Peruvian ingredients,"' said Carla.

They were still making up their minds when the waiter reappeared.

'We've no idea yet,' said Peter. 'What would you recommend?'

'Is it your first time here?' the waiter asked.

Peter nodded.

'Then I would recommend our signature dish, black cod in miso,' the waiter told them.

They all ordered the cod and a bottle of the recommended wine to accompany it.

Erika, studying the other diners, couldn't help but giggle. 'This place makes me feel like a country bumpkin.'

'Nonsense,' her mother responded, 'you look as smart as everyone else here. With the exception of that lady over there, perhaps.'

They all looked to where a tall, blonde woman had just risen from her table and, accompanied by a man, was making her way towards the exit.

'Isn't that our mayor?' Erika's mother remarked. 'And that must be his wife. Such a handsome couple, don't you think?'

Erika and Peter didn't respond. Peter felt Erika stiffen beside him and he nearly had a panic attack at seeing Doctor Wagner here. In a flash, he understood she would discover the connection between him and Erika. If she had already read the article, she would understand Erika had told him much of what was in it. The woman mustn't see them together.

He got up quickly, muttered "excuse me," and dashed towards the toilets where he locked himself in one of the cubicles and looked at his watch. He decided to give it at least five minutes. Had she seen him? Recognised him from his journo headshot at the foot of the article? He hoped not. After five minutes he spent some time washing his hands, then returned to their table. Claudia and Thomas Wagner were nowhere to be seen.

'Are you all right?' Erika asked. Her parents looked concerned.

'I'm fine. Fine.' Peter changed the subject quickly. 'I'm sure you'd all like to know why I have invited you here. To find out, you need to go to the internet on your phones and bring up today's issue of *Die Tageszeitung*.' Erika and Berndt did so, with much surprised laughter. 'Got it?' Peter asked. They nodded. 'Now go to page three. I would have preferred to show you the printed copy, but didn't think bringing a pile of newspapers to the restaurant was a good idea.'

'*Have Hamelin's children returned and are they living among us?*' Erika read aloud.

'By Peter Hahn,' her father continued.

Congratulations followed and the mood turned cheerful. Erika and her parents read the article until their food arrived and everyone tucked in.

Walking back to their flat afterwards, Erika put her arm through Peter's. 'It's a good thing it's not published locally, but in the '*taz*' instead. That way, the connection between you and me might remain unnoticed.'

Peter thought, you've no idea how close we came tonight to being recognised and the connection made between us.

Erika continued. 'I just dread to think what Doctor Wagner's reaction would be if she were to read it.'

'I hope it will be read not just by the general public, but especially by those in the health sector,' said Peter. 'There must be someone whose job it is to inspect the klinik, who can't be bought or persuaded by Claudia Wagner. I want the existence of those patients in the secure unit for thirty-three years to be out in the open and questioned. Not by me, but by the authorities. That's what I hope the effect of the article will be.'

When Peter woke the next morning, he found a message on his phone from his contact at *Die Tageszeitung*. It read:

> Someone phoned about your article. She says she has important information and wants to talk to you.

A Hamelin phone number and a name followed. Alana Friedrich.

THIRTEEN

Erika slid her bike into the metal rack, secured the lock and entered the Koppenberg Klinik via the side entrance. In the locker room she took off her coat, deposited her bag and was pulling a comb through her hair when Astrid, Doctor Wagner's secretary, came in. Astrid's face bore a more serious expression than usual as she walked right up to Erika and spoke in a hushed, almost conspiratorial voice.

'Be careful. Wagner is in a terrible mood. She's furious and looking for a scapegoat.'

The warning surprised Erika. They usually only exchanged small talk and pleasantries.

'Why? What happened?'

'A patient in the secure unit died overnight and another one has been taken to hospital in a critical condition.'

'Who?' Erika felt appalled at the news, since every patient in her unit had been in good health when she'd finished her shift yesterday.

'I don't know their names, but I'm sure they'll fill you in once you get there. All I'm saying is: tread carefully. Everyone's on tenterhooks.'

As Erika hurried towards her unit, anxiety snaked through her. She opened the staffroom door and found her colleagues gathered in the small space, subdued, their faces grave as they listened to Nurse Bauer. This was unlike other mornings, when the atmosphere was relaxed and chatty, especially when the senior nurse wasn't around.

'Ah, Nurse Kramer, I'm glad you could join us,' Nurse Bauer interrupted herself.

Erika glanced at her watch. She was on time. Then what was with the sarcasm? In her mind, she went over her actions at work yesterday. Had she forgotten something? Made some mistake? She couldn't think of anything. Mindful of Astrid's words in the locker room, she quietly joined the others to listen to what Nurse Bauer had to say.

'As I was just saying to your colleagues, Erika, sadly our chap Martin passed away overnight and Tobias, who also became critically ill, was transferred to St Agnes' Medical Centre. There will be an inquest today because Martin's death was unforeseen. He showed no signs of illness yesterday, I've been told, and we will get to the bottom of what caused it.'

At the mention of Martin's death Erika felt indescribably sad. Her eyes welled up. She took deep breaths and blew her nose.

'We don't want the other patients to find out yet,' Nurse Bauer continued. 'It'll only upset them. We can tell them at a later date if necessary. Go about your duties as normal, and remember to keep quiet about this when patients are present.'

Nurses and therapists dispersed, to start their morning rounds, as did Erika. She couldn't help thinking of Helga Dietz and her suspicion that Katrin's sister, Trude, had died during drug trials. Some patients were treated with a new medicine these last few days. Should she mention that to someone? But who? Not her supervisor. She knew how Bauer would react.

She would accuse her of spouting fairy tales and tell her that she, Erika, was unqualified to question Doctor Wagner, an esteemed and brilliant psychiatrist.

That there was going to be an inquest into Martin's death was reassuring. If there was anything wrong with the new medication, surely they would discover that. Too late for Martin though: harmless, childlike, moon-faced Martin. Hopefully they would be able to save Tobias' life. Was it worth saving? Not for the first time, Erika wondered about the quality of life her patients had. Sure, materially, they didn't suffer. All had a decent room, plentiful food, and some gentle pastimes and therapies were provided to compensate for the mind-numbing monotony of their existence. But they were sleepwalking, suspended between life and death. Now in their forties they were still children who knew little about the real world, apart from what they saw on television.

She unlocked the room of her first patient that morning. Pale-faced Dagmar had puffy eyes as if she'd been crying. She wasn't dressed yet and her breath smelled stale. Her lank hair was uncombed and fell in greasy strands over her pink dressing gown.

'Something terrible has happened,' she wailed as soon as she saw Erika. 'Tell me what it is.' In her round face, her eyes brimmed with tears.

Taken aback by Dagmar's words, Erika was speechless for a few moments. Patients were supposed to not know about Martin and Tobias. How had she found out? Had anyone told her? Erika tried to think of an answer that would not be a lie, yet would tell Dagmar nothing, as instructed. In the meantime, she handed Dagmar tissues and a glass of water and tried to calm her down.

'There's no need to be upset, Dagmar. I see you haven't had

your breakfast yet. Come, have some muesli. You'll feel better with something in your stomach.'

Dagmar pushed away the bowl Erika put in front of her.

'I'm not hungry.'

Erika tried a different tactic. 'What do you think happened that was so terrible? Why don't you feel like eating?'

Dagmar dabbed her eyes and blew her nose. 'I don't know, but it was a bad night. I couldn't sleep and I felt so sad.'

Erika stayed until her patient calmed down and was willing to eat a little. As she went from one patient to the next, she discovered that they all knew. Not that one of them had died, and another had been taken critically ill, but that something bad had happened during the night.

One of them, Arno, needed a bandage for his head, as he'd banged it repeatedly against the wall during the night, then passed out.

'Why didn't you ring the bell?' she asked as she treated his wound and changed his bloody pillowcase. 'Someone would have responded. There was no need to bang your head.'

'I did. I wanted to know what was happening, but everyone was busy. I heard them, running and shouting, but they didn't hear me.'

He didn't look at her as he spoke and his speech was indistinct as some of his teeth were missing. Finally, he repeated Dagmar's words. 'Something bad happened.'

They were the very words every patient had voiced that morning. It was uncanny, as if they had spoken to each other. Erika felt a shiver running down her spine.

Katrin was the last patient on her round. Erika unlocked the door and opened the curtains. Katrin was still in bed, but awake and watching Erika.

'Morning,' said Erika with a brightness she didn't feel. 'How did you sleep?' There was no answer. 'Are you all right to get up?' Again, no answer. Katrin stared steadily back at her, with an almost hostile expression on her face. 'Bad dreams?' Erika tried again, but it was no use. Finally, she left, promising to return soon, in the hope Katrin would be more willing to talk.

Back in the staffroom, she sat down with a coffee to fill in the details of her patients' early morning check-ups. She hadn't been writing long when Yann, one of her colleagues, came in. He was a big man, with a red stubble beard and moustache but thinning fair hair on top of his head. He took a paper bag with buttered pretzel rolls from the fridge, stacked them on a plate and placed them in the centre of the table.

'They're for everyone. My treat.'

'Lovely. Thanks.' Erika took one; breakfast seemed hours ago. Yann grabbed a coffee and sat opposite Erika at the table.

They munched their pretzel rolls, lost in thought, until Yann abruptly broke the silence. 'It's no use telling us to keep quiet about what happened during the night. They already know.'

'Yes,' Erika nodded, 'but how did they find out? The doors are locked and those walls are virtually soundproof.'

At that moment another nurse, Hedwig, returned from her patient round and joined them. She was relatively new to the unit, and still settling in.

'God, I'm starving,' she said, hungrily gazing at the plate of pretzel rolls. 'I should have brought something to eat with me.'

'Help yourself,' Yann gestured.

Between bites, Hedwig was eager to talk about patients, since she too had noticed they knew something had happened overnight and were asking about it.

'I think they sense it, like animals do. My dog, you can't keep anything hidden from him either. When something's wrong, or when there's any kind of danger, he knows. He's got this acute sense.'

'They're not animals though, our patients.' Erika frowned.

'No, but they're not quite like you and me either, are they? They're more... like children. And young children have it too, this sixth sense.'

Erika could have reacted with scepticism at the concept, but kept quiet. She was in no mood to argue. Besides, she had suddenly remembered Martin's secret pet snail, and resolved to release him in the garden.

Erika went to check on Katrin again after lunch. A tray with soup and a chunk of bread was left untouched on the table. The soup felt nearly cold when Erika cupped her hand around the bowl. Katrin was dressed and sat on the bed with her back against the wall, and her knees drawn up against her chest. She hugged her knees on which her chin rested. When Erika came in, Katrin looked away, out of the window.

'Won't you tell me what's wrong?' Erika asked. Silence and a head that remained stubbornly turned. 'Okay. We don't have to talk. How about a walk in the garden for some fresh air and exercise? Who knows, you might get your appetite back afterwards.' It looked as if Erika's suggestion would have no effect. 'Did you know the crocuses are out and I've even seen the first daffodils? I'll show you if you like,' Erika tried one more time.

Finally, a small victory. Katrin stood up from the bed and went to get her coat. Although she still wouldn't speak, Katrin nodded after their walk when Erika suggested she try the soup and went to reheat it in the staff microwave. As she stood waiting for the "ping", Nurse Bauer came in.

'There's a special staff meeting with Doctor Wagner at four, after the inquest. I'll see you there.'

Erika's shift finished at four and her hope to get away early dissolved. On the other hand, she was also anxious to hear the result of the inquest.

The meeting took place in the conference room next door to Doctor Wagner's office. Erika had never been in there. Staff meetings were usually held in their unit. She went along amongst her colleagues and took her seat at the conference table, as did the others. Conversations stopped abruptly when Doctor Wagner arrived with a document which she placed on the table and cleared her throat.

'Thank you all for coming,' she began. 'I thought you might like to know the results of the post-mortem on Martin's body. I have them here.' She picked up the document. 'I'll read them out to you.'

The medical terms translated in plain German as anaphylactic shock.

Doctor Wagner put the document away and looked at the faces around the table. 'Martin died between eleven thirty and midnight last night of a severe reaction to something he was allergic to, which caused his immune system to release a flood of chemicals and consequently go into shock. Death must have occurred within minutes. No staff on the night shift heard the alarm go off and when they checked patients at midnight, they found his lifeless body. I've spoken to night shift staff earlier today and they're understandably upset. But there was nothing they could have done for him.'

Erika studied the woman's composure and the tone of her

voice, which was grave, with a touch of regret and empathy, but mostly professional and detached.

'Do we know what caused the allergic reaction?' one of the nurses wanted to know.

'Not exactly,' said Doctor Wagner. 'As you all know, anaphylactic shock could have been caused by something in the food he ate, sometimes it's caused by certain nuts, or by bee stings, or–'

'Medication.' Erika realised she'd said it aloud, not just thought it, when all eyes turned towards her.

Doctor Wagner glared at her before continuing. 'Nothing unusual was found in his stomach contents, so we might never know what triggered that reaction.'

Someone asked if there was any news about the other patient, Tobias, who had been taken to hospital.

'Yes, some good news. Tobias' condition is no longer life-threatening and he has been transferred to a regular ward,' was the answer.

'Did Tobias have the same symptoms as Martin?' Erika asked.

'He did, but fortunately he was taken to the hospital in time, where he was given an injection of epinephrine, which saved his life.' Doctor Wagner rose, indicating that the meeting was finished.

As everyone trooped out of the conference room, Erika remained seated. Beside her, Yann was getting up and putting on his jacket. Erika looked up at him.

'Am I the only one who feels there is something wrong with, "We might never know what triggered Martin's death"? It's like, "Nothing to see here!"'

She hadn't been aware of the open door. Before Yann could answer, Doctor Wagner turned in the open doorway.

'Erika, can I see you in my office? Now.'

Doctor Wagner closed her office door behind them. This time, she didn't invite Erika to take a seat on the swanky pale grey leather sofa. Erika stood awkwardly and waited for her employer to speak. She didn't have to wait long.

'I don't like it when a member of staff is stirring.'

'I wasn't aware—'

'What else did you think you were doing?'

Erika decided to be straight with her employer. 'I didn't mean to undermine you. I was just wondering whether Martin's death could have been caused by something in the new medication administered to him yesterday. Tobias also took it.'

In the few seconds the psychiatrist took to coldly observe her, Erika felt herself shrinking.

'These medicines have been used for years,' Claudia Wagner stated. 'Hundreds of patients have benefitted from them. Do you think I would have prescribed them to our patients if there was any risk involved?'

'N-no.'

'Then why not leave decisions about patients' medicines to me? Nurse Bauer told me you're causing a certain... *discord* amongst staff with your doubts and questions. You're free to find employment elsewhere if you're not happy, but if you want to stay, just do your job. Is that understood?'

'Understood,' said Erika, and left the room trying to hold on to the shreds of her self-esteem.

She returned to her unit. An idea had occurred to her during the meeting and taken shape in Doctor Wagner's office just now. She entered the empty staffroom and took the keys to the small room where all medication was kept. There, she opened a drawer and took out a strip of pills, the same medicine Martin and Tobias had taken the day before. She put the strip in her coat pocket, locked up and returned the keys to the staffroom. In all that time she did not encounter another member of staff. The corridors were deserted. Then she left the building.

As she cycled home, she considered how she might have the pills analysed and checked, and establish whether these drugs really had been used by hundreds of patients for years, as Doctor Wagner claimed.

At home, Erika found little food in the fridge other than a few leftovers. She made a shopping list and went on foot to a nearby Edeka. On her return she prepared an *auflauf*, a layered oven bake using up leftovers. Combined with a fresh green salad and a bottle of Pinot Grigio, it made for a tasty dinner.

Afterwards, while they finished off the wine, she told Peter what had happened at work that day, then went to retrieve the strip of pills from her coat pocket and placed it in front of him on the table.

'This is the medication I was telling you about. These were given to Martin, who died, and to Tobias, who was taken to hospital severely ill. I want to know if that had anything to do with these pills. But I don't know anyone who could analyse them for me. Do you?'

'Not really, no. But I might be able to find someone. Leave it with me.'

'Not just anyone, though. It has to be someone we can trust not to go running to Wagner to tell her that I have stolen these pills from the Koppenberg.'

Peter agreed.

Erika emptied the last of the wine into their glasses. 'What was your day like?'

'Not as dramatic as yours,' Peter told her. 'I've been trying to get hold of a certain retired police inspector here in Hamelin, but apparently he's on a cruise or holiday. The social worker I spoke with referred me to him.'

'What's his name?' Erika asked. 'I could mention it to Katrin. It might trigger a memory.'

'His name,' said Peter, 'is Klaus Lenau.'

FOURTEEN

The allotments were situated along the railway on the outskirts of Hamelin and separated from the train tracks by a fence of wire mesh. Peter had often noticed the "little gardens", as they were known locally, from the window of a train compartment, but had never been there.

'Look for plot number twenty-three,' Alana Friedrich had told him on the phone, when they had arranged to meet. 'The numbers are painted on wooden posts in the corner of each plot.'

On his motorbike, Peter slowly cruised along the plots until he found number twenty-three. He swung his leg over the saddle and pushed the heavy bike along the path towards a wooden hut among the cultivated soil. The other plots had lawns, flowerbeds and garden furniture. Here, there was none of that. Every scrap of earth was used to produce vegetables or fruit. Peter spotted peas, tomatoes and courgettes, gooseberries and blackberries. Before he reached the hut, he caught sight of a bent figure among rows of beans.

He stopped and called out. 'Hello!'

A woman straightened and turned. Her hair was white and,

as she came closer, he noticed her weather-beaten face and faded dungarees. She put the hefty metal watering can down, wiped muddy hands on her dungarees, walked up to Peter and shook his hand.

'Peter? I'm Alana.' Her handshake was firm and the eyes that scanned his face were a piercing blue.

She showed him where to park his motorbike and went off to make tea in the hut.

'Come and get the chairs,' she called from inside. 'We'll sit outside and enjoy this fine weather.'

The chairs were foldable aluminium-framed garden chairs, placed against a wall just inside the hut. As Peter stepped inside, the overall impression, even in the dimly lit space, was one of frugality and neatness.

A strip of pavement in front of the hut offered a level surface for the chairs and after he sat down and prepared his phone to record their conversation, he was joined by Alana, who handed him one of the mugs of tea she was carrying.

'It must be rewarding to eat something you've grown yourself. Is it hard to do?' Peter remarked by way of a conversation-starter.

She chuckled. 'Depends on the weather.'

'Oh, I think it's a bit more than that. I know enough about gardening to see you've invested an immense amount of work. Do you grow all this on your own or do you have help?' He wondered if there was a Mr Friedrich.

'It's just me, by myself.' It sounded matter-of-fact, with no trace of pride or self-pity.

'What do you do with all the produce, apart from using it for your own consumption?'

'I eat just a small amount myself. Most of it I sell at the Saturday farmers' market in town. I have a stall there and regular customers. People like buying fresh, organic food.'

'So does my fiancée. She's into health foods and all that. I'll tell her about the Saturday market and your stall.'

After what Peter felt was a respectable amount of small talk, he broached the real reason he was there. 'When we spoke on the phone you mentioned you wanted to talk to me regarding my article about the lost children of Hamelin.'

'Yes, it brought it all back to me, you see. Memories either forgotten or buried, I don't quite know which. It's so long ago, nearly a lifetime.' She sounded eager to tell him something but struggled to put her half-formed ideas into words. He waited while she gathered her thoughts. 'In 1945 I was eight years old. The war had just finished and large parts of the country were reduced to rubble and ruins. I was found wandering around Hamelin on my own, lost, not knowing where I came from or where I was going. I wasn't the only orphan, far from it. But all that is vague. It's what I've been told. I can hardly remember anything from that period. Even less what happened before that day. But I do know that like the children in your article, I woke up in a mountain cave. There were tremors in the earth I was lying on. I got up with a few other children who'd woken up too, walked towards the light, left the cave and just... kept walking.'

Peter gently prompted. 'What happened to you after you were found?'

'I was adopted by the Friedrich family. They gave me my name: Alana. After their daughter Alana who died during the war.'

'What was your name before you came to them?'

'I honestly can't remember.'

'Were you happy with the Friedrich family?'

'Happiness is not a word I would use to describe my childhood and upbringing. It was such a different time compared to the present. Austere, and everyone I knew was poor. The Friedrichs were strict, but so were everyone else's parents. Strict but fair, and I have no doubt they loved me, in their own way. *Content* would be a better word to describe how I felt most of the time while growing up, had it not been for the dreams that recurred regularly.'

'You had nightmares?'

'I wouldn't call them nightmares, because they weren't frightening. On the contrary, they painted a world that was at the same time different and familiar.'

'What do you mean?'

'In the dreams I lived with another family and I didn't go to school. We spoke a different language. I helped the woman I called "Mother" to spin and weave. I wasn't an only child, either. I had many sisters and brothers. My "father" had a workshop where he made clogs and shoes for rich people. In the real world my father was an accountant. Yet, the world of my dreams felt as familiar as my life with the Friedrichs. I felt as if I belonged there, as if these were more than dreams.'

'Did you talk about it with your parents, the Friedrichs?'

'I tried, but they told me my dreams were just the product of a lively imagination. So I stopped talking about them and only wrote about my dreams in the diary I kept at the time.'

'For how long did you have these dreams and write about them?'

'A few years, perhaps. By the time I was thirteen I stopped having them and stopped writing about them. Then I just forgot about it all. But your article made all that surface again.'

'I'm sorry.'

'Don't be. In a way, your article was of great comfort to me. There were periods in my life when I wondered if there was something wrong with me, just like those poor souls in that hospital you're describing. You seem to think otherwise.'

'Yes. My fiancée is a nurse who cares for these people. Like you, they believe they were asleep in a mountain cave before they came to Hamelin. They also believe they are lost children who were led away by a stranger, hundreds of years ago. It sounds bonkers but Erika, my fiancée, says they seem perfectly normal people, just institutionalised and a bit *odd*, which is understandable. They've never been part of the outside world.'

'I don't think it sounds bonkers,' Alana replied, apparently carefully choosing her words. 'If these people are mentally ill, then so am I. Because waking in a cave surrounded by sleeping children, leaving the cave with a few others who were awake and walking towards this town, I thought that was a dream but now I think perhaps it was a memory. Perhaps the other "dreams" were memories too. So, you see why I contacted you. So much of what you wrote about these patients is part of my story, too.'

'Only, it happened to you in 1945. For them, it happened in 1978.'

For a time, they were both lost in their own musings. Peter reflected that this was either a scam or something huge: the possibility of time travel, which until now had always been part of science fiction. This old lady didn't seem the type to conduct a scam. For one, what would be her motivation? This was someone who preferred to live a quiet life and remain anonymous. Still, he had to proceed rationally and practically.

'Did you remain in contact with the other children who left the cave with you in 1945?' he asked.

'Not after I went to live with the Friedrichs.'

'How many others were there? Do you think it would be possible to find them?' Peter decided that should be the next step: to try to find the others, to confirm Alana's story and prove the patients in Erika's unit were anything but mentally ill.

'There was only a handful of us. Five or six. The others were boys. I don't know where you could find them, or if they even remained here in Hamelin.'

After they'd agreed to keep in contact, Peter thanked Alana for her openness and left.

Back at the *DeWeZet*, as he parked his motorbike, he felt, for a moment as if he was being watched. When he looked round, he didn't see anyone. He'd probably imagined it.

Peter was keen to discuss his visit to Alana with Erika when he got home. There was no one else he could tell, without risking being laughed at. He especially wanted to find out what she thought about Alana's "dreams" of another time and being part of another family. Also, that she too had woken up in a mountain cave, just like Erika's patients. But he had to wait until nearly midnight when she returned from her late shift looking wrung out, all her usual bounce and energy evaporated.

'I need to tell you something,' Peter said, sitting up in bed while Erika stepped out of her nurse's uniform.

'Can it wait till the morning? I've a headache and really need to sleep. I've got tomorrow off, we can talk about it over breakfast, okay?'

The next day was Saturday and Peter wouldn't have to work either. The familiar buzz of her electric toothbrush was the last sound he heard before he drifted off.

When Peter returned from the bakery the next morning with fresh rolls in a paper bag, Erika was up making coffee and scrambled eggs. Over breakfast, he told her all about his visit to Alana Friedrich the previous afternoon.

She thought for a moment. 'Do you think she might have a photo of when she first came to the Friedrichs? If so, I could show it to Katrin and see if she recognises Alana as a child. If Katrin recognises her from before they were taken, it would confirm their story, wouldn't it? About the cave.'

'Excellent idea! Why didn't I think of it? I'll phone her after the weekend and ask.'

'Ask her about the diary she kept as a child. The one in which she wrote down her dreams. See if she still has it and is willing to share that, too. It could provide more information, more pieces of the puzzle.'

'You're right. It's a private diary, though. I doubt she'd show that to anyone, let alone a stranger.'

Peter phoned Alana Friedrich early on Monday morning, to catch her before she went to work on her allotment. He didn't mention the diary, just asked about the photo. He would ask about the diary when collecting the photo, perhaps. She told him she would look for a photo of herself, aged eight or nine, that there might be some in the family photo albums. They arranged for Peter to come to her house at four o'clock the next day.

Because the address Alana had given him was near to his work, Peter decided to walk. After hours of sitting behind the computer, he could do with the exercise. Outside, a man was loitering on the pavement opposite. Peter might not have noticed him, had he not turned away as soon as Peter glanced in his direction.

When he stopped in front of Alana's house in a quiet street, he became aware of having heard the same footsteps following him all the way. He turned sharply, to see the man he'd previously observed across the road from the *DeWeZet* offices, now standing a short distance away from him. Peter saw the man was at least in his seventies. He was poised to go up to him and ask what he wanted, but at that moment Alana opened the front door and invited him in. After a slight hesitation he responded to her welcoming words and entered.

The house was a modest bungalow with a large garden at the back.

'Do you grow fruit and vegetables here as well?' Peter asked, seated on a faded sofa with flattened cushions that had once been plump.

'Only flowers,' Alana gestured towards a vase with daffodils and yellow tulips on the coffee table. 'And then there are the beehives and chicken coops.'

'You've got plenty to keep you busy.'

'I'm used to it. My dad always kept bees and chickens in the garden and I liked helping him. Nowadays, I put the honey and eggs up for sale in my stall on Saturdays and keep the beeswax for candles to sell at the Christmas market.'

'Do you make enough to live on?' It popped out before Peter could stop himself.

She didn't seem offended by his directness. 'Just about. I don't need much and, when my parents died, they left me the house as well as a small sum of money. When that was gone, I got my state pension.'

The interior of the bungalow bore the same characteristics of simplicity and neatness as that in the allotment hut. Apart from the sofa and coffee table, there were two easy chairs. There was no television, but a cast-iron wood stove stood in the corner.

From the bulging bookcase, which lined one of the walls, Alana took an old-fashioned photo album and a thick notebook, placed them on the table and pushed them towards Peter.

'I found these. The photos you asked for, and the diary I wrote my dreams in.'

The cover of the diary was decorated with hearts, flowers and butterflies as well as names of fifties' film stars in different styles of lettering. Peter was relieved he didn't have to ask her for the diary and surprised she was so forthcoming.

'You don't need to remove any photos from the album,' he explained. 'I could just take some snapshots of those with my mobile.'

Together, they leafed through the album of tiny black and white photos. They were mostly holiday snaps of Alana playing on a beach somewhere, taken from far away. There was a school photo, too.

'That one will do,' said Peter. 'How old were you then?'

'I must've been nine then, or ten, perhaps.'

Peter had told her about Erika's patient, Katrin.

Now Alana said, 'You can take the diary, but don't let it fall into the wrong hands. Give this only to Katrin to read. The name sounds familiar.'

'That's a promise. I'll make sure you get it back soon.'

As he stepped outside to walk back to his office, he looked around for the old man who had followed him there and was almost disappointed when there was no sign of him.

FIFTEEN

What made Katrin stand out from the other patients in the closed unit, Erika reflected as she cycled to work that morning, were her small acts of rebellion. Refusing food or not speaking but wrapping herself in a defiant silence. And then there were her eyes, curious, intelligent and aware of what was going on around her. Perhaps because Erika was gradually reducing her medication, but even before that there had been that difference.

The other patients in the unit were not fully present. What consciousness they'd once had was lost in time. They were empty husks, as they moved slowly from the garden to the physio- and occupational therapy rooms, as if moving underwater.

The shoulder bag in Erika's bicycle basket contained the diary as well as Alana's school photo. Peter had printed the photo from his phone. Thinking about how to get these to Katrin without her supervisor or colleagues noticing, Erika had put the dustcover of one of her books around the diary, which turned out to be a perfect fit. That way, she could always say she was lending Katrin the book. It was a well-known fact amongst staff that Katrin was an avid reader.

As it turned out, no one stopped or questioned her as she took the book from her shoulder bag in the locker room, carried it with her to her unit, unlocked and knocked on Katrin's door.

Seated at the table, Katrin was having her breakfast while listening to a radio programme. She had not spoken to Erika or, as far as she knew, anyone else since the night Martin died.

'There's something I'd like you to have a look at.' Erika placed the "book" on the table in front of Katrin. She went on to tell her about Peter meeting Alana, before taking the photo from the diary.

'Take a look at this photo. Do you recognise the girl in it?'

As Erika said it, she heard Katrin's sharp intake of breath.

Katrin lifted the photograph to take a closer look.

'You do, don't you? You *do* recognise her,' said Erika.

Katrin studied the photo and at last whispered, 'Yes.'

'Who is she and where do you know her from?' Erika could barely restrain her excitement.

Katrin placed the photo carefully down on the table.

'Her name was Lena. She was my best friend when I was a little girl.'

'Do you remember anything else about her?'

Katrin thought for a moment. 'I remember her hunger. She was just this scrawny little thing, one of the youngest in that family. At mealtimes the older siblings would grab most of the food, not leaving enough for her and the other little ones. My mother once caught her stealing a handful of plums, but instead of punishing her she gave her some more to eat, which she wolfed down. I've never seen anyone eat so fast.'

Erika had an idea. 'Would you mind if I wrote that down?'

Katrin ignored the question and continued. 'I remember too how we made dolls from stray pieces of wool and linen her mother had no use for anymore. Her mother was a weaver and she could spin too. There was a loft in their house where we played with our dollies during bad weather.'

Erika's pen hovered above the paper she was writing on. 'Anything else?' Katrin shook her head. 'Perhaps you'll remember more after you've read this.' Erika took the diary from the book cover and pushed it towards Katrin, who turned to the first page and started reading.

At that moment a student nurse rushed into the room. 'Erika, can you come? Otto has locked himself in his bathroom and refuses to come out. I'm worried he'll do something to himself.'

Erika got up to leave.

'Her left arm was badly burned when she fell in a basin of boiling water,' said Katrin, quietly.

Erika turned. 'Your friend, Lena? Did the burns leave scars?'

'Yes, very bad scars.'

As she left the room, Erika made a mental note.

Erika phoned her fiancé during her lunch break. 'If Alana's left arm shows burn scars, she must be the Lena who was Katrin's friend when they were small children,' was Peter's reaction. 'It proves they are telling the truth.'

'It proves they knew each other as young children and they lived in a rural community, not necessarily the Hamelin of the thirteenth century. Time travel is fiction, not fact,' Erika responded. After a pause, she resumed. 'So, what do we do now?'

'I'll phone Alana and arrange another meeting. Perhaps you should come too.'

As soon as they arrived at her house, Alana was keen to learn more about Katrin. Erika told her everything Katrin remembered of their shared childhood, leaving out the accident with the basin of scalding water.

Moments later Erika, in her role of nurse, turned to her fiancé. 'Could you give us a minute? I need to ask Alana something.'

Peter, who knew what was coming, left to take a look at the garden, while Alana raised her eyebrows but didn't say anything.

Treading carefully, Erika asked Alana to show her her left arm.

Alana stiffened and her face lost the animated expression of moments before. 'Why?'

'There was just something Katrin mentioned about her friend Lena,' Erika explained apologetically. She wasn't happy about putting Alana on the spot.

Alana reluctantly rolled up the left sleeve of her dress. The bare arm showed little regular skin, rather a patchwork of blotchy reds and purples where deep dimples alternated with smooth, shiny and hairless bumps. The association that sprang to Erika's mind was that of craters and mountain ranges on the surface of some distant planet.

These were the worst burn scars Erika had seen and she had to restrain herself from showing signs of pity. 'Does it hurt?'

'Not at all.'

'This proves you are the Lena Katrin told me about.'

'Lena.' Alana lingered over the sounds with her tongue and teeth.

Erika went into the garden to find Peter and tell him Alana's arm was indeed covered in burn scars. On their return to the sitting room their hostess had rolled the sleeve down again.

'So, what did Katrin tell you about my arm?' Alana asked. 'Does she know how I got these scars?'

'Do you not remember?'

Alana shook her head and Erika repeated what Katrin had told her about the accident. 'When can I see Katrin? I want to see her,' said Alana.

Although it was a reasonable question, Erika didn't know what to say. 'I don't know,' she stammered. 'I'd have to discuss it with my supervisor. You see, it was always presumed Katrin and the other patients in her unit had no family or friends. No one has ever visited or enquired after any of them.'

'It's a good idea, though, for you to visit Katrin,' said Peter, 'but we need to work out a plan before you do, and concoct a credible story. If you turn up at the klinik unannounced and ask to see Katrin they'll probably send you away.'

The three of them thought for a while.

'What's the most accepted theory about the background of those patients?' Peter asked Erika. 'Where they're from, I mean.'

'The most common explanation is that they were children of a secret cult who escaped from their parents. So traumatised were they by the abuse they survived, they couldn't talk about it, despite all efforts to try and find out where this cult was based. It was in the seventies, and it was probably some hash smoking hippie commune.'

'Then we stick to that story. Alana and Katrin knew each other from the days they spent in that commune and they both escaped.'

'But Katrin is in her forties and Alana is ...'

'... in my seventies,' said Alana. 'So, we could not have known each other as children.'

'Perhaps you were a family member – a sister of Katrin's mother, a kind aunt, who helped the children escape and then lost contact,' Peter thought aloud.

'That might work,' said Erika, 'but how did Alana find out about Katrin residing at the Koppenberg Klinik?'

There was another lengthy silence while the three of them

thought how to answer the question. Alana went out and returned with a fresh pot of tea.

'I might have an idea, but it would take some time,' Peter said finally. 'I could do a feature about Alana for the *DeWeZet*. You know what I mean: elderly citizen, very active, contributing to her community, growing organic fruit and veg. The article could be illustrated with a few photos of Alana at various ages. After publication you, Erika, happen to leave that particular edition of the *DeWeZet* in Katrin's room. Having read the article, she'll tell you she recognises Alana from a photo. When Katrin was a child, she knew her. Then Katrin asks to see Alana, not the other way around.'

After outlining his plan Peter looked expectantly at the two women.

Alana looked thoughtful and turned towards Erika. 'What do you think?'

'I can't think of a better plan.'

It was agreed and the couple left, Peter promising Alana he would return soon for his feature about her.

Katrin could barely control her excitement once Erika had told her about Alana's burn scars.

'What did she say after you told her about me? Does she remember me? What is she like?'

Erika responded with a question of her own. 'Would you like to see her?'

'Of course. More than anything in the world.'

Then Erika told her about the plan hatched at Alana's, to organise a visit.

'It's going to take some time, though. It might be a week or two before the feature about Alana appears in the *DeWeZet*.

That's not Peter's decision, but his editor's. We'll have to go about this carefully and patiently.'

'I've waited years for anything that could make this confinement more bearable or end it altogether. I can wait a few more weeks.'

And a few more weeks was what it took for Peter's feature about Alana to appear in the *DeWeZet*. To Erika's surprise, when she finally took the newspaper to Katrin, her patient's reaction was very different from the one she had expected.

'I'll read the article, but I don't want Alana to come and visit me here.'

Erika knew how much Katrin had been looking forward to the visit.

'What changed your mind? Why don't you want to see her?'

'Of course I want to see her. That's not the point. I just don't think it's going to happen. They'll never give permission for the visit. And I don't want to get Alana into trouble. I might need her, in case I manage to ...'

'Manage to?'

'Escape.'

Before Erika could respond to that, Katrin continued. 'I need to get out of here. I don't want to die, like Trude. Like Martin and Tobias.'

It was true. Tobias, who was taken to hospital on the night Martin had died, had slipped into a coma and died a few days later. Members of staff knew, but how Katrin had learnt the news was a mystery to Erika; staff policy was to keep quiet about it.

She tried to reassure Katrin. 'Just because these rare accidents occurred to Trude, Martin and Tobias, doesn't mean that would happen to you.'

'And Else. Before your time. She died, too. Too many in too short a time. I don't want to be next.'

It was on Erika's lips to say that of course Katrin wouldn't be next, but she stopped herself just in time, realising the emptiness of those words. Why *wouldn't* Katrin be next when another new batch of medicines was being tested?

Erika was still trying to think of something positive to say, when Katrin spoke again. 'There's no hope of any of us ever getting out of here, is there? We will be imprisoned until the end of our days.'

'Doctor Wagner doesn't think you would be able to live independent lives in this society,' Erika said quietly, fed up with telling lies or giving false hope.

'I would. I know I would, from what I've seen on television. I would only need a little help to begin with. I'm sure Alana would help me. There are jobs I could do. I could be a gardener or do what Alana is doing, growing and selling fruit and vegetables.'

Katrin is right, Erika thought. She most likely *could* be independent that way. Especially if Alana would help her. None of the other patients would manage; they'd be lost in the outside world.

'That's why I think you should ask permission for Alana to visit you,' she tried again. 'Then, after a few more visits, we might suggest you visit Alana, followed by a short stay at Alana's to gradually expose you to twenty-first century living.'

But Katrin stubbornly shook her head. 'They won't let me go. And if they know about Alana, that would be the first place they'd come looking for me, if I decided to run away. I'd have nowhere to go to.'

'But how would you get out of here? There are stringent security measures in place.'

'I'm working on it.'

'You probably shouldn't say that to me. I would have to

report that,' Erika said with a faint smile. She wouldn't and they both knew it.

Arriving home after her shift, Erika found Peter standing beside the large window, in their living room in the near dark, half-hidden in the curtain. He was peering out but clearly didn't want to be seen. There was something faintly comical about the way he stood, a bit-part player in a spy movie.

'What are you up to?' Erika barely suppressed the laughter in her voice.

'Remember I told you about the old man who was following me? If you come and stand beside me, you'll see him. There, looking in the shop window of the tobacconist. Wait until he turns round, then you can get a better look at him.'

At last, he turned and looked up at their apartment.

'But I know that man, or rather I've seen him before,' Erika exclaimed.

'Where?'

'Let me think.' Erika racked her brains, but it wouldn't come to her. 'No. Give me a minute.'

They stepped away from the window and went to the kitchen to cook supper. As she was putting a handful of dried spaghetti into the pot of boiling water, Erika remembered.

'He's one of the cleaners in the klinik. A friendly old codger called Bodo. He hasn't been with us long, just started in the job last week.'

She ran to the living room window, to see if he was still there, but found him gone.

'Why would he follow you?' she wondered aloud.

'I have every intention of asking him that next time I see him.'

SIXTEEN

Later that evening, Peter's phone rang. The brightly lit screen showed him it was Dirk, a former housemate during his university years. While Peter studied journalism, Dirk had attained a PhD in biochemistry.

Peter hoped Dirk could tell them more about the medication Erika wanted analysed. So far Peter had been unsuccessful in contacting him and had left various messages. This was Dirk finally responding.

Peter picked up the phone and, after some initial banter, got to the point. 'There's something I meant to ask you, for an article I'm working on. If I wanted some medicine analysed, how would I go about doing that?'

'You go online and put it through a pill identification tool. On the site, they'll ask you to identify the colour, shape, and imprint on the pills. Once you've found a match, you'd be able to link to a detailed description of that particular medicine.'

'Sounds simple enough. I'll try that.'

'Let me know how you get on. If you need any further information, text or email me.'

Peter thanked him and they finished their conversation. He

then asked Erika for the strip of pills she had taken from the klinik. Following the instructions on the website, Peter noticed that the letters, numbers and markings on the back of the blister pack strip differed from the ones on the actual pills. Puzzled, he tried to enter first one code, then the other. Neither provided him with any results, which left him feeling that the website was inaccurate or he'd done something wrong. He'd try again in the morning.

When the morning attempts brought no different result, Peter texted Dirk to ask for further advice.

> There's a fail-safe method to identify and analyse a wide variety of chemical compounds. It's called mass spectrometry.

Dirk texted back.
Peter responded:

> Sounds expensive. How much would that cost?

> Thousands. Who's the manufacturer of the pills?

Peter looked in vain for a name on the foil strip, then asked Erika, who didn't know.

'It was probably on the box I took it from,' she said. 'I should've looked for it. I didn't think of it.'

Dirk texted, a little later:

> Find out and let me know. The company I work for has connections with lots of manufacturers in the pharmaceutical industry. Perhaps I can provide contact details for someone who works there, so you could use your journalistic skills to interview them.

'I can find out at work,' Erika assured him. 'It shouldn't be hard.'

But when Erika returned after her shift that day, the news wasn't good.

'I looked through the drawer in our medication room where those tablets were kept, and where I took that strip from. They were no longer there. Because I searched for so long, Bauer came and asked what I was looking for. I had to fob her off with an excuse. Afterwards, I asked some of the other nurses. Discreetly, of course, I didn't want to raise anyone's suspicions. But no one could give me a name. Someone said the missing pills were either returned to the manufacturer or to our pharmacy.'

'What's the difference between the medicine storage room and the pharmacy?'

'Every nurse at our unit has access to our medication room. It stores the medicines we currently dispense to our patients. We receive them from the pharmacy, which is managed by a pharmacist and has medication for all units, not just ours.'

'You couldn't go and chat to the pharmacist, could you, to get the manufacturer's name?'

'I would, if the woman in question wasn't close friends with Bauer. She would most definitely mention it to our senior staff nurse. No doubt about it. Bauer might tell Wagner, too. I could either get another lecture or the boot.'

'Is there a time when the pharmacist isn't there?'

'Between six in the evening and eight in the morning. But then the pharmacy is locked.'

'Who has access to the key?'

'Senior nurses, I should think. Night cleaning staff, perhaps. I don't know. Why? You're not thinking of breaking in, are you?'

'Not really. I'd do a lot to obtain information, if I think it's important, but breaking in isn't one of my preferred methods.'

About a week later *Skyfall*, the latest Bond film, was released. Peter and Erika had been looking forward to going and seeing it.

After the film, as they were about to leave the *Astor Kino*, a cinema not far from their apartment, they paused in the foyer. Outside, torrential rain was scouring the streets of an already-washed-out world.

'It's just a shower. Let's wait until it's over.' Erika was reluctant to get her new shoes soaked through. She loved beautiful shoes. Peter often teased her about it, saying she collected shoes like other people gathered CDs or books.

'I mostly buy them in the sales,' Erika would say defensively.

Staring out at the drenched high street, where snack bars, ice-cream parlours and coffee shops bumped hips with chemists, jewellers and fashionable boutiques, Peter's eyes were drawn towards the bus shelter across the road. Everyone in it huddled close. Everyone except an elderly man, who stood at the bus stop alone, seemingly indifferent to the rain. There was something about the old geezer that looked familiar. Peter kept staring until he recognised him as the man who had been following him for weeks. Peter marched out of the glass doors of the cinema, which opened automatically, and stormed towards the old boy.

'Hey!' he shouted, as rain pelted his head. 'Were you following me? What do you want?'

At that moment the bus arrived and the old man disappeared from view as the people waiting in the bus shelter swarmed around him. By the time Peter had dashed across the road and arrived at the bus stop, the door of the bus was closed and the bus pulled away from the pavement. Frustrated and soaking wet, he returned to Erika, behind the glass doors of the foyer.

'Bastard got away before I could get to him,' Peter fumed.

'If anyone shouted at me like that, I'd run a mile, too.'

'You know he's been stalking me. I just want to know why.' Peter dried his face with the tissues Erika handed him. He combed his hands through his hair to remove the wet strands plastered to his face.

'You could have asked him nicely. No need to go at him so aggressively. On those few occasions I've come across him at the klinik, he hasn't seemed the type to bother anyone. Are you sure it was the same man? It was definitely Bodo this time?'

'No doubt about it,' said Peter, gruffly. 'Let's go home. The rain seems to have stopped.'

They walked home, with a strained silence between them. Usually, after the cinema, they'd go for a drink and discuss the film in great detail. Not this evening. Peter's mood had soured and Erika made no attempt to lift him out of it.

Peter waved at Alana, who straightened from a row of ripening vegetables at her allotment garden. She left the green beans she was picking and came towards him.

'I've come to return these to you.' Peter held out her diary and the photo, tucked inside.

'Did Katrin read it?' Alana asked, as they walked towards the wooden hut.

'I think so. Erika says Katrin made a drawing from the photo, which has place of honour on her bedroom wall. According to Erika, she often talks about you and can't wait to see you.'

Alana smiled. 'Now you've mentioned old friends, I've just reconnected with another one. I'll tell you all about it. First, let me wash my hands.' She disappeared inside the hut.

Meanwhile, Peter organised the garden table and chairs as he'd done on his last visit and somewhat later they each sat behind a tall glass of craft beer, which Alana poured from a brown glass bottle.

'I've really developed a taste for this particular beer,' she told him.

'It's good,' he agreed and took another sip. 'You said you've recently reconnected with another old friend?'

'Yes! As a matter of fact, when I saw you just now, because of the distance between us and my failing eyesight, I thought you were him. But he's a lot older than you. He's my age and he's ... one of us. One of the other children who returned to Hamelin when I did, in 1945.'

Peter instantly became more interested. 'You lost contact?'

'Yes. I never saw him again after the Friedrichs adopted me. He wasn't as lucky as I was, and had to stay in an orphanage, before being adopted. He told me he vowed never to set foot in Hamelin again. I think those years in the orphanage scarred him, probably for the rest of his life.'

Peter remembered what Erika's dad, Berndt, had told him about the orphanage. He could only imagine the cruelty and inhumane treatment endured by the orphans.

'But now he has returned to Hamelin. What made him change his mind?' he asked, intrigued, and at the same time thinking: the more people we find like Alana, with the same story to tell, the more believable it will be and the more likely we are to prove patients like Katrin are not delusional, or at least don't belong in a psychiatric hospital.

'He's staying in a mobile home for the moment. We met when he came to the farmer's market. I didn't recognise him after all these years, but he knew who I was. He said he'd come back to Hamelin because of your article in *Die Tageszeitung* and that he'd like to talk to you about it.'

'I'd like to meet him.'

'Then you're in luck. We agreed he'd come this afternoon, and if I'm not mistaken, that's him over there.'

Alana pointed towards the path where a lone cyclist was slowly approaching. As Peter got a clearer view of him, he realised that the person he was looking at was his stalker.

'I was waiting for the right moment to talk to you. It never came,' Bodo replied. The three of them were seated around Alana's garden table. Peter had asked the old man why he hadn't just contacted him instead of following him around.

Although the answer didn't quite satisfy him, Peter decided to let it rest and asked why Bodo wanted to speak to him.

'Because of what you wrote in the newspaper. Those patients believing they're Hamelin's lost children, waking in a mountain cave after a long sleep? They're not delusional. Or, if *they're* delusional, then so am I, and so is Alana. Same thing happened to us, only longer ago. Do you believe Alana is delusional?'

'Of course not.'

'Well, neither am I. Nor are those patients locked up in the secure unit of the Koppenberg Klinik. They're the same as us. So why have they been kept there for such a long time?'

'That's something I would like to find out, too,' Peter said.

'I took the job of night cleaner so I could get close to those patients, who I believe were my childhood friends. But so far I haven't been given their unit to clean,' said Bodo.

'Even if you had, I doubt you would've learned much about them,' Peter said. 'They're drugged to the eyeballs. Most will have forgotten their past lives. I know that, because my fiancée works in that unit. I believe you've met. Her name is Erika.'

The more they talked, the clearer it became to Peter that they were on the same side as far as the patients in the secure unit were concerned. He told Bodo about the deaths, possibly caused by a drug trial gone wrong. At that point, an idea struck him. 'When you clean at night, do you also clean the pharmacy?'

'Sometimes.'

'Do you have a mobile phone?'

Bodo shook his head.

'If I gave you a disposable camera and told you what to look for, do you think you could take some photos?'

'What are you looking for?'

'The name of a pharmaceutical company. I'm sure Erika could tell you precisely what to look for.'

Bodo hesitated. 'I've only just started working there. If they catch me, they might fire me and my chance of contact with those patients is gone. And with it, my plan to help them get out and live a normal life.'

'I'm not asking you to do anything but take a few photos.'

Bodo relented and so it was agreed. They might yet discover the name of the manufacturer of the tablets Peter had not been able to trace. The tablets that had allegedly killed Martin and Tobias.

A few days later the sound of a doorbell ripped through the quiet dawn. Peter opened his eyes and, still half asleep, looked at the radio alarm beside the bed. Ten to six. Who the hell...?

'Go and see who it is, would you?' Erika mumbled, sleepily.

Another long, persistent ring got Peter out of bed. He added tracksuit bottoms to the T-shirt he was wearing and padded barefoot towards the front door. The moment he recognised Bodo, he remembered they'd agreed he would come and find them if he succeeded in his mission. During an earlier visit, Erika had instructed Bodo what to look for.

'Morning.' The grin on the older man's face suggested success. Or perhaps it was because of Peter's early-morning appearance.

'Morning,' said Peter. 'Come in. I was just about to make breakfast. Want some?'

'I wouldn't say no.'

In the kitchen, Peter put the coffee machine on. 'I'll go and get Erika.'

When he returned with Erika, Bodo had placed the camera on the kitchen table.

'Did you manage all right?' Erika asked. 'They didn't catch you?'

'They didn't. I was in there, alone, for at least twenty minutes. They thought I was mopping the floor, but I skipped that. I don't think anyone would notice, though. It wasn't very dirty. Instead, I did what you instructed me to do. I think I did all right. I checked and there wasn't any CCTV.'

The photos showed a box of medicine and the name of the manufacturer printed on it. *Hamburg-Pharma AG*.

SEVENTEEN

'Mind if I smoke?' Bodo asked over the remains of breakfast, consisting of rye bread with ham and eggs followed by more rye bread with honey, washed down with a pot of strong, black coffee.

'Not at all.' Peter avoided Erika's frown. Bodo took a tobacco pouch from his pocket and his hosts watched him roll the tobacco into a cigarette.

'I used to be part of this gang at school who smoked roll-ups and thought it was cool.' Peter smiled at the memory.

'It's cheaper than buying cigarettes,' Bodo said.

'There's nothing cool about smoking or lung cancer.' There was disapproval in Erika's voice.

'You better watch it, Bodo,' Peter said lightly. 'She persuaded *me* to stop and a non-smoking journalist is an odd thing.'

Erika changed the subject. 'Did you know a girl called Katrin, before you fell asleep in the mountain cave?'

Bodo looked pensive.

'She had a younger sister called Trude,' Erika continued. 'Their parents were farmhands. They lived in a cabin on farmland just outside Hamelin and the children helped out on the land.'

'I do remember Alana and her family, but Katrin and Trude, no, the names don't ring a bell,' Bodo said apologetically.

'That's a shame. Because if you want to contact my patients, Katrin is your best bet. She's the most lucid of all. After years of medication, the memories of the others are practically non-existent and they're having trouble forming and expressing coherent thoughts and ideas.'

'Will you let me speak to Katrin?' Bodo asked.

'I might when I'm on nights, next time. But that won't be for a while. Besides, they haven't given you our unit to clean yet, have they?' Bodo shook his head. 'I'll tell you what,' Erika said, 'why don't you write to Katrin? I was going to suggest the same to Alana. Write her a letter. Tell her you're a friend of Alana, describe what you remember from growing up in Hamelin before you disappeared into the mountain cave, and explain why you came back to Hamelin and now work at the klinik as a night-time cleaner. If you give me the letter, I'll make sure she'll receive it and I'll tell her to write back. That way, at least you get some form of communication going even if you can't see each other in the flesh.'

'Excellent idea,' said Peter.

Bodo agreed, then stubbed out his cigarette, thanked them for a wonderful breakfast, promised Erika he'd write the letter the same day and left.

Later that morning, Peter tried once more to contact retired Chief Inspector Klaus Lenau. Nurse Domin's friend, Regina Montag had mentioned the policeman to Peter, as someone who could tell him more about Katrin and her companions' first appearance in Hamelin in 1978.

Peter had made several efforts to contact Lenau but never received a reply to his emails. At the police station he was refused Lenau's phone number, but he found it by googling.

He went a few times to the address mentioned online, but no one answered the doorbell. Trawling through social media yielded no results. Lenau wasn't on Facebook, Twitter, LinkedIn or Instagram.

It was time to pay the police station another visit. Perhaps Lenau had changed his email address, or Peter might get lucky and encounter a more helpful front desk officer.

The receptionist at Hamelin's main police station was young and female. Peter launched a charm offensive when he approached her.

'Let me see if I can find out for you, just a moment,' she said briskly, clearly unimpressed.

While she was gone, the queue of people behind him grew longer and more disgruntled. He tried to ignore the impatient sighs and restless mutterings behind his back.

When she finally returned, the receptionist was accompanied by a stout, middle-aged man in plain clothes, possibly CID.

The detective took Peter aside. 'Did you ask about DCI Lenau?'

'That's right.'

'What did you want from him?'

None of your business, Peter thought. 'Information.' Before the other man could ask what kind of information, Peter quickly added, 'I have his email address and home phone number. But so far, he hasn't responded to either.'

'Perhaps he doesn't want to.'

Peter decided to ignore the dig. 'Can I just check whether I've got the right email address?'

The email address was correct.

'Is there a mobile phone number for DCI Lenau?' Peter asked casually, but without much hope.

The detective ignored the question. 'Look, DCI Lenau is retired. If it's police business you want to discuss, you can speak to me.'

Peter had no wish to speak to anyone but Lenau. Regina Montag had told him Lenau had been kind to the children. He had tried his best to do the right thing. The children trusted him, according to Paula Domin.

'Thanks, but I'll wait.' Peter turned to leave.

The detective changed tack. 'You might have to wait a while. They're on a round-the-world trip, him and the missus. They went immediately after he retired.'

No wonder I didn't get any response, Peter thought. 'D'you know when he's due back?'

'No. No idea.'

Something about the detective's tone suggested he was lying, but Peter thanked him anyway and left.

Back at work, Peter tried to concentrate on other newsworthy stories for the rest of the afternoon. But his thoughts kept wandering, mulling over what Alana and Bodo had told him. He believed their story as far back as 1945. But what to make of their claim they had been part of a group of children who had followed a stranger into the mountains around Hamelin a long, long time ago, centuries possibly, then fallen asleep in a cave? He had always thought that was only a story, not something that had really happened.

Were he and Erika too gullible, too easily conned? Either these two, Alana and Bodo, were as mad as Erika's patients and should be in the Koppenberg Klinik's special unit, or they spoke the truth and Erika's patients didn't belong there.

But that would mean the impossible: that they'd slept for hundreds of years and woken up in the same place. Hard evidence was what he needed. And even if that part was fake, why detain patients, even patients with a mental illness, for thirty-three years?

Alana and Bodo proved confinement was unnecessary. True enough, they lived at the fringe of society, but they weren't the only ones who did. They were independent, needed no one, made a living and a life for themselves.

After a long and entirely unproductive afternoon Peter was glad when it was time to go home.

Dirk, true to his word, had given Peter an email address for someone at Hamburg-Pharma AG. A certain Jens Hagedorn. By the time Peter got home, Hagedorn had replied to Peter's email requesting a meeting.

'Lunch at Hamburg *Tierpark*. Wednesday, 13.00 hours.'

Peter wondered why Hagedorn wanted to meet at the zoo, but agreed. He'd take the day off and travel to Hamburg by train; it was quicker than the car journey and he wouldn't have to worry about parking.

Peter deliberately took an early train, in case of delays, but the journey was uneventful. At Hamburg *Hauptbahnhof* he smelled the fresh sea breeze and its salty tang. Peter took a taxi to the zoo and arrived an hour before the appointed time.

He hadn't visited a zoo since he was a young boy, and he walked around for a bit. The place was immense, it would be easy to lose yourself in it. He found the map, which showed at least three eateries. One was a Coffee Corner, another a McDonalds and the third was called The Garden Restaurant. Peter assumed the latter was the one where Jens Hagedorn wanted to meet.

On his walk there, he saw a hippo surface from its pond, while at the water's edge a duck stood, sentinel-like, beak and breast thrust forward. Heaving itself out of the water, the hippo tried to climb on land, but the duck challenged him. Amused, Peter got out his mobile to take a picture of the duck with attitude, before the vast mass of hippo retreated and dropped back heavily into the water.

Further along the path he noticed dwarf antelopes making their shy appearance round shrubs and bushes. Slender, fine-boned creatures, the size of dogs, but more delicately built and moving with a grace which ballet dancers only dreamed of. Moving on, he passed a tiny lizard hugging a tree trunk, seemingly inert like all reptiles. No camouflage colours for this little fellow, but an exuberant display of emerald green.

Arriving at the restaurant, Peter looked at his watch. Twelve forty. Another twenty minutes to kill. Should he wait in the restaurant? He spotted a bench, where he sat to watch people go by. Since this was a weekday and off-season, the zoo wasn't busy. Most visitors looked to be grandparents with pre-school children.

At twelve fifty-five, Peter entered the restaurant, which did indeed have the look of an indoor garden, with its rattan tables and chairs, its abundance of tall potted plants and a vine-clad pergola forming a roof overhead. Only a few other guests were there. The waiter who met him at the entrance made a wide, inviting gesture, instead of steering him towards a table, meaning "take your pick."

Peter chose a table near the window with a view of the entrance. He felt slightly on edge. Had he done the right thing in taking the day off and coming all this way? He hoped it would be worth it. At one o'clock precisely, a tall man, in his fifties or thereabouts, walked in and looked around. Peter noticed the thin fair hair, the square, steel-framed spectacles, the expensive charcoal suit and hoped this wasn't his lunch appointment. If this was Jens Hagedorn, he looked anything but congenial. The feeling was confirmed when the man steered towards him, asked if Peter was *Herr* Hahn, introduced himself as "Doctor Hagedorn" and used the formal form of "you". It wasn't going to be a cosy chat, Peter concluded. Hagedorn took the seat across from Peter.

'Just out of interest,' said Peter, 'why the zoo?'

A shrug. 'It's opposite my office.'

They ordered. A salad niçoise and a Perrier water for Hagedorn, and a sausage roll and lager for Peter.

'What is this about?' Hagedorn asked, as they waited for their drinks to arrive.

Peter dug out the strip of tablets Erika had given him and put them on the table.

'I was hoping you could give me some information about these tablets.'

His companion frowned, took the tablets from the table and studied the code on the aluminium side of the strip for a moment.

Then he placed them back. 'I can't help you, I'm afraid.'

'They are manufactured by your company, though,' said Peter. 'I have the photos to prove it.'

He tapped on the screen of his mobile until the photos

which Bodo had taken of the medicine boxes appeared – with the name of the company on it as well as the code.

Jens Hagedorn only took a perfunctory look at the photos. 'How did you get hold of those?'

'I can't reveal my source, *I'm afraid*,' Peter used the tone Jens Hagedorn had used, 'but I can tell you that the photos were taken at the Koppenberg Klinik in Hamelin. Ring any bells?'

Hagedorn remained silent, with his mouth set in a thin line. His eyes blinked more rapidly.

'The tablets are nowhere to be found on a pill-identification website,' Peter continued. 'They're not licensed or labelled. Are they part of a clinical trial?'

Could the man stiffen any more? Peter wondered. There was something robotic in Hagedorn's manner and speech.

'It's possible. We have a good many clinical trials running, all over the country and abroad.'

'And to your knowledge, are all your participants doing these on a voluntary basis, having previously signed a contract?'

'Naturally.'

'Then you'll be sorry to hear these are being tested on patients, allegedly suffering from a form of delusion. I say "allegedly" because I have reason to believe they're not delusional. They had no say in the matter and two of them at least died after swallowing these tablets.'

Hagedorn abruptly pushed his chair back and stood up, although most of his salad was uneaten.

'I've listened long enough and I've nothing to say to you. I'm a very busy man, so if you'll excuse me–'

Peter didn't let him get away that easily. 'What compounds did you use in manufacturing these tablets? Do you have a contract with Doctor Wagner to run trials on her patients? How much are you paying her? I'm sure my readers would be interested to learn of any deals between Hamburg-Pharma AG and the director of the local psychiatric hospital.'

Hagedorn turned around sharply to face the journalist. He took a few steps towards Peter and leant over the table. 'You try that and I'll take you to court,' he spat. 'My lawyers will make mincemeat of you. You'll be finished, jobless, penniless. I can guarantee you that.'

With that he stalked away, leaving Peter outwardly calm but inwardly shaken, to finish his lunch.

During the return journey to Hamelin, Peter reflected on having been unfortunate enough to speak to the wrong person. He'd expected to speak to an employee: an analyst perhaps, or even better, a disgruntled employee.

Instead, his lunchtime appointment had been with a chief executive. He berated himself for not checking out the name online beforehand. He hoped the man's threat would prove empty.

Peter couldn't afford an expensive lawyer or a costly court case. He'd tell Erika there was no point in pursuing the matter any further.

Except, something Erika mentioned that evening gave Peter a new idea. Late afternoon she sent a text:

> Going to be late. I'm wiped out, can we get a pizza tonight? I won't feel like cooking dinner.

After work, before going up to the flat, Peter nipped into the pizzeria downstairs, ordered and paid for an extra-large Napoli, a salad and a bottle of Chianti Classico, to be collected when Erika got home.

The evening was warm enough to eat on the small balcony outside their bedroom.

'This is nice.' Erika sighed with satisfaction after the last mouthful of their anchovy pizza had disappeared from her plate. 'We should do this more often.'

She stretched as languorously as the rickety garden chair would allow and Peter refilled both their wine glasses. They watched as the sun went down. The front of the apartment looked out onto a busy shopping precinct, but here at the back, the view was that of the park. Apart from an occasional pedestrian hurrying home, the park was deserted. The only sound they could hear was birdsong.

'Bad day?' Peter asked.

'Always is on a quality control day. It's a nightmare for patients and staff alike.'

'Why is that?'

'Everything has to look picture perfect, so Doctor Wagner can show off her impressive achievements. The wards need to be clean, aesthetically pleasing and friendly-looking. The caring and helpful staff are expected to have a broad smile plastered over their faces. Patients are too drugged to move or answer any questions while their rooms are unlocked, doors open and nurses are expected to answer questions only in a positive way.'

'And this quality monitoring is carried out by whom? An external organisation?'

'Yep. Some external body.'

'Do you know its name?'

'Not really. But they're doctors, the ones that visit. Doctor Wagner keeps calling them "dear colleagues" or even "esteemed colleagues".'

Peter scoffed. 'I'm sure she does.'

They finished their wine, lost in their own thoughts. It was nearly dark and getting colder when they went inside. Erika put the dirty dishes and glasses in the dishwasher while Peter prepared to take the rubbish downstairs for the early-morning collection.

'Would it be possible to find out who exactly does the quality control at the klinik?' Peter said on his return. 'Preferably names of the "esteemed colleagues".'

Erika's eyes widened in bemusement. 'Sure, no problem. Why don't I also find out who's been having an affair with whom, out of that lot?'

He grinned at her sarcasm and kept looking at her, appealingly.

'Why do you want to know? We have no evidence of anything illegal going on at the klinik. All we have are suspicions.'

'At this moment we haven't any evidence, but that might change and then it's handy to know where to go with that information. So, could you?'

'I'll see. I'm not promising anything.'

EIGHTEEN

Most days, a deep pocket in Erika's uniform hid a letter from Bodo or Alana to Katrin and vice versa. After suggesting the correspondence, Erika had provided Katrin with a stack of envelopes and a notepad. Though Erika had no idea of the content of the letters she carried and delivered because they came in a sealed envelope, she noticed their effect on Katrin. Unfortunately, Erika wasn't the only one. Bauer too had noticed.

'Katrin looks a lot happier these days,' the senior staff nurse observed, after the letter exchange had been occurring for a couple of weeks. She and Erika were in the staffroom updating patient files.

'With this fine weather lately, she enjoys working in the garden. That way at least she feels productive. She hates feeling useless.' Erika was careful to steer away from the real reason for Katrin's smiles and lively chatter these days.

Nurse Bauer didn't buy it. 'Nah,' she said, 'I don't think it's anything to do with gardening. She's been gardening for years. I know she enjoys it, but I've never seen her like this. So lively, almost exuberant, one could say. It's so unlike her. I wonder... does she still take her medication?'

'Of course.' Erika hoped her voice sounded indignant enough.

'And there's no way she could have avoided swallowing them?'

'None at all, she's always supervised while taking the medicines.'

Which, hypothetically, wasn't a lie, Erika thought. I'm the one who started flushing them away.

The senior nurse gave Erika a long sceptical look before she returned to her files.

'We have to be more careful,' Erika warned Katrin later that day. 'Bauer mentioned earlier how much you have changed lately. She was wondering why you seem so happy nowadays.'

'Was I that noticeably glum before?'

'Not so much glum as dispirited.'

'Wouldn't you be, wouldn't anyone, after thirty-three years of incarceration, your sister's death and nothing to live for, or look forward to?'

'You're right. I can't even begin to imagine what that's like. That's why I'd like to help you, and it's also why I'm warning you to be careful. We don't want anyone to find out about the letters. It's those letters that have brought on this change, isn't it?'

'The letters give me hope. We're making plans for me to escape. If you really want to help me, you could be part of our plans.'

'If that's what's in the letters, all the more reason to be

careful. Not only could Bodo and I lose our jobs, we could be arrested and charged for a criminal act.'

'What do you suggest I do? Apart from hiding the letters where no one can find them?'

'Try not to show your feelings. You don't have to pretend, just tone it down a bit. Behave more like the other patients, so you don't stand out.'

'You mean I should behave like a zombie? Moving around as if sleepwalking?'

'Well, Bauer did ask if you were still taking your medication.'

'What did you say?'

'I said yes, of course.'

Katrin smiled her crooked smile. 'Don't worry. I'll be careful. And anyway, as long as Bodo isn't cleaning here in our unit at night, nothing is possible yet. I'm practising patience for now.'

Thinking about how to obtain contact details of representatives from the quality control organisation who had recently visited the Koppenberg Klinik, Erika came up with a plan. Before going ahead, she discussed it with Peter. 'One of the representatives, a woman, talked to us nurses about a course in the treatment of psychiatric patients. A refresher course is being offered by her organisation, for those already working in the profession. At the time I didn't think it was for me. I've only just completed my training. This was for those who have worked in the profession for years and want to find out about the latest trends and medicines. I could pretend to be interested and ask our receptionist for contact details. They would probably give me their email address. Is that enough?'

'It's a solid start. From that, we can find their website. The website might have further information: names, phone numbers.'

The receptionist, after listening to Erika's request, couldn't provide her with the information, but referred her to the klinik's administration team, where a member of staff wrote the email address down for her.

After work, Erika googled the address on Peter's laptop and the name came up as The Institute of Quality Psychiatric Health. On their website, in amongst the contact details, was a phone number.

'So what do we do now?' Erika asked Peter after he arrived home.

'Now we phone them.'

'And say what?'

'I'll think of something. What did that doctor or psychiatrist look like, the one who spoke to you about the course?'

'Medium height, medium build, middle-aged, short dark brown hair going grey. She wore tortoise-shell glasses and she looked Italian or Greek.'

Peter tapped in the number and Erika listened.

'Afternoon, my name is Kramer. I'm a nurse at the Koppenberg Klinik. We recently had an inspection from your representatives. One of them mentioned a refresher course for those working with psychiatric patients: a lady doctor with tortoise-shell glasses. Short dark hair, possibly Mediterranean.' Peter waited briefly, then continued. 'That's right. Doctor Polat. Now I remember the name. Could you send me an email with information about the course?'

He finished the conversation. 'She's from Turkey originally,' he told Erika. 'You nearly got it right.'

It didn't take them long to find her on LinkedIn: Doctor Azra Polat, psychiatrist.

'That's her.' Erika recognised her from the photos.

Peter took screenshots of some of the photos and saved them. 'Might be of use one day.' He thought, briefly. 'Let me know when that course is, will you?'

'Why?' said Erika. 'I'm not going.'

'I know. But it might be an opportunity to speak to Doctor Polat.'

'Don't even think about it. We were going to file her name away for later, in case we needed to contact the authorities, only if we discover more about deaths due to unlicensed drugs used for unauthorised drug trials. Leave it alone for now.'

A few days later, Erika entered the staffroom just before seven thirty. She was told there would be a morning briefing as soon as all six nurses were there. They didn't often have briefings, only when Nurse Bauer had an important announcement to make.

'What's this about?' Erika quietly asked Irina, one of her colleagues, 'and who are we waiting for?'

Irina shrugged and pulled a face. 'Uzo, of course. Who else?'

'He can't help it.' Erika felt she needed to defend him. 'He has four young children and his wife doesn't always cope and is frequently ill. It's not an easy situation.'

Irina scoffed. Just then, their colleague arrived, panting.

'Talk of the devil,' Irina muttered under her breath.

Erika frowned.

'Apologies,' Uzo called out towards Bauer.

She ignored him and, clutching papers under her arm, addressed the small gathering. 'I've decided to shake things up a bit,' she started brightly. 'You've all cared for the same group of patients these past six months.'

Everyone went quiet and Erika listened with a sinking feeling in her stomach.

The supervisor continued. 'It's time you all took charge of a different group of patients. It's very simple. From today, Doris will swap her patients with Uzo's, Ingo will swap with Dagmar and Erika will swap her patients with Irina. This morning you'll visit and introduce your patients to their new nurse. I also want you to take some time to brief each other on your patients' symptoms and care plans. Any questions?'

Erika put her hand up. 'Some of our patients are likely to be upset with the change of nurses. They trust us. And now they have to rebuild that trust with another nurse. That'll take time. If nurses are being changed frequently, they might feel they're being treated like a case instead of a human being.'

Erika was glad to see some colleagues nodding or make noises in agreement.

'They'll get used to it,' Bauer said. 'Now, if no one else has a question, I suggest you all get started.'

Of all her colleagues it had to be Irina to replace her, Erika thought. Irina, whom Erika had caught mocking patients with crude imitations. Irina, who had shown little compassion when Martin died. To Irina, members of staff were "us" and patients were "them".

With a heavy feeling, Erika reflected on her patients' probable reactions to being cared for by Nurse Irina. Sigi and Carla might be okay; they didn't notice what was going on, anyway. But the others? Ilse and Bettina would be distraught. Any change to their daily routine upset them. For Rolf and Heiko, the change of nurse could cause problems and they could become aggressive. And what about Katrin? How could she help Katrin now? They'd come so far, she was nearly off her medication and was doing so well, healthy in mind and body and hoping to leave this place behind. What was to become of *her?* Forced to take her medication, she wouldn't be able to think about or remember any of her plans. The medicines might even make her ill, after taking only very small doses these past months.

Erika's train of thought came to a sudden halt when Irina approached her. 'What shall we do first, briefing or patient visits?'

I need to speak to Katrin, Erika thought, and tell her I'll still come and see her, might still be able to slip the letters underneath her door. It doesn't have to mean the end of her dreams.

'Will you excuse me for a moment?' she replied.

Without an explanation, Erika rushed off towards Katrin's room. There, she didn't linger for a moment, but hurriedly explained what was going to happen to a stunned Katrin. She finished her account with a warning. 'Be careful. I hate to say this about a colleague, but I'm not sure you can trust Irina.'

'What about...?' Katrin began.

Erika cut her off. 'I have to go back now. We'll speak later. I'll come to you as soon as possible.'

Irina looked up from the files she was studying, when Erika returned to the staffroom.

'I thought I'd better have a look at these, while waiting for you to come back.'

She sounded annoyed. Erika noticed the files were those of her patients. Now *ex*-patients, she thought miserably.

'Good idea. I'll read those of your patients and then we'll talk through each of them.'

Cycling home after her eight-hour shift, Erika thought of that time in the staffroom, reading files and discussing patients, as the calm before the storm. She had expected patients to be upset by the change of nurses, but upset wasn't the word. Some cursed, threw food around and shouted at them. Others sobbed, rocked back and forth or punched themselves in the face, signs of distress Erika had not seen before in her patients.

Katrin, who was the last patient they visited, refused to acknowledge their presence after Erika and Irina entered her room. She didn't look at them or speak at all. Erika had not been able to see Katrin on her own as promised, and now cycled home with the weight of guilt on her shoulders. Perhaps all this was her fault. She remembered Bauer asking if Katrin was still taking her medication and the sceptical expression on her face when Erika confirmed. What if Bauer didn't trust her, somehow suspected the truth and therefore had implemented this change, this swapping of patients?

As if Erika wasn't feeling miserable enough it started to rain, lightly at first, but by the time she reached home it came down in solid sheets. Soaked through, she put her bike in the shed round the back and climbed the stairs to the apartment.

As Erika took off her dripping coat, guitar chords sounded from the bedroom revealing that, unusually for him at this time, Peter was already home as well. In the bathroom, she dried her face and wrapped a towel around her hair before entering the bedroom.

Peter, sitting cross-legged on the bed, stopped in the middle of an instrumental rendition of a popular song and looked at her. 'You're early.'

Erika was on the cusp of telling him all about her disastrous day.

'I've lost my job,' Peter said, before she could do so.

'What? Why?'

Peter put his guitar down and opened his arms. 'Come here.'

After she'd sat down and nestled in his arms, she noticed the letter lying on the bed beside him.

He handed it to her. 'You'd better read this.'

The letter, from the distinguished law firm "Mayer &

Partner LLP, threatened to sue Peter for libel if he published anything more about the Koppenberg Klinik, its patients or Doctor Wagner. Peter waited until Erika had finished reading.

'They sent the same letter to my editor. She was furious and gave me my notice there and then, but I persuaded her to let me work from home and publish articles or features under a pseudonym. Nothing about the Koppenberg Klinik, of course. If I want to continue my investigation, I'd have to try and publish it in another newspaper, under a different name.'

'Forget about it. Stop the investigation. It's not leading anywhere. I don't want you to make it any worse for yourself. It's not worth it.'

'Not worth it? What about justice for Katrin and her fellow patients? What about the possibility of stopping illegal drug trials?'

'Katrin is no longer my patient.'

And Erika started to tell Peter what had happened that day at work.

Two days later, Erika finally found an opportunity to visit Katrin alone. She had seen her a few times, but always with Irina or another nurse present.

'Katrin? I'm sorry I didn't come sooner, I...'

The room was dark and the curtains closed. Erika switched the light on. Katrin, still dressed in pyjamas, was lying in bed. A sour smell pervaded the room and when Erika came closer, she noticed that dried vomit had spilled from Katrin's mouth onto the pillow and sheets. It was in her hair as well. Erika initially thought Katrin was asleep. She was lying motionless, but her eyes were open and stared into space. Her usually expressive face was blank.

'Katrin, it's me, Erika. Let's sit you up.'

She helped Katrin to sit up, needing all her strength for a body that was like a dead weight. She washed Katrin's face and hair with a flannel. After transferring her former patient to a chair, Erika changed the bedding and tried to explain why she hadn't been able to visit her sooner.

'Katrin? Won't you say something? Tell me what you're thinking or feeling. If you're angry with me, or disappointed, can we at least talk about it?'

Erika reassured her, pleaded with her, urged her, but not a word escaped Katrin's lips and the eyes that looked at Erika didn't acknowledge her. She remained unresponsive. She doesn't recognise me, Erika thought, and wondered how long Katrin had been lying on the bed in her own sick. Her gentle patience with Katrin was in sharp contrast with the way she pummelled the pillow, now with a clean pillowcase, into shape with her fists. They had no right to treat Katrin in this way. Katrin had been happy, healthy and sane before the change of nurse. Now look at her. She had become like the other patients, or worse.

The hopelessness of the situation and her own powerlessness was almost too much to bear. Erika took Katrin's hand and gently squeezed it. They sat like that for a time without speaking or looking at each other.

Erika didn't see Katrin again until a few days later. She'd just finished her morning round and was wheeling her medicine trolley back to the medication storage room when, passing Katrin's room, she became aware of a commotion behind the door: screaming and loud, harsh voices.

Thinking she might be able to calm Katrin down, Erika

went in to find Irina wielding a syringe, while a robust student nurse pinned Katrin down on her bed. Katrin was kicking, screaming and wrestling to escape the student nurse's grip. Horrified, Erika could only stare.

Irina glanced up. 'Erika, can you sit on Katrin's legs while I inject her? She's refused to take her medication these last few days and as you can see, she's fighting like a wildcat to avoid the injection. Was she always like this?'

Only when I first saw her, Erika thought, reminded of that occasion when Bauer had forced her to hold Katrin down.

'I never had any trouble administering her medication. Why don't you let me try, without the needle?'

Grudgingly, Irina complied. She and the student nurse stepped back while Erika took the pills and glass of water from the medication trolley. Katrin sat up and stared at Erika with eyes that were pools of hatred.

Erika leaned towards Katrin, making sure she blocked the patient from view, before handing her the glass with a wink and emptying the cup containing a mixture of pills into her sleeve.

'Well done. Now swallow,' Erika said soothingly.

When Katrin did so, the other two nurses looked surprised.

'How did you do that?'

'I just calmed her down, that's all.'

Erika prayed fervently the pills would not fall from her sleeve, as she made to leave.

'Perhaps you should administer her medicines from now on. I've found it an impossible task,' said Irina.

'No problem,' Erika smiled, 'just call me and I'll do it.'

That same evening, she wrote Katrin a note. *They will let me give you your medication. Pretend to swallow them and act as if you have. I will get you out of there, I promise. Destroy this note.* She would push it underneath Katrin's door tomorrow, just as she had done with Bodo's and Alana's letters.

NINETEEN

Peter counted himself lucky to find a parking spot right opposite the Institute for Quality Psychiatric Health, from where he could watch Doctor Polat leaving the building.

Erika wouldn't like what he was about to do and he hadn't told her. On this particular Thursday in November, the refresher course for mental health nurses ran from 19.30 to 22.00 and Erika's shift would not finish until midnight.

Peter had decided to wait until the course finished and catch Doctor Polat on her way out. He hoped the doctor would be interested in what he had to tell her. She might not be, of course. There was no way of knowing, but he felt he needed to take that risk. If anyone could order an investigation into Doctor Wagner and the Koppenberg Klinik, she could.

The clock on the dashboard indicated it was now ten o'clock. He didn't expect Doctor Polat to leave immediately; there would be questions to answer or the session might overrun. He kept a steady eye on the gate. Ten minutes later it opened and from it emerged small clusters of people. Some climbed straight onto their bikes and pedalled away, others stopped on the pavement to chat. Another ten minutes went by before he recognised the woman with tortoiseshell glasses coming through the gate, whose face he had memorised from photos on her social media.

In a blink he was out of the car, crossing the road and striding towards her.

'Doctor Polat? Azra Polat?'

She stopped and turned to face him with a smile. 'Yes?'

'My name is Peter Hahn. Do you have a minute? I have some information that might interest you.'

She dropped the smile. 'Information? To do with what exactly?'

'Regarding the Koppenberg Klinik. The same klinik to which you paid a quality control visit about a month ago.'

She frowned. 'Do you work there?'

'No. But I know someone who–'

'Why don't you email your information to the institute and we'll see what we can do? Good night.' She walked away.

Peter, instead of going back to his car, kept walking beside her, trying to hand her his card.

'Here are my contact details. If not now, could you let me know when would be a good time to talk?'

'I told you what to do with your information. Email us.'

'Aren't you even the slightest bit curious to find out what I have to tell you?'

'Please leave me alone or I'll contact the police.' By now she had arrived at her car, a cream Mercedes, and after some digging around in her bag she pulled the car keys from it.

'Did you know there's a large group of patients in a closed unit who have been incarcerated there for thirty-three years?' Peter said.

She didn't reply, but tried to put the key in the car door. Her hand was a little shaky and the key fell. Peter heard the tinkle as it hit the ground. They squatted in unison to pick it up. While they searched for the key in the dark, Peter kept talking. 'Some of those patients died after new medicines were tried out on them. No one is being held accountable. No one is considered responsible for those deaths. Did you know that?'

Just then, he spotted the key. As he handed it to her the tone of his voice changed from accusatory to persuasive. 'They are locked away, these patients, because they believe they are the original lost children of Hamelin. The ones who followed the piper into the mountains. There are others, you know, who are not locked up. People who swear they were amongst the ones who followed a musician into the mountains and disappeared.'

If he'd hoped to convince her, her reaction suggested he'd done the opposite. She straightened and her face showed what she thought. He was the one who needed to be locked up. He was the crazy one.

He made a final effort to make her listen. 'I've met them. They live a perfectly normal life. I could introduce them to you and you'd see they're not crazy.'

As she hurried into the car, Peter became aware that they were alone in a deserted street with hardly any streetlamps. No wonder there'd been fear in her eyes.

'That went well,' he muttered to himself, as he walked towards his car.

Peter liked to visit the farmers' market on Saturdays, during the late afternoon when market vendors were packing up. If he went earlier, the place would be heaving with customers and Alana and Bodo, who was helping her, would be too busy to chat.

As Bodo and Alana served their last customers, Peter surveyed the remaining fruit and vegetables.

'Hello, Peter,' Bodo said, after his customer left. 'What will it be?'

Other than potatoes, onions, carrots and tomatoes, Peter also bought a jar of set, pale amber honey.

'Best honey we've had in years,' he told Alana, who joined them. 'It's delicious. We finished that jar you gave us in no time.'

Alana smiled and nodded. 'I made plum jam, but they've all gone. Pity. I wasn't sure you were coming today, or I would've kept a jar for you.'

'I've had some good news,' Bodo told Peter. 'Starting on Monday I've been given the special unit to clean at night. The one where Katrin is. We've been writing letters to each other.'

'Excellent,' said Peter, 'so now you can finally meet face to face. That is what you wanted, isn't it?'

'Actually, I don't think that's a good idea. It'll be night time and discovery by members of staff might get me fired. Also, I'm working on a plan to help Katrin escape and any connection between us would raise suspicion. Especially just after I start cleaning her unit.'

'What's the plan?'

Bodo hesitated and looked around, making sure they weren't overheard. 'It's very simple, but I think it could work. I'd need Erika's help, though. It would involve giving me the combination for the lock on Katrin's door and the one for the door to the garden. Also, I need Erika to leave a nurse's uniform in Katrin's room. Katrin, dressed in nurse's uniform, could walk through the garden towards the bicycle racks, take Erika's bike out and walk with it through the gate.'

'Does Katrin know how to cycle?'

'I'm sure she doesn't, but she doesn't have to. Katrin could walk, bicycle in hand, to the end of the street. Round the corner, Erika or you would be waiting to drive her to Alana's. The bike is only a means to make Katrin's getaway appear natural. As well as hiding her problem leg. I mean, who at the gate is going to look at a nurse with her bicycle?'

'Sounds like a good plan to me,' Peter said, 'and I'm sure Erika would participate. She's been worried about Katrin since she started working there. When were you thinking of carrying it out?'

'Not this week and perhaps not the next, but the week after that. We have to make sure Erika and I won't be suspected of helping Katrin escape. At least, no more than any other member of staff. It'll be difficult enough for both of us to pretend we weren't involved.'

'Have you told Erika your plan, yet?'

'I haven't had an opportunity to speak to her lately.'

'Then I'll tell her and I'll let you know next Saturday, when I visit the market again, what she thinks.'

To his surprise, when Peter returned home, he found an email from Doctor Polat, agreeing to meet. She suggested the Eichendorf Hotel, the following Wednesday afternoon at four. He was to ask for her at the reception desk in the lobby.

The Eichendorf was the smartest and most expensive hotel in Hamelin. Situated in the centre of town, the hotel, with its elegant Art Nouveau façade, had been built in the late nineteenth century and had survived the wars.

A valet service was offered in the car park at the rear of the Eichendorf but, because the hotel was not far from his apartment, Peter arrived on foot and entered via the front entrance. Though he'd changed into 'smart clothes': leather shoes, tan chinos, white shirt and a black leather jacket, the doorman looked at him like something that the cat had dragged in.

He crossed the marble floor of the lobby towards the reception desk, past expensively dressed guests lounging on sofas and a medieval tapestry depicting a large group of children marching cheerfully behind a brightly dressed flautist. Crystal chandeliers dangled above his head. The air was heavy with the scent of fresh flowers in vases perched on coffee tables. The reception desk was made of mahogany and had a dark-green granite top. To attract the attention of one of the receptionists, Peter had to speak up and cut through the hubbub of voices. 'Can you tell me where to find a Doctor Polat? I have a four o'clock meeting with her here.'

Unexpectedly, a gentleman who hovered near the reception desk with the authoritative air of a manager, answered his question instead. 'Ah, yes. I'll show you, if you will follow me.' He led Peter through a set of double doors to a small table in a secluded bar. The bartender was the only other person present. 'Can I get you a drink while you're waiting?' the manager-type asked.

'Just a coffee, please.'

A coffee was ordered from the bartender and Peter was left by himself.

The coffee came with a small glass of water and a heart-shaped gingerbread biscuit. It tasted Italian.

Once again, Peter wondered what had made Doctor Polat change her mind. He was inwardly rehearsing what to say to her, when the door to the lobby opened and the mayor, Thomas Wagner, came in and made a beeline for him.

'Peter Hahn? You are expecting Doctor Polat?'

'Yes.'

'She's not coming. Instead, you and I will have a little chat.'

Momentarily lost for words, Peter waited, realising Doctor Polat had not changed her mind at all. She had been asked to send him that email. Why? What could the mayor possibly have to say to him that was different from the letter he'd already sent Peter via his lawyers?

'You see, Azra Polat is a very good friend of my wife's,' Thomas Wagner began, amiably enough. 'After you accosted her in the street late last Thursday, she phoned and told us about it, clearly upset. Said you wanted to tell her something about the Koppenberg Klinik. Doctor Jens Hagedorn, too, is a good friend of ours and we know all about your meeting with him at Hamburg Zoo. We know you also had a conversation with Christa Sachs at the department of social services. All that digging and for what? What are you hoping to find out?'

'Evidence that patient deaths were caused by unlicensed drug trials on patients who had no say and no choice about taking part. Patients who have been incarcerated for thirty-three years, without any assessment by mental health specialists other than your wife and her friends.'

Peter held Wagner's eyes without blinking or looking away. It was the mayor who broke off their staring contest and emitted a short, harsh laugh. 'Ridiculous! Where did you hear such fabricated nonsense? Who fed you these unfounded fairy tales?'

For one breath-stopping moment Peter feared Wagner knew about his relationship with Erika. But she hadn't been mentioned yet.

'You know I can't reveal my sources,' Peter said as he stirred his coffee.

'Ever the journalist, I suppose.'

In the silence that followed, Peter thought he could almost hear the mayor's thoughts spinning like the cogs in a Swiss clock.

'Must've been hard to lose your job at the *DeWeZet*,' Wagner said finally. 'A bright young reporter like you, hoping to make it big time in the media.' Peter didn't react. He didn't want to give anything away. Wagner continued casually. 'What if I told you I could possibly get you a job writing for the nationals? I happen to know the editors of *Die Welt* and the *Frankfurter Allgemeine*. Send some of your articles and I could put in a word for you. They owe me a favour.'

The offer was so unexpected, Peter sat dumbfounded for a moment, his thoughts racing. Writing for one of the national newspapers had been his ultimate goal, ever since studying journalism. Working for the *DeWeZet* was always supposed to be a stepping stone, an apprenticeship on his way there. He knew how hard it was to get a foot in the door. Too much competition. A chance like that hardly ever came along and should be seriously considered if he wanted to fulfil his dream. No doubt there was going to be a price to pay, though.

Wagner leant towards him. 'Refrain from writing about the Koppenberg Klinik, its patients or staff, and I'll be on the phone to the editors in question to suggest they give you a chance.'

When Peter stalled, considering his answer, Wagner got up. 'You need time to think about it. I understand. Let me know when you've made up your mind. But I wouldn't take too long if I were you, in case I change my mind first.' He gave Peter his business card and left.

Over a late home-cooked supper of roast chicken and stuffed peppers, Peter discussed the matter with Erika, who became quite excited.

'It's what you've always wanted.' They sipped their wine, lost in thought for a moment. 'It's too good an offer to ignore,' Erika suggested. 'I'd say, let's get Katrin out of there, then leave it alone. Don't write about it. Accept his offer.'

Peter didn't immediately respond.

'What?' Erika exclaimed, slightly impatient.

'What about the other patients? Do we just ignore them? Just put up with them continuing as guinea pigs for the pharma companies? So that I can pursue a glittering career?' The last words rang with an undertone of cynicism.

'Consider the alternative,' Erika said. 'You don't accept the offer. You keep writing about the Koppenberg from our bedroom. You even manage to get your article published in the *Tageszeitung*, just like you did last time. The Wagners will accuse you of defamation and take you to court. After losing, you will have to pay the costs, which you can't afford.'

'Only if we have no evidence. I won't publish anything until we have evidence. Or until an authority believes us and can look into the matter. That's why I went to Doctor Polat.'

'You did what?' Erika looked startled at first, then furious.

In the heat of their discussion, he'd forgotten he hadn't told her about his meeting with the psychiatrist.

'I thought, perhaps, I could persuade her to investigate what's going on at the klinik. It turns out, she's a friend of Claudia Wagner.'

Erika was still annoyed with him when they went to bed. A sleepless night ensued and early the following morning, Peter sent Thomas Wagner a short email.

```
Thank you for the offer, but I have
decided not to accept it. I would prefer
a  job  offer  based  on  merit,  not
someone's recommendation.
```

TWENTY

'Put these in the back of your wardrobe.' Erika handed Katrin a plastic bag containing a nurse's uniform, a short, woollen jacket and a scarf.

Katrin peered inside the bag, took out a delicately patterned *crêpe de chine* dress and held it up. 'What's this?'

'That was my sister's. She wanted to throw it out. I put it on top in case anyone asked who the bag was for and what was in it. They know I sometimes bring you clothes.'

'Did anyone ask?'

Erika shook her head. 'There's still one thing missing though. The right kind of shoes, like the ones we nurses wear. What size do you take?' She stepped out of her shoes. 'Try mine.' Katrin did. 'Can you walk in them?'

Katrin took a few steps up and down her room. 'They're a bit tight.'

'You don't need to walk far. I do have an older pair. They're more worn so might be slightly wider. I'll bring them in tomorrow. Wrap the scarf around your head, like so.' Erika demonstrated how. 'Make sure you cover as much of your hair with it as you can. You'll need a bag, too. A nurse going home without a bag doesn't look right. I'll bring a large shoulder bag. You can put some of your personal belongings in it. They have to be small items, though. Things you don't want to leave behind.'

Katrin nodded. 'Anything else?'

Erika thought for a moment. 'Just look confident. As if you've walked out of that gate hundreds of times, like I have. Say "night night" to the guard as you pass him, but in an off-hand way.'

Katrin grimaced. 'The closer the night comes, the more nervous I feel.'

'That's understandable. It's a big adventure for you, and a big risk for you to take as well. But remember: once you've walked through the gate, we're not far away. Peter and I will be waiting for you round the corner to take you to safety.'

'To Alana's house?'

Erika smiled. 'She can't wait to see you.'

Breath steamed up the windows of their car, as Peter and Erika sat in the dark, waiting for Katrin to appear around the corner. Peter had parked in a quiet residential street some twenty minutes ago. Neither was in the mood for talking or listening to music and as the minutes passed, Erika, in the passenger seat, felt more and more on edge.

According to the digital clock on the dashboard it was a quarter past midnight. The plan was for Katrin to leave her room just after midnight. From the gate of the Koppenberg Klinik to where they were parked was no more than a ten-minute walk, at a slow pace. Both kept their eyes glued on the spot from where Katrin would emerge.

A few more minutes passed, during which Erika inwardly

listed everything that could go wrong. What if, for some reason, a member of staff had injected Katrin with medication? What if Bodo had been assigned somewhere else to clean tonight? What if he'd been seen while unlocking the door to the garden or Katrin's room? What if Katrin had been caught leaving via the garden door?

What if she hadn't been able to unlock the bike? She had forgotten to tell Katrin the bike wasn't essential. It was just a nice touch to make her getaway look more natural. She could leave it in the bicycle rack and do without. What if the guard started to chat and became suspicious? All these possibilities went through her head, although she had rehearsed most of those with Katrin and discussed what to do in each case.

Not being able to contain herself any longer, Erika pulled her beanie further down over her head and pushed the door handle down. 'I'm going to have a look.'

'Don't. If you and Katrin are seen together, your career is over, and they'll find Katrin and take her back to the klinik. She'll never be free.'

'Perhaps she got lost between the Koppenberg and here. What if she's wandering around, looking for us? I need to get out and see if she's all right.'

Erika opened the car door and moved to step out when Peter's voice stopped her. 'Look! There's someone with a bicycle. Is that her?'

Erika thought at first it was an attempt to prevent her from leaving the car. She saw neither woman nor bike in the distance. But as she kept staring, the darkness revealed the shape of a small woman pushing a bike along by its handlebars.

'It is. It's Katrin. Your eyesight must be a lot better than mine.'

Peter flashed the car lights once, a signal they had arranged earlier, so Katrin would know where to find the car. Erika saw

Katrin walk as fast as her leg would allow, with purpose. As she got close, both Peter and Erika jumped out. Peter took the bike from Katrin and strapped it to the bike rack attached to the back of the car, while Erika shepherded Katrin onto the back seat and fastened the seatbelt for her.

All this was done silently and at great speed, so they could vanish in a flash. After getting back in the car herself, Erika turned and smiled reassuringly at Katrin, who was holding on to her seat with a tight grip.

'You're doing fine. We'll be at Alana's soon; it's not far. We'll talk there. You can tell us all about your escape.'

With hardly any traffic on the roads, they reached Alana's ten minutes later.

Before Erika, who led the way, had a chance to ring the doorbell, the front door opened and Alana appeared on the doorstep.

'You made it then,' she greeted them in a low voice, to avoid waking the neighbours.

'Lena... Alana?' Katrin, behind Erika, stepped forward.

The two women hugged in a tearful reunion. Childhood friends, whose only recent contact had been through letters furtively delivered to Katrin by Erika. On recovering, Alana invited the three of them in.

'I can make tea,' she said, leading the way, 'but perhaps something stronger is called for. I know I need it. Let me see what I've got.'

She returned a minute or two later with a bottle of sherry and four glasses, and put them on the table. 'To celebrate.'

No one declined. Not even Peter, who still had to drive home. 'One small glass won't get me fined.'

Katrin had never tasted sherry before.

'It burns in my throat,' was her reaction.

'Drink it slowly in small sips,' Erika advised her. 'It'll relax you. You'll see.'

It loosened Katrin's tongue as well. Asked to narrate the details of her escape, she elaborated. 'Everything went according to plan, until I got to the gate, when the guard stopped me and said he'd never seen me before. I nearly burst into tears. My legs were shaking. I had trouble keeping the bike upright. But he only thought I was a recently employed nurse. He just wanted to chat. I think he was bored. I said I was keen to get home, and that I could hardly keep myself awake, just like you told me to.'

Erika finished her sherry. It was time for her and Peter to go home. 'I'll see you in a few days. Enjoy your reunion. You'll have so much to talk about.'

The next morning Erika felt a swirling in her stomach and a headache threatened. She nibbled on her toast and honey, trying to get some breakfast inside her.

'I feel sick.'

Peter, tucking into a bowl of cornflakes, looked up from his Twitter feed. 'Don't go in to work then.'

'I have to. It'll look suspicious if I don't. They'll think I had something to do with Katrin's disappearance.'

Peter agreed. 'Text me when you have time. Let me know how the situation is over there. It might not be too bad.'

Oh, but it was bad. It was very bad, Erika realised, as soon as she entered the klinik. Staff members looked up to stare at her or whisper, their heads close together as she passed by. In the staffroom, when she looked at the schedule to see where she was assigned and what her role would be for that day, Nurse Jaeger intercepted her. 'Erika, you're wanted in Doctor Wagner's office. You need to go immediately.'

'Why? What's happened?'

'If you don't know yet, you'll soon find out. Go. Now.'

On her way, Erika nearly bumped into Doris, a colleague, in the corridor.

'Have you heard? Katrin has disappeared.'

Erika summoned as much astonishment as she could in one word. 'No!'

'Yes! Overnight. Hermann went to check on her at ten thirty last night and she was still in her room. But when Irina came to bring her breakfast this morning, she was gone. Bauer immediately organised a search before Doctor Wagner arrived. Katrin was nowhere to be found. Bauer then had to go and tell Doctor Wagner, who had a hissy fit. Apparently, you could hear her screaming at old Bauer two doors along the corridor. Now she's interrogating everyone who was frequently in contact with Katrin.'

'That'll be me,' said Erika. 'I'd better go.'

'Rather you than me. Good luck.'

As Erika sped towards the director's office her mouth felt dry and it was hard to swallow. A gallon of water would not have quenched her thirst.

She knocked on Doctor Wagner's door and Nurse Bauer opened it. 'Come in.'

Erika had never seen Bauer like this. Her supervisor looked older, deflated, her usual confidence gone. Did she just get the sack? Erika wondered. She hoped not. She wasn't fond of the woman but wouldn't want her to lose her job because of Katrin's escape. At Bauer's age it would be near impossible to find another one.

'Sit down, Erika.' Doctor Wagner, behind her desk, had dropped her usual charm and pleasant manners. Her chin, above a clenched jaw, jutted sharply forward, lending her face a more angular appearance. Erika took the seat facing her in front of the desk.

'Shall I leave you to it?' Bauer turned towards the door. She sounded as if she was desperate to get away.

'No. Stay.' But Wagner didn't offer Bauer a chair.

'Nurse Bauer tells me you have a close relationship with Katrin,' Claudia Wagner began.

'It was always a professional relationship between nurse and patient, but yes, we got on well during the time she was my patient, which is no longer the case.'

'I changed that,' Bauer, hovering between desk and door, interrupted. 'I could see Katrin and Nurse Erika were getting too familiar. Erika went out of her way to favour Katrin over her other patients. She bought her clothes, lent her books and spent more time with her than anyone else.'

'I felt sorry for Katrin. She was more conscious of her situation than my other patients. She needed someone to talk to. The others didn't.'

'Did your feeling sorry for Katrin extend to helping her walk out of here?' Wagner asked. 'Your colleague, Nurse Irina, revealed that, although Katrin was no longer your patient, you still administered her medication every day. She says you two talked a lot. What did you talk about?'

'Katrin didn't want to take the medication. She thought she would feel better without it. I persuaded her to take it anyway. That took time and much talk from my side.'

'Katrin could never have run away without help from staff. She could not have opened the doors by herself. So, I'm asking you again: did you help her? Did you open the doors for her?'

Erika's heart pounded in her throat and her headache by

now was so bad, it felt as if someone drilled into her temples. But she managed to appear calm when she looked straight at Doctor Wagner. 'No, I didn't. I'm not working nights at the moment. You can check that.'

'You could have returned during the night.'

'Someone would have seen and recognised me.'

Claudia Wagner changed tack. 'Where do you think Katrin went?'

'I have no idea.'

'She must have mentioned places she would like to visit.'

'I don't think she had any hope of leaving the Koppenberg. We didn't discuss it.'

Wagner gave her a long, hard look. 'That's all for now. I've informed the police and they'll be here this afternoon. They will want to question you. Do not leave until they have done so.'

Erika left the office and went straight to the staff toilet, where she splashed cold water on her face and gulped some down too. She was shaking and breathing unsteadily, while now and then a sob escaped her.

'Get a grip,' she told herself. Erika remained in the cubicle until someone banged on the door and asked if she was all right.

Somehow, Erika managed to get through the next few hours doing her regular duties, checking on patients, updating charts, delivering lunch trays and after lunch, accompanying patients to various therapy sessions.

Around three o'clock, Bauer came to tell her the police wanted to see her in the conference room. There were two of them, both in uniform, an older officer and a youngish one. They sat side by side behind the conference table that filled the room. Erika remembered the last time she'd been here, when Doctor Wagner and staff members discussed Martin's sudden, unexplained death.

The officers told her to take a seat and commenced their

interrogation. The older man asked the questions and his colleague made notes. How well had she known the patient who disappeared last night? What were the symptoms of Katrin's mental illness? Had the patient been unhappy lately? Had she talked with Erika about running away from the Koppenberg? How difficult was it for patients to escape?

'Extremely hard. Even if her door had accidentally been left unlocked, she'd still have to get through the door that gives access to the unit and walk out of the main entrance of the klinik. Both are secured. She would have been seen by staff on night shift, too.'

Erika purposefully avoided mentioning the side door to the garden.

'So how do you think she did it?'

Erika shrugged. Then she feigned an idea. 'Perhaps the security system went down last night?'

The older man shook his head. 'We checked that. There was nothing wrong with the security system. Also, there was a guard on duty at the gate. He would have seen her leave. He says he didn't. Her escape can't have been a sudden impulse. Everything points towards a well-thought-out plan. Your chief psychiatrist suspects Katrin had help.' He studied Erika with a penetrating look, then leaned forward. 'Tell me, which members of staff are familiar with the security code? I take it you change it every day?'

'The code does change daily. As far as I know, only qualified and permanent staff have the code.'

'What about cleaners?'

It was the first time the younger officer had spoken, and the question rang so close to the truth, Erika experienced an involuntarily sharp intake of breath followed by a sense that her mask of detached innocence had momentarily slipped and visible underneath was... what? Nervousness? Guilt? Because now they homed in on her. *Did* she know any of the cleaners?

Erika was desperate to leave Bodo out of it. 'I only know the cleaning staff in passing. We say good morning or good evening, that's all.'

'Everyone we talked to told us how close you were to this patient. You were concerned about her; you defended her; you spent a lot of time together. Are you telling us you really don't know anything about her escape or where she went?'

Erika would have liked to tell them the truth. She didn't like lying. But Katrin's freedom and Bodo's anonymity were more important now than her own feelings.

She shook her head. 'I wish I could help because I worry about her, being alone, somewhere in the outside world.'

'Are you sure about her being on her own?'

'I don't know, but I guess so.' Erika had nothing more to add. 'We're understaffed at the moment, so if you have no more questions for me...' This was not strictly true, but she was desperate to get the ordeal over with.

The older officer sighed. 'All right, we'd better let you get back to your patients. But we might ask you at a later date to come to the station and answer more questions.'

'No problem.' Relieved, she got up and left.

Erika heard the key in the front door turn, then the door opened and closed and Peter's voice sounded in the passage.

'Erika?'

By candlelight, Erika luxuriated in a bath of lavender-scented bubbles, with a mug of herbal tea resting on the edge of the tub. She lay back listening to the soothing strains of Enya playing through a Bluetooth speaker.

'I'm here. In the bathroom.'

The door was unlocked. Peter pushed it open. 'How did it go?' Erika told him. 'You poor thing. That must have been hard, having to lie to the police.'

'Far harder to lie to Wagner. Gave me a sense of what the inquisition would have been like.'

'On another note, I have some news,' Peter said.

'Is it good news? Otherwise, don't bother. This has already been one of the worst days of my life.'

'It *could* be good. Do you remember I tried to contact that Inspector Lenau? The one who was on a worldwide trip with his wife, after he retired.'

'Remind me why you tried to contact him?'

'Because he met the "children" when they first came to Hamelin in 1978. Well, he's back now. He just emailed me and agreed to meet.'

TWENTY-ONE

'I can't believe it really *is* you. I wouldn't have recognised you if I passed you in the street,' Erika told Katrin as she hugged her. After the Sunday church service Alana, Bodo and Katrin had been invited to Peter and Erika's for coffee and cake.

'That was the plan. We don't want Katrin to have to stay indoors. She's done that for far too long. We want her to go out without being recognised.' Alana removed her coat and hung it on the coat stand.

Erika couldn't take her eyes off Katrin as they made their way to the living room. Her ex-patient had been a brunette with long, thick, straight hair, often gathered in one plait. Now, she had turned into a platinum blonde with short, curly hair, pink lipstick, mascara and eyeliner. Katrin had never worn make-up at the Koppenberg. Her coat and dress were new and so were the ankle boots. She looked fuller in face and figure, no longer the rake-thin wraith from the psychiatric hospital.

Erika hadn't seen Katrin since she and Peter left her at Alana's just over three weeks ago. With colleagues absent because of colds and flu, Erika had worked many extra hours. Another reason she hadn't visited Alana was the fear she might be under surveillance and Katrin's whereabouts revealed. They had talked on the phone instead.

'*Baumkuchen* or plum crumble tart?' Erika asked her guests. After everyone was settled with coffee and a piece of cake, Katrin took a small flat object wrapped in gift paper from her shoulder bag and handed it to Erika.

'I never thanked you and Peter for what you've done for me. I made this for you both as a thank you.'

Erika unwrapped the present: a framed pencil drawing of Peter and herself.

'Did you draw this from memory?' Peter looked impressed.

'From Alana's computer,' was the answer.

'I found a photo of you both online,' Alana explained.

Erika asked Katrin what places she had visited since her metamorphosis, other than the church that morning.

'I've been to Alana's allotment and we've been to Edeka for groceries and Karstadt for clothes and shoes.'

'Katrin helps out at the allotment, for which I pay her. We've also been to the arts and crafts shop to buy pencils, water colours and a sketchbook. But we're taking it one day at a time. It's hard not to feel overwhelmed or panicky after thirty-three years of incarceration,' Alana added.

Unexpectedly, Bodo, usually a listener rather than a talker, spoke up. All eyes turned towards him. 'Thirty-three years to the day next Sunday, the 21st of December. Sixty-six years for Alana and me. Midwinter's day.'

'D'you think...?' Peter's words hung in the air, inviting Bodo to continue.

'According to Katrin there were more of us, asleep, when she and the others left the cave. So, yes, I think it's possible. There could be another group walking out of that cave next Sunday.'

'If the cave is still there,' Erika said.

It was Katrin who spoke next. 'The cave closed after we left. Trude and I went back with a police inspector. That's why no one believed us. They thought we were lying. Is it still closed?'

The question was directed at Bodo, who nodded. 'It is. The spot where the cave was isn't far from my mobile home. Lately, I've been on daily walks in the area. There's no sign of it. It looks as if there never was a cave in the rock face.'

'It seems too much of a coincidence, children walking out of that cave on Midwinter's day, with a thirty-three year gap between groups... and it will be exactly another thirty-three years since Katrin's group this Midwinter's day. I don't know about you, but I'd like to be there on that day,' said Peter.

'Me too,' said Erika.

'Let's all meet at dawn next Sunday at my caravan and walk to where the cave opening was,' Bodo suggested.

Everyone agreed.

Lenau scrutinised the young man sitting on the battered old sofa in his study. He was fond of that sofa. It was comfortable, even if the cracked, worn leather of its sagging cushions showed small rips and its once bright tawny colour was now bleached by the sun streaming in through the window. His wife wanted him to replace it with a new one, but so far, he'd refused to let it go.

Lenau was impressed with the young reporter's frank, intelligent questions. Peter Hahn explained he was researching the appearance of a group of unaccompanied minors in Hamelin in 1978. Was it true Lenau had been the investigating police inspector at the time? Lenau confirmed that had been the case.

'Do you know what happened to these children? Where they ended up?' The journalist asked.

Lenau recounted how he'd first met them in the city hospital, as part of his investigation into a traffic accident. After a couple of days, they were moved into the orphanage, from where adoptive parents would have been found, or if not, foster families.

'Would it surprise you to learn that all of them, since then, have been in the closed unit of a psychiatric hospital, locked away from the outside world and isolated from one another, conditions even convicted criminals aren't subjected to?'

Lenau was speechless for a moment. It sounded so far-fetched.

'Of course that surprises me. I mean... why? ... What happened? Are you sure they're the same children?'

'They were taken from the orphanage to the Koppenberg Klinik by a Doctor Claudia Wagner, chief psychiatrist at the klinik. That's where they've been these last thirty-three years. I was hoping you could help me with the whys and wherefores of what happened in 1978.'

'After the children were given a temporary home at the orphanage, social services took over and we were no longer required. But why don't you ask Doctor Wagner? She should be able to answer your questions far better than I can.'

'I've tried. She doesn't want to speak to me. Can you think of any reason why she kept these people locked away for so long? I mean, it's costly.'

'I don't think I... unless it's something to do with the whistling?'

'The whistling?' Peter's eyes widened.

Lenau continued. 'Yes. I'd forgotten about that after all this time, but I've just remembered. There was something peculiar about those children. On occasion, they would gather and whistle a tune, and anyone who heard it became paralysed. Turned to stone, almost. They did this a few times and tried to run away. We only caught them because we wore ear defenders.'

'That might explain why they are kept segregated from each other,' Peter mused. 'But they would have led separate lives too, had each lived with a different family. No need to put them in a mental hospital. So, why was that decision taken?' The tone of his voice changed, as he continued with more urgency. 'Actually, for now there's something more important. May I ask how many children there were when you met them in 1978?'

'About thirty-five, I reckon.'

'Only, just over half of that number are at the Koppenberg Klinik now.'

'The others were released?'

'No. One of the nurses told me that, considering their age, a surprising number of deaths have occurred since she started working there. The cause of these deaths is always listed as "unexpected heart failure" or other undetected health conditions. What's more, the medication these patients are taking appears on no list of licensed, off-label or unlicensed drugs.'

'You think the medicines caused these deaths?' Lenau released a long, low whistle. 'That's a very serious allegation. I'd be careful not to mention that in your article without solid evidence.'

'I'm aware of that,' Peter said. 'That's partly why I came to you. I can't get the evidence, but a chief inspector of police could.'

'*Former* chief inspector. I'm retired, remember?'

'You have experience, police contacts, more resources.'

Lenau thought it over. He'd promised Gisela he'd clear out the garage now that they were home. She also suggested they needed a new carpet in the bedroom and was making plans for an extension. None of that appealed to him just now.

'All right,' he said slowly. 'I'll see what I can find out.'

Could there be any truth in it? Lenau was left to wonder, after Peter left. He distinctly remembered those children. They'd been so different from his own two, or their little friends, who were the same age as the foundlings.

As young as they are, children have their individual looks and distinguishable personalities. Not those children. There was something almost herd-like about them. They looked strangely identical. He remembered thinking they must all have been family. Siblings or cousins. They had the same straight brown hair, large eyes in pale, grave little faces and small, wiry bodies. When he got to know them better, it had turned out most were unrelated. He didn't think he'd ever heard them laugh or joke.

Could they really have been taken to the Koppenberg Klinik and kept there ever since? He should check it out and the person to approach first would be Christa Sachs, the social worker in charge at the time.

Over the years he'd been in professional contact with her more than once, as well as seeing her at PTA meetings. Their children had attended the same school. He knew the area she lived in and, after a quick online search, located her address.

That evening after dinner, Lenau put his coat on, told Mrs Lenau he was going for a drink with a former work colleague, and set out to pay Christa Sachs a visit at her home.

Christa Sachs looked surprised when Lenau appeared on her doorstep. 'What is this about? We have friends over for dinner. Can't this wait until tomorrow and we can discuss it in my office?'

'It won't take a minute. I need to verify something about an old case we both worked on, then I'll let you get back to your guests.'

A thin veneer of courtesy barely covered her obvious

displeasure when Christa Sachs led Lenau through the hallway into a small sitting room.

'What is it you want to ask and what's the urgency?'

'Do you remember that large group of foundlings we dealt with back in 1978?'

'How could I forget? That was one hell of a job and I had hardly any experience at the time. It was at the beginning of my career.'

'What happened to those children?'

'They were looked after by the Sisters of Mercy at the orphanage on Hanover Street. There were plans for the orphanage to be demolished. It was extremely run-down, but we had no other place to put them up. There were just too many of them. It wasn't ideal, but it was only a temporary arrangement.'

'I know all that,' Lenau said. 'I'm more interested in what happened to the children after the time they spent at the orphanage. Where did they go from there?'

The woman opened her mouth to say something, then closed it again. Her hands fluttered towards the scarf she was wearing. Flapping like a fish on dry land, Lenau thought. 'Well?'

When she found her voice, he noticed she opted for attack, as the best form of defence.

'Only one question, you said. You've had your question and I really need to go back to my guests.'

Lenau remained unperturbed. 'The one question is: where did those children go when they left the orphanage?'

'It's so long ago. I would have to look it up in our files. Come to my office tomorrow and I'll tell you.'

Lenau didn't let up. 'You see, I know they were taken to the Koppenberg Klinik and locked away and they're still there, after all these years.'

Lenau was bluffing. He hadn't fully believed Peter Hahn

and there was still room for doubt, but Sachs' reaction suggested there was at least some truth in Hahn's account.

She nervously pulled on the delicate scarf around her neck.

'They were dangerous,' she suddenly burst out. 'Anyone who saw what happened when they started their bizarre whistling would agree with me. You saw it. The longer they stayed at the orphanage, the more of a problem it became. In the end, the nuns didn't want to look after those children any longer. According to Doctor Wagner they were a danger to society and she offered them treatment before introducing them to foster families.'

'Only she never did introduce them to foster families. They're still in the Koppenberg Klinik.'

'I didn't know. Perhaps they never adjusted.'

'Hmm. Did you never follow up to see how they were doing? Not one visit?'

'We were seriously understaffed and swamped with new cases.'

Sachs refused to give Lenau any more information. For that, he'd have to speak to Claudia Wagner herself.

Lenau chose not to visit Claudia Wagner at home or in her office, but to corner her somewhere a little less advantageous for her. The information Lenau needed to plan this, the colour and make of her car and the time she usually went home, he obtained from Peter, with some help from Erika.

It was nearly five o'clock on a Monday afternoon when Lenau parked his car alongside Claudia's in the Koppenberg Klinik's parking area and settled down to wait for her as daylight turned to dusk. During the next ten minutes his eyes were fixed on the main entrance from which he expected her to emerge.

When he heard the boot of the car beside his being opened and shut, he looked round. There she was. He recognised her, even though so much time had elapsed since he saw her last: the same tall, straight figure, the same immaculate hairdo.

He ducked so she wouldn't notice him prematurely. Her car door opened and slammed shut. He got out of his car quickly, opened her door on the passenger side and, taking the seat beside hers, shut the door behind him and turned to face her.

'Good afternoon, Doctor Wagner.'

In the process of fastening her seatbelt, she froze and gasped audibly at his sudden appearance in her car.

'What do you want from me?' Her voice caught in her throat and was barely audible.

'We've met before, though it was a long time ago, so you might not remember.' Lenau hoped she would not know about his retirement. 'Chief Inspector Lenau. A little chat is all I want.'

'What about?' Already, she had recovered from the initial shock and sounded calm and in control.

'About a group of unaccompanied children found wandering around Hamelin in 1978 and given a home and education by the Sisters of Mercy at the town's orphanage.'

He paused for her reaction.

'And?' Cold tone, cold stare.

'Word is, you took them from the orphanage to the Koppenberg Klinik, where they remain until this day.'

She scoffed. 'Who told you that? Was it that journalist? You'd be wise not to listen to that lying news monger. It's a hoax.'

'If it's a hoax, as you say, you'll have no objection to giving me a tour of the klinik at this moment, including any closed units.'

She sighed. 'All right. I took those children to the Koppenberg because they couldn't stay at the orphanage and they weren't ready to face a normal life with adoptive families. They were delusional and dangerous. I thought, if I treated them at the Koppenberg, with the right medication and the right therapy, social services could start looking for placements.' She paused.

'Go on.'

'It didn't work out that way. Their condition only worsened. As time went by their disorder grew stronger.'

'Funny, I don't remember those children as suffering from any mental illness. To me they just looked disorientated and scared.'

Doctor Wagner raised her eyebrows. 'They never stopped believing they're the lost children of Hamelin who, in 1284 followed a stranger, a musician into the mountains and disappeared. Do you dispute my professional diagnosis?'

'Not at all. There were about thirty-five children in 1978. That's quite a large group to take in. Must be expensive to look after so many, the Koppenberg being a private clinic.'

'We manage. We are lucky to have some very wealthy donors and I do a yearly lecture tour at US universities.'

'Drug trials are a good source of income, I hear.'

Lenau felt rather than saw her barely controlled anger.

'Then you heard wrong. We don't put our patients through drug trials. We only use licensed medication and their treatment is mostly behavioural therapy.'

Curiosity got the better of Lenau. 'And the whistling? Are they still–'

'Of course not,' Claudia Wagner snapped. 'They're kept in separate rooms for that reason.'

'Isolated? For thirty-three years?' The cruelty of it, Lenau thought.

'We couldn't take the risk. And they see nurses, therapists and carers all the time.'

'And their future? What are your plans for their future?'

'To look after them as well as I can, for as long as it takes. You have to understand, by now these poor things are so institutionalised, it would be impossible for them to live in today's society. They'd be as helpless as babies.'

Lenau had heard enough. He needed fresh air and, without so much as an '*Auf Wiedersehen*', he opened the car door and got out.

TWENTY-TWO

Sunday morning, 3am on Midwinter's day. Erika's sister, Ulrike, woke up and needed to go to the bathroom. She threw off the duvet, rose and wrapped her dressing gown around her. Careful not to disturb the sleepers in the house, she opened the bedroom door and padded across the landing towards the bathroom. A sound stopped her in her tracks. She stood and listened, her heart beating faster. There was someone downstairs. She heard sliding over parquet, as if a piece of furniture was being moved. Turning back towards the bedroom to wake her husband, she noticed Jonas' bedroom door was ajar. She opened it further. Jonas wasn't in his bed. Relieved not to have to face a burglar, she quietly slipped downstairs where, underneath the door of Andreas' office, a strip of light was visible.

When Ulrike swung the door open, Jonas froze in the middle of the room and dropped the tablet computer he held in his hands. A heavy chair was still positioned in front of the bookcase on top of which, earlier, she had placed the tablets. Her fury evaporated when she saw Jonas' stricken face, his tousled hair and rumpled dinosaur pyjamas.

Instead of shouting or threatening punishment she decided

to try and talk to her son. She sat on the couch and patted beside her. 'Come here.'

Jonas picked up the tablet from the floor and joined her with a guarded expression.

'Couldn't you sleep?' Ulrike began.

A shake of the head.

'So, what's this game you can't stop playing, then?'

The answer came hesitantly. 'It's called Follow my Leader.'

'Go on, show me.'

Jonas didn't move. 'You wouldn't like it. It's not for adults.' He clasped the tablet in his arms against his chest. He wouldn't let it go without a fight.

Perhaps she should tell him how she felt, Ulrike thought. 'What happened to the boy who never had secrets from me? Never before shouted, slammed doors, called me names or went on a hunger strike because you could not play with a toy? I worry about you and your sister.'

He shifted uncomfortably beside her, hung his head and was quiet.

'It's not just that,' Ulrike went on. 'You and Suzi are growing more tense by the day. More nervous. It's almost as if you're expecting something to happen. Or waiting for something or someone. Tell me if I'm wrong.' No answer. 'I'm your mum. You can tell me anything. I won't shout at you or laugh, or tell anyone else, I promise.'

Another long silence.

'You're not wrong,' Jonas mumbled eventually.

'Not wrong in assuming that...?'

'We're waiting.'

'What are you waiting for?'

'The leader.'

'What do you mean?' Ulrike felt icy cold and not just because of the temperature in the room.

'We follow the leader. That's the game.'

Ulrike sat rigid and her hair stood on end. 'And who is the leader?'

Jonas shrugged. 'His name isn't important. We'll know him by his music, not his name.'

Sunday morning, 4am. Midwinter's day. Erika and Peter, after a hasty breakfast of coffee and a thick slice of buttered muesli bread, quietly left their apartment and drove under an inky sky through deserted shopping streets with brightly lit windows.

Soon enough, they reached the outskirts of Hamelin and turned into a country road, depending more and more on the car's headlights to see where they were going. Two pairs of eyes searched the woodland on the left-hand side for the path that would lead them to Bodo's caravan and the mountains behind.

Erika straightened and pointed. 'There. That's it.'

Just in time Peter turned off, slowly drove the car a little further and switched off the motor before unbuckling his seatbelt. 'Let's go on foot from here. The path is getting too narrow to drive any further. Anyway, Bodo said it wasn't far from the main road.'

Erika got out and peered through the darkness. 'We should have brought a torch.'

It wasn't just that it was pitch black, as they followed the path, it was freezing as well. Erika, in her woollen coat, shivered as the path forced them to climb.

'How does Bodo get about from here?' Erika wondered aloud, avoiding the grasping branches on both sides.

'He cycles.'

Bodo had been right. It wasn't long before the path opened and became a clearing. The caravan was made of wooden slats and partly covered in green mould. They were greeted by Alana and Katrin, whom they found looking in through the unlit windows. They turned at Erika and Peter's approach.

'It looks like Bodo isn't here,' Alana said.

'We knocked but he's not answering,' Katrin added.

'Did you try the door handle?' Peter asked.

'We did. It's locked.' Alana frowned.

They called without any response or movement from within.

'What do we do now?' Erika asked.

'Let's wait,' Peter suggested. 'He might turn up shortly.'

On the eve of Midwinter's day, Lenau and his long-time friend and former colleague, Stefan Brückner, enjoyed a beer in Adler's, a bar which had always been and still was a favourite haunt of police officers for an after-work swift one. Or two. The pub was decorated with the usual Christmas paraphernalia and bar staff were serving and collecting glasses, wearing bright red Father Christmas hats hemmed with white fake fur.

After a long swig of the amber draught, Lenau put his glass down, wiped his white foam moustache and exhaled with intense satisfaction.

'Missed that during your round-the world-trip?' Brückner, opposite him, grinned.

'And how.'

A group of customers seated around a long table linked arms and swayed rhythmically from side to side belting out the words of: '*O, Du lieber Augustin*'. It was near impossible to have the conversation Lenau was hoping for. He rolled his eyes and took another swig.

'I take it you didn't miss *this* old-fashioned national pastime, then?' Brückner shouted close to Lenau's ear.

Lenau laughed. 'Never been a fan.'

When the singing died away, they talked about the trip for a while: the sights that the Lenaus had seen, the food they'd tried and the encounters they'd had.

When the subject came to its natural end, and before Brückner could broach another matter, Lenau decided to get to the point. 'There's something I'd like to pick your brain about.'

'Shoot.'

'D'you remember those unaccompanied children who appeared in Hamelin in 1978?'

'The ones who whistled and made everything freeze to a halt? Hard to forget something like that.'

Brückner, now Chief of Police in Hamelin, had been a young officer assisting Lenau at the time.

Lenau nodded. 'Any idea what happened to them?'

Brückner shrugged. 'I suppose they went into care. Why?'

Lenau took another sip of beer. 'According to a reporter who came to see me, they were taken into care, all right. Taken to a psychiatric hospital. And they're still there.'

'What?' Brückner's face showed disbelief. 'You mean they've been there all this time, since 1978? What was wrong with them?'

'They believe they are the Hamelin children who followed the piper into the mountains and disappeared in 1284.'

'To be fair, that is bonkers. It's only a fairy tale.'

'Oh, it's more than that. The story everyone knows is based on historical facts. A hundred and thirty children really did go missing from Hamelin on the same day. Midsummer's day, as a matter of fact,' said Lenau, who was familiar with the different theories, written by well-known historians, regarding what had happened to the children.

'Still, it's not possible to disappear in 1284 and reappear in 1978. Anyone believing that is not in their right mind.'

'Or has been brainwashed. I've always suspected these children of having run away from some cult or sect. We never did find the parents, remember? Whether we had or not, there should have been deprogramming measures in place to help them adjust to society. That's no excuse to keep the children locked up in a psychiatric ward for thirty-three years.' Brückner gave Lenau a sceptical look. Lenau continued. 'There's more. This journalist knows one of the nurses who works there. According to her, the medicines tried on these patients are unlicensed, nowhere to be found on lists of legitimate medication. There have been a number of unexplained deaths amongst these patients and she suspects drug trials might have something to do with it.'

'Really, Klaus, I never thought of you as being gullible. Where are your critical faculties? He's a news hack. Spinning stories is his trade. Conspiracy theories, that's all they are.'

'That's why I did some investigating of my own. I interviewed the social worker who dealt with the children at the time, and talked to Claudia Wagner, who assessed the children's mental state in 1978. She is now the chief psychiatrist at the Koppenberg Klinik, where the children allegedly still are. Both behaved as if they had something to hide. Both were reluctant to answer my questions. My request to visit the hospital and meet these patients was bluntly refused.'

'Apart from a nurse's suspicions and uncooperative interviewees, is there any evidence that something fishy is going on?'

'No hard evidence, but if there was nothing "fishy" as you call it, going on, why are these women so unwilling to cooperate and let me speak to the patients?'

'I don't know. Same again?' Brückner asked, taking Lenau's

empty beer glass and getting up to walk towards the bar. Brückner returned with two cold lagers, the tall glasses filled to the brim with frothy foam collars. 'I suppose you were going to ask me for a warrant to enter the psychiatric hospital?'

'M-hmm.'

Brückner looked regretful. 'I'm afraid that's no longer possible. Regulations have become a lot stricter since you retired. There just isn't enough evidence for a warrant. Besides, Claudia Wagner's husband is our mayor and I have enough problems keeping him on our side as it is.'

Lenau left it at that and their conversation shifted back to harmless gossip about mutual friends and acquaintances.

Driving home afterwards, Lenau was convinced he could do no more for Peter and resolved to contact the reporter the next morning to let him know his findings. At home, he found himself in the doghouse for keeping Mrs Lenau waiting, with dinner ruined, according to her. He didn't think it tasted that bad.

The phone rang, interrupting the meal. It was Stefan Brückner.

'Have you changed your mind about the warrant?' Lenau half-joked.

'Actually, Klaus, I need to ask you a favour and perhaps we can review the warrant decision afterwards.'

'How can I help?'

'A few weeks ago, a patient in the secure unit of the Koppenberg Klinik, that psychiatric hospital you were talking about earlier, disappeared. She could not have done that all by herself. It happened during the night, when patients are locked in, so she must have had help. Naturally, we interrogated all members of staff but were unsuccessful in finding a suspect. That is, until today, when we took into custody a cleaner who was at work in the unit that night and whose behaviour during his last interview was suspect, to say the least.'

'Suspect? In what way?'

'He won't admit to helping the patient escape and keeps shtum when being questioned, but he's an eccentric old codger who lives by himself in a mobile home.'

'You want me to interrogate him? Why? You have plenty of people there who have the skills.'

'No one like you, though. You always got more out of suspects than anyone else. And, I don't know why, but I have a hunch this old bloke might open up to you. If he does, you might find out a bit more about these patients you're so keen to speak to.'

'When do you need me?'

'A car is on its way to you now.'

'All right.' Smiling to himself, Lenau put the phone back in its cradle.

Lenau felt as if he'd come home as he shook hands with former colleagues at the station. He teased one of them who had just married, joked with another whose first child had recently been born and congratulated a third who got promoted, before he stepped into Brückner's office.

'Can you tell me what we already know about this suspect?' Lenau began.

Brückner handed Lenau a slim file. 'His name is Bodo Freitag. Everything we know about him is in here.'

It only took Lenau a few minutes to read the file's contents. Freitag was apparently an elderly loner, living in a ramshackle caravan in the woods just outside Hamelin. The caravan had been searched, in vain, for traces of the missing psychiatric patient. The old man had no computer and wasn't on any social networks. There was no online footprint. Rare these days. He mostly worked nights as a cleaner at the Koppenberg and had no friends at the klinik. Staff there said he kept himself to himself.

'No surveillance notes?' Lenau asked Brückner.

'Let's see what you can find out first, before we go down that road.'

Lenau entered interview room one, where the suspect waited for him. The former chief inspector dropped the file on the table, dismissed the young officer standing guard, took the seat opposite the old man and switched the tape recorder on.

'Mr Freitag, my name is Klaus Lenau, retired chief inspector. I'm here to ask you some questions regarding the disappearance of a female inpatient at the Koppenberg Klinik three weeks ago.'

Lenau's tone was friendly but professional. Wearily but not unwillingly, his suspect answered the first routine questions. Yes, he was employed as a night-time cleaner at the Koppenberg Klinik. Yes, he had been at work on the night the patient disappeared. Yes, he had hoovered and mopped the corridors of the secure unit. No, he did not know the patient who had disappeared. No, he had never spoken to her. No, he had not helped her to escape.

Lenau tried another approach. 'Tell me a bit about yourself.'

Disapproval showed in his interviewee's eyes. 'I can't see how that would help your investigation. Do you have any evidence to justify keeping me here? Because if not, I'd like to go home.'

'Indulge me a little longer. You seem an interesting fellow, but an enigma. Have you always lived in Hamelin?'

As Lenau waited for an answer in the silence that followed,

he sat back and studied the man opposite him. He guessed him to be in his seventies. Stocky yet wiry, he still exuded strength despite his advanced years. His striking features, combined with a mop of thick white hair tied in a bunch, would make him a good subject for a portrait artist. The clothes he wore were frayed at the sleeves, probably second-hand, but clean, and so were his nails. Square nails on a firm, square hand.

'I can tell you some things about yourself. Although you look like a hippie, an artistic type, you're actually rather practical and grounded. I suspect you have a connection with the earth element. I would have thought you'd rather be a landscape gardener or a farmer than a cleaner.'

For the first time during their meeting, the man opposite him looked surprised and less in control.

'How...?'

'Your hands. Earth hands.'

'You know about palmistry? Remarkable for a policeman.'

'I would say: of course a policeman like me would be interested in palmistry. It's not all that occult, you know. It actually tells you a lot about someone.'

'I know,' Bodo said. 'There was a time, at a much younger age, when I used to read as much about it as I could lay my hands on. Then I'd go out and study people's hands.'

'You see, now you've told me something about yourself. That wasn't so hard, was it?' Although the words were meant to sound light-hearted, the moment he'd said it, Lenau regretted it. It was as if a door that had just opened a little, firmly slammed shut again.

Lenau switched off the tape recorder, leant forward, lowered his voice and spoke confidentially. 'Before we go any further, let's go off the record for now. Perhaps we would both feel freer that way. I have a feeling we have more in common than an interest in palmistry. I'll start, shall I?' Though he remained silent, the eyes of the man opposite him widened in interest. 'You see, I'm very interested in the Koppenberg Klinik,' Lenau told him. 'Not long ago I was asked to investigate why certain patients have been residing in the secure unit since 1978. Also, why there were more deaths that occurred than could reasonably be expected.'

Surprise flickered in the man's eyes. 'Who told you that?'

'A young reporter. Goes by the name of Peter Hahn.'

'You know Peter?'

Lenau nodded. 'You know him too, don't you?'

The man confirmed this, but wouldn't say anything more.

Lenau started to talk about events in 1978. How, when he was a young detective inspector, he had known Katrin and her sister Trude. How the two little girls had wanted to show him the mountain cave from which they had appeared. The mountain cave could not be found, though. Even so, he had never thought of the children as being delusional or dangerous, and they certainly didn't need lifelong incarceration in a psychiatric hospital.

'My theory has always been that the children ran away from a hippie commune, which would not have been unusual at that time. That they were brainwashed to believe certain things and were, therefore, unworldly, and unprepared for mainstream society. How does that sound to you?' Lenau didn't expect an answer.

'You're wrong,' the man sitting opposite him responded. 'The "children", as you call them, spoke the truth.'

'You mean when they said they're the same children who were lured away from Hamelin by a rat-catching, pipe-playing stranger in 1284? You know as well as I do that's impossible.'

'They didn't lie and they are not mad. If you don't believe

me, come with me tomorrow morning, when the cave will open again and another group of us will walk out.'

'Us?' This time it was Lenau who was taken by surprise.

'You heard me.'

'But you're so much older...'

'We were the first group to have woken up and walked out, I believe. Not in 1978, but in 1945. There were only a few of us then.'

'If I come with you tomorrow morning, will you tell me where Katrin is?'

'I won't need to tell you. She'll be there.'

It took a good deal of persuasion for Lenau to convince Brückner it would be safe to let the suspect leave the following morning. Lenau was to stay with him at all times and deliver him back to the station when it all proved to be a hoax. Which it undoubtedly would, Brückner told him.

'You need a weapon in case he tries to escape,' said the chief as he slid a stun gun across his desk towards Lenau.

Lenau gave him an exasperated look. 'For goodness' sake, Stefan. He's an old man. He's hardly going to be a faster runner than me, is he?'

'Even so,' Brückner insisted.

At Bodo's caravan, Erika, Peter, Alana and Katrin watched the dawn sky. Peter looked at his watch.

'Something must have happened to him,' Alana said.

'An accident?' Erika wondered.

'I've no idea. I only know it's unlike him not to turn up, or not to let us know what's going on. He's always been reliable.'

'Perhaps he's already gone to the cave,' Katrin suggested.

'Then why don't we go there now and find out?' said Peter.

'Katrin, Alana, you know where it is, don't you?' They nodded. 'Then lead the way. There's no point in waiting any longer and we might see Bodo there.'

The women agreed and the four of them set off, with Katrin and Alana in front, followed by Erika and Peter.

TWENTY-THREE

As luck would have it, Alana and Katrin had thought to bring a torch. Thick clouds had kept the moonlight hidden throughout the night and at this early hour, visibility was still a problem.

Erika wrapped her shawl around her head as she carefully picked her way behind Alana and Katrin along the woodland path. Even then, the chill seeped in and her skin felt raw. Freezing air forced its way into her lungs and stung her eyes.

The rutted footpath intertwined with knotted tree roots. Bare branches arched over the path from both sides, as it led them deeper into a thick maze of woodland where densely packed trees stood starkly in the early, winter morning.

Trekking through the gloom, Erika felt her senses sharpen. She noticed the different hues of brown bracken, the smell and feel of decomposing leaves under her feet and the outlines of trees gradually becoming clearer.

Only an hour ago, when she and Peter had arrived at Bodo's caravan, the blackness of the sky had been absolute, but it had now turned the colour of slate. The quiet, too, was something she was acutely aware of. The only sounds were the cracking of small twigs underfoot and the rustling of bushes.

Though none of the others spoke much, Erika was glad of their company. Had I been on my own, she thought, I would have been scared stiff.

As they came out of the forest and onto the track that would take them up to the mountain, each footstep cost more strength. Where the soil was soft, the track grew wide, but in the rocky passes it narrowed. Erika steeled herself to keep moving as they encountered loose rocks on the way; she braced her feet, attempting to guard against the scree inevitably rolling in random directions.

'Are you sure this is the right way?' The question, coming from Peter, who was behind Erika, was meant for Katrin who led them.

Katrin stopped and so did the others. 'It's a long time ago, but I think the cave was up this mountain. Bodo would have known with absolute certainty. I don't. I just hope I'm right.'

'Did you ever return after you left the cave as a child?' Erika asked.

'Only that time with the policeman, when the cave opening had disappeared,' was the answer.

'You, Alana?'

Alana shook her head. 'Too far from where I grew up. Anyway, I tried to forget about that part of my life.'

'Shall we walk on?' Peter suggested and the small group continued its climb. Moss-covered boulders lined both sides of the path that wound steeply upwards towards the peak.

Under the winter rains the mountain track had become slippery, a muddy brown ribbon on which the four of them trudged in single file as the sky turned to ash.

Erika was startled by the sound of a human voice interrupting the quiet of early morning. Someone shouted. It didn't seem to come from far away.

She turned to Peter. 'Did you hear that?' They had all heard and halted to listen. 'Could it be the children Bodo expects to walk out of the cave?' Erika asked no one in particular.

The thought renewed their energy as they walked on.

'If I remember rightly, we should get to the plateau and the cave soon,' Katrin told the others.

Just before they did, voices were heard again, this time not shouting but talking loudly.

'They're on the plateau in front of the cave,' Katrin commented.

'It must be the other children,' said Erika, fizzing with nerves and excitement.

'Hang on a bit,' Peter said. They halted. 'Let's be careful. Let's not just walk up to whoever is there, but watch and see who they are first. Those weren't children's voices. Children sound higher pitched than that.'

Just before the path widened at the top into a plateau, the four of them crouched down behind the bushes that grew on both sides.

Erika drew in breath sharply and stared aghast at the spectacle in front of them.

Bodo had been right. Today at sunrise, after thirty-three years, children once more spilled from the cave. Children with dishevelled hair and pale unsmiling faces. Little ones, their small bodies covered in mere scraps of crumpled clothing. Children shivering in the wintry air, blinded even by this dim light, taking faltering steps, like newly born calves walking for the first time.

It wasn't the sight of the children though, that horrified Erika. It was the adults, waiting by the mouth of the cave with blankets and leading them towards a different path from the one Erika and her friends had taken towards the plateau. There was no doubt who the adults were. She recognised most of them: her colleagues, as well as Claudia Wagner, Nurse

Bauer, Doctor Azra Polat, and a handful of people she didn't know.

Behind her, Peter touched Erika's shoulder and whispered in her ear. 'How did they know?'

'I've no idea. What are we to do now? They're so many and there are only four of us. They're taking the children and we won't be able to stop them.'

From behind the bush on the other side of the path Alana dashed across and crept behind Peter and Erika. 'Under no circumstances must they see Katrin, or they'll take her too and we can't stop them.'

They looked on as more children appeared, hesitantly, from within the cave opening and were accompanied towards the path that would lead them down the mountain.

'What can we do?' Erika whispered. Beside her, Peter had brought out his phone and was busy taking photos. There was another movement from the other bush, and Katrin materialised behind the others, her face wet with tears.

'Don't let them take the children.'

That did it as far as Peter was concerned. 'I might not be able to physically stop them, but I can go and talk to them. I have photos and I will make this public.'

'I'm coming with you,' said Erika, in a tone that suggested she wouldn't take no for an answer.

'You might lose your job,' Peter reminded her.

'I don't care. This is more important.'

'I'm coming too,' Alana added. 'I'll tell them I was such a child once and lived my life without mental illness. That it's perfectly possible.'

Erika and Peter managed to persuade her to stay with Katrin though and, while Katrin and Alana moved back behind denser shrubs, Peter and Erika stood up and walked onto the plateau.

At the sight of them, Nurse Bauer dropped the blankets she was carrying and watched the couple approach. 'Have you two come to help?'

'Help the children, if that's what you mean.' Erika was unable to restrain the contempt in her voice.

In the moments that followed, they were joined by Claudia Wagner who, after briefly scrutinising Peter, turned towards Erika. 'I wondered where or who that young man got his information from about the patients in our secure unit. It was you, wasn't it?' Erika ignored her question. Doctor Wagner continued. 'Tell me, were you also behind Katrin running away? *Was* it you who helped her? Not that it matters anymore. As you can see, we'll have new patients. Oh, and consider yourself fired.'

'I've taken photos of what's going on here and sent them to my newspaper contacts,' said Peter calmly, before she could walk off. 'This time you can't hush up what you're doing. It's already out in the open, it'll be in at least four newspapers tomorrow after I've told them the story behind the pictures.'

Claudia Wagner's lips curled into an unpleasant smirk. 'Surely, the photos only show how my nurses took good care of these poor foundlings, by wrapping them in warm blankets? What is so bad about that? And after physical and mental examinations, if it turns out these unaccompanied children suffer from certain delusions, the Koppenberg Klinik will be able to provide a treatment plan and a place to stay. No one could find fault with that. No one will believe you. Now hop along. We've got work to do.'

Something Peter had asked earlier now became a question that burned on Erika's tongue.

'How did you know?'

'Know what?' Claudia Wagner sneered as she gestured the

nurses to continue taking the children towards the edge of the plateau and the path that would lead them down.

'How did you know the cave would open today and another group of children would walk out?' Erika replied.

At that moment Thomas Wagner appeared on the path used to take the children down from the cave.

The mayor walked up to his wife. 'What's this?'

'These two don't approve of us taking care of the children. They've had their say and they're about to leave.'

'No, we're not.' Peter shifted his weight and planted himself even more firmly on the ground he stood on.

Thomas Wagner gave him a searching look. 'Didn't we have a conversation in the Eichendorf Hotel? Aren't you that reporter who's been making up stories about the Koppenberg Klinik?'

'Not stories, but facts witnessed by my fiancée, while working in the secure unit of the klinik. We'll make damn sure an independent enquiry will take place about what happens to these young children from now on,' Peter replied.

Wagner's still handsome features twisted into an ugly expression as he took a few steps towards Peter.

'You forget who you're speaking to. There won't be an enquiry as long as I'm mayor of this city. You, on the other hand, will hear from my lawyers, as soon as you get home today. Expect a court summons for libel to follow. You won't ever be able to write for a newspaper or magazine again.'

'That goes for you too, Erika,' Claudia Wagner added. 'You carry out your threats and I'll make sure you won't work as a nurse again.'

Barely had she finished speaking when the Wagners averted their eyes and stared intently at a spot behind Erika and Peter.

'Oh no,' Claudia Wagner's voice grew gradually to a scream. 'Oh, no, no, no, NO!'

Peter and Erika turned.

From the path, where previously they had been hiding behind the bushes, two figures approached. Katrin walked slowly but purposefully towards the group gathered on the plateau. Alana followed, hesitantly, at a distance.

Erika's ears picked up a tune trailing through the air. A tune as simple as a folksong. She wasn't quite sure where it was coming from until Katrin and Alana were close and she noticed how their lips were shaped in a funny way. They were whistling! That was odd. Stranger yet was how an unnatural stillness descended onto the plateau. Normally a breezy place, now the air seemed motionless. Before rigidity took over Erika's body, she noticed something else. The children from the cave seemed to know the tune and joined in the whistling. As the whistling grew to a chorus, Erika felt as if her feet were growing roots and someone was pouring concrete over her. It became impossible to move. She was paralysed and it looked like everyone else was too, except for Katrin, Alana and the children.

And Thomas Wagner.

Unlike his wife and her helpers, the mayor wasn't immobilised at all. The mayor had joined in with the chorus of whistlers.

Her body might have turned to stone, but Erika's mind was agile enough as she watched Katrin leading the children back into the cave. Alana followed and so did Thomas Wagner. She noticed how all the whistlers looked as if they were in a trance. Certainly, Katrin and Alana didn't seem themselves. The spell of the piper, whispered a thought in Erika's mind. Where did that come from?

As soon as the whistling grew quieter, then became inaudible, movement in Erika's limbs returned and those around her stirred. Doctor Wagner found her voice and ordered Nurse Bauer and her group of nurses to go after those in the cave.

'And make sure you bring them back out here.'

As the police helicopter flew over buildings shrouded in early morning mist, Lenau turned towards the other passenger. He wanted to reassure Bodo, who looked ill at ease, but the sound in the tiny cabin was deafening. Like the pilot, they both wore headphones.

It had taken him a long time the previous night to persuade Bodo to travel by helicopter to the cave. 'It'll be so much quicker. I know where we're going. I've been there. It's a hell of a climb.'

'The helicopter will scare the living daylights out of the children when they leave that cave.'

'*If* they walk out of that cave.' Lenau doubted it. He had doubted the existence of the cave ever since Katrin and Trude had taken him there to show him and found no trace of it.

The pilot pointed at a spot below and spoke through the microphone. 'We'll soon be landing. There's the plateau.'

As they came closer, Lenau noticed clusters of people sprinkled in front of a large opening in the mountain.

'The cave,' Bodo said quietly and with a note of wonder in his voice. 'It's open. Just as I thought it would be.'

From the plateau all eyes turned towards the helicopter as it landed noisily but gracefully on rocky ground. Someone waved from that small crowd. Lenau thought he recognised Peter Hahn, the journalist and, after the motor was switched off and the door thrown open, he heard the young woman beside Peter call out. 'Bodo! Thank God you're here. We were wondering where you'd disappeared to.'

After stepping down from the helicopter, Lenau and Bodo

walked up to the young couple. 'What are *they* doing here at this hour?' Lenau indicated Doctor Wagner and her helpers.

The young woman beside Peter replied, 'They're here for the same reason we are. Only, we want to protect the children. They want to lock them up and declare them mentally unfit for society. Delusional.'

'Inspector, I didn't expect you here either. This is Erika, my fiancée,' said Peter. Lenau shook Erika's hand.

'Where are Alana and Katrin?' Bodo asked.

'They're in the cave. But what happened to you? We were worried when you weren't at the caravan.'

Bodo explained briefly.

Amongst the waiting adults, Lenau recognised two familiar faces. One belonged to Christa Sachs, the Social Services Director, and the other to Claudia Wagner. He hadn't recognised her at first. She looked very different from the last time they'd met. Her confidence seemed to have evaporated. Her tall figure was slumped on a large rock near the cave opening, into which she dolefully stared. Her hands had disappeared into the pockets of her camel coat and a cashmere scarf covered the lower half of her face.

'What's up with her?' Lenau nodded towards Doctor Wagner.

'Her husband went into the cave,' Peter said.

'The mayor? Is he here as well? Did he go after the children?' Lenau reacted.

'No,' Peter said, 'he didn't go after them. He went *with* them, whistling as well. It was odd. Very odd. Never expected that to happen.'

Bodo, who had been quiet for a while now, spoke up. 'You know that can only mean one thing, don't you?'

'That he's one of them. One of the children,' said Peter, slowly.

'But he's old,' Erika said.

'Not one of these children,' Bodo explained, 'but one of those who came out of the cave with Alana and me. In 1945.'

They all stared at him, speechless.

'That makes sense, I suppose,' Erika said finally. 'Thomas Wagner is about your age.'

'It doesn't make sense at all,' Peter spoke with passion. 'Claudia Wagner has always claimed the children who walked out of this cave in 1978 are mentally ill and dangerous. She locked them away and no one questioned her. Now it turns out her husband, the mayor of this town, is another of these children.'

'Not only that,' Lenau added, 'he's the very evidence that these people don't belong in a mental institution and can live a successful life.'

TWENTY-FOUR

Erika watched a reluctant Nurse Bauer enter the cave to pursue the children, Katrin, Alana and Thomas Wagner.

Almost immediately, Bauer returned. 'It's impossible to see anything inside. Did we bring torches?' she asked Doctor Wagner.

Claudia Wagner ordered the nearby waiting nurses to see if there were any in the vans below, where some of the children had already been taken. 'But do hurry. We don't know how long the cave will remain open and we don't want anyone to be stuck inside.'

None of the nurses moved. They looked at each other, muttered a few words and remained in place.

'Well, what are you waiting for?' Claudia Wagner snapped.

A red-haired nurse Erika didn't know by name because she didn't work at the same unit replied, 'It's too risky to go in there. Torch or no torch.'

Emphatic nods from the other nurses.

'Perhaps we should wait,' Nurse Bauer intervened. 'Once they get bored with their whistling, the mayor will take charge and bring the children back out.'

Doctor Wagner stalked off.

'D'you think she knew her husband is one of the original lost children?' Erika asked her companions who, like her, had noticed the nurses' defiance.

Peter, Bodo and Lenau glanced across at Claudia Wagner hugging herself, a solitary figure enthroned on her rock. Nurses in small groups congregated at a safe distance. Erika couldn't read Doctor Wagner's face, but the psychiatrist's deflated posture said enough.

'Even if she did, she knows it's over,' Lenau said. 'Whatever she had planned to do with these young children, it's not going to happen. I'll take care of that.' He walked back to the helicopter.

'He'll contact the police from there,' Peter indicated the helicopter. 'They'll be swarming all over this place soon.'

'I hope so,' Erika said. 'But what can we do apart from hang around and wait for everyone to come out of the cave?'

'They might not,' Peter said. 'Katrin and Alana don't know help is on its way. They'll try to protect the children inside the cave.'

After a while, Lenau returned. 'I've spoken to Police Chief Brückner. He will send as many helicopters as he can organise. They'll be here soon.'

Bodo, who hadn't said much, now voiced his concerns. 'What if it's too late? What if the cave closes with them inside before the police arrive? We can't let that happen. We need to get them out.'

'How do you suggest we do that?' Peter asked. 'If we enter the cave, Katrin and Alana might not realise it's us. They could immobilise us.'

'I've an idea.' Lenau walked off towards the aircraft, to return a little later with three sets of headphones as well as a torch.

'These will block out the tune. It worked in 1978. We could try this again to go and talk to your friends and persuade them to come out with the children.'

'Are there only three sets?' Peter asked.

'It's all right. I'll stay here. Just make sure you all come back before the cave closes.' Erika, with her fear of being stuck in small, enclosed spaces, was relieved to leave it to the three men.

Lenau walked towards Claudia Wagner and told her he'd notified the police and they would soon be here. She gave him a hard stare but didn't reply.

'Let's go,' Lenau said, and the three men fastened their headphones, entered the cave and disappeared from sight.

With nothing else to do, Erika decided she might as well go and talk to her colleagues. She didn't blame them for being here, suspecting they had no idea what this was all about. They might have been bullied into it by Nurse Bauer or Doctor Wagner. Besides, they had refused to enter the cave and capture the children.

The nurses seemed happy to talk and were full of questions. Who were these children? Where did they come from? And those women, who started the whistling, did Erika know them? They hadn't recognised Katrin, Erika concluded.

'Wasn't that creepy? I couldn't move and couldn't even blink.' One of them looked at Erika as if she expected an explanation.

Erika decided to tell them as little as possible. Instead, she tried to find out what reason her colleagues had been given for coming here.

'No reason. We were told an explanation and bonus would follow afterwards. It's all very secretive and I can think of better ways to spend my Sunday morning.'

Whoever said it, sounded resentful. Erika hoped they wouldn't ask her what had brought her and Peter here. To avoid the question, she talked about what the men going into the cave hoped to achieve. She told them one was a former police inspector and had notified the police, who were expected to arrive at any moment to sort things out.

Somewhere above them a whirring sound was heard. Everyone looked up towards what appeared to be a swarm of giant locusts approaching from the air.

'I think that's them now,' Erika said.

Before they landed, Erika, alerted by sounds from the cave behind her, turned to see Lenau emerging from the cave with a toddler in his arms, closely followed by Peter carrying another. Next came the two women holding hands with little ones, then Bodo and a group of older children behind him. Last to appear was Thomas Wagner, heading towards his wife, who turned her head away. He crouched in front of her and talked quietly but fervently.

Peter set down the child he was carrying. 'This is everyone. If there are more, we didn't find them.'

Lenau, who noticed the helicopters landing on the plateau, also put down the child he had carried and made his way towards the aircrafts.

Katrin wandered over to Erika. 'I'm sorry to have done that to you. The whistling, I mean. I had no other option. I could not let her take these children as well.'

'Whatever that was, you did the right thing,' Erika reassured her, and then, like an afterthought, 'it certainly was a powerful weapon.'

'That's why they always kept us separated at the Koppenberg Klinik,' Katrin explained. 'Together we have this curious power, when we feel we're in danger. We could have paralysed everyone and walked out. Doctor Wagner knew this.'

Lenau returned with Chief Brückner and uniformed police.

When Brückner asked who was in charge, Claudia Wagner stood up. 'I am.'

'What is it exactly you are doing here?'

'Do you know who you're talking to?' Doctor Wagner replied. 'I won't answer your questions, but will speak to your superiors instead.'

'Then I suggest we take everyone to the police station and sort it out from there,' Brückner said calmly.

'There are more children and nurses down that path with the vans the Koppenberg staff came in,' Erika said quickly. 'If they're not still there, I expect you'll find them at the klinik.'

Transporting the children and adults took the rest of the morning. The Wagners refused to cooperate and threatened to use their influence with politicians and police bigwigs.

Erika and Peter were on the final flight of the last helicopter that would take them to the police station. They'd stayed behind to help supervise the operation to the end.

At the station, they waited to make their written statements.

'I think Thomas Wagner knew another wave of children would come out at dawn on Midwinter's day,' Peter said. 'He worked it out, just like Bodo did. That's why they were there, on the mountain.'

'Did they say anything to each other while you were in the cave, Bodo and the mayor? They must have known each other in the past.'

'I didn't hear it. But Bodo told me Thomas Wagner has always been a bully. Even in 1945, when apparently he was only three or four.'

'In 1284? Does he really remember that?'

'Alana too had some memories of that time.'

'I suppose so.' Erika thought for a moment. 'Claudia Wagner claims she kept Katrin and her companions imprisoned for thirty-three years because they spoke about what they believed: that they're the original children from Hamelin who followed the Piper into the mountain cave and slept for hundreds of years. How does that hold up, now it turns out her husband is one of them?'

'It doesn't,' Peter said. 'And if he tries to deny he's one of the original children, there were witnesses, the two of us amongst them.'

By the time Erika and Peter arrived home that afternoon, so much had happened and they'd been up so early, it felt like a whole day had passed already.

'I'm going to take it easy for the rest of the day.' Erika yawned and stretched. 'Have lunch, listen to music and read my book.'

'I wish I could do the same. But my article won't write itself and neither do my emails. Fingers crossed some national newspaper will publish it.'

The bell rang and Peter went to the front door, returning a few moments later in the company of Alana, Katrin, Bodo and Lenau. As they entered the living room Erika caught a fleeting look of surprise on Lenau's face as he noticed the ancient sea chest which served as a coffee table, the rainbow fairy lights and the red leather car seats turned into a sofa.

'We've come with a special request for Peter,' Bodo explained.

Erika put the kettle on.

'I assume it's something important, otherwise one of you would have phoned or texted me,' said Peter, once everyone had a mug of coffee in front of them.

'You're right. It's something that needs careful discussion,' Bodo answered.

'The suspense is killing me.' Peter smiled. 'Out with it.'

'We don't want our background and history known about by the general public,' Katrin blurted out quite suddenly. 'At least not the part that deals with what happened before we walked from the mountain cave to Hamelin: that part of our lives when we lived in Hamelin before Midsummer's day 1284.' She ended on a more thoughtful note.

'You don't want me to write that you are the original Hamelin children who were lost and have been found in our time?'

'No,' Alana said emphatically.

'No,' Katrin repeated.

Bodo shook his head.

Peter frowned. 'May I ask why not? It's the biggest news story of this millennium. Scientists have been discussing the possibility of time travel for centuries. You are the evidence that it is possible. Shouldn't the general public be informed about this discovery?'

'What do you think will happen when you write about us being born centuries ago?' Bodo held Peter's gaze while putting the question to him calmly.

Peter thought for a moment, before answering. 'Scientists would want to meet and interrogate you, I suppose, and so would the media.'

'Journalists and photographers would camp outside their houses for God knows how long.' Lenau, who had been quiet until then, now spoke up. 'I'm sorry, Peter, but you know as well as I do that's exactly what would happen. Not just the German press, but foreign media too would descend on them like flies on a steaming pile of horse shit. There'd be a barrage of requests for television appearances. They'd be celebrities, picked apart on social media. Frankly, it's going to be hard enough for them to adjust to modern life without all that.'

'That's right.' Katrin spoke from experience. 'There's so much to learn.'

'And it would distract from the real issue here,' Alana added.

'But *isn't* that the real issue?' Peter argued. 'There is enough evidence now that you didn't lie and were never delusional, so there was no reason to lock you up for thirty-three years. I thought that's what you wanted: for the truth to come out.'

'What we want most of all,' Bodo said, 'and I think I speak for all of us, is to be left in peace and to get on with our lives, out of the limelight. In anonymity, but free, not imprisoned.'

Erika saw Peter's disappointment. She knew he considered this his story, his scoop. It could have been his big break to be taken seriously as an investigative journalist, writing for the national newspapers.

'Without divulging their origins, there remains much to write about,' she suggested. 'What Alana means by the real issue is the grave injustice done to the children in 1978, and about to be repeated at present to these little ones we've just fetched from the cave: incarceration and unlicensed drug trials for the rest of their lives. For no other reason than that they have no one to speak up for them. That should make a big news story.'

'Where are the children now and what's going to happen to them?' Peter looked at Lenau. It was a distraction from having to answer the 'special request'.

He needs time to think about it, Erika thought.

'When we left, they were still at the station while a youth hostel was being prepared for their stay. Authorities will need a day or two to decide what to do,' Lenau told him.

'We promised we'd go back immediately after we'd spoken to you,' Alana said. 'Apart from Bodo, Katrin and me, no one speaks their language.'

'No one except Thomas Wagner,' Peter said.

'Don't worry,' Lenau reassured them. 'He won't have access to the children, not after my statement, and neither will his wife.'

'I'm glad to hear it,' said Erika. 'Speaking of the Wagners, what will happen to them? Will there be an investigation into what went on at the Koppenberg Klinik?'

'I've been assured by Chief Brückner that there will be an investigation by the national organisation of psychiatrists, and not the one Doctor Polat belongs to. In fact, she will be investigated too, as will Christa Sachs, the social worker. When that's done, there will likely be a court case. I will make sure Katrin and her fellow patients have the best lawyers to represent them. But that'll be a while away yet.'

'I'm keen to go back to the children.' Katrin stood up and went to take her coat from the coat stand. The other visitors followed suit.

'At least think about it,' Bodo said to Peter as they were leaving.

It wasn't until much later that evening, as they were getting ready for bed, that Erika brought up the subject again. Earlier, Peter had worked on his article practically non-stop.

'Is it finished?' she asked, rinsing her toothbrush under the bathroom tap.

'As a rough draft. It still needs some editing tomorrow morning.'

'Will it include the origins of the children, or will you let it go, as you were asked to do this afternoon?'

'I've been thinking about what you said. You were right. There are plenty of other issues to write about. Unnecessary incarceration and illegal drug trials, to name but a few. I'll show you tomorrow.'

Relief flooded through Erika. 'I'm glad. I worried about the consequences. I don't think people would have believed that part of the story, anyway. You, as well as the children, could have been at the receiving end of mockery or vile comments on social media. I don't think it would have done your career much good, either. I doubt editors would have printed the article for that reason.'

Peter turned the shower on and Erika went to bed. She was still awake when he joined her.

'What's happening tomorrow? With your job, I mean?' he asked.

'I'd booked the day off. But Wagner fired me today, so now I don't know. I'll phone tomorrow morning to find out.'

At coffee time the next morning Erika was reading Peter's finished article, when her phone rang. The lit screen showed no name. She answered.

'Nurse Kramer? Doctor Pletscher here. You rang earlier to inform us that Doctor Wagner released you from your employment at the Koppenberg, yesterday. I have temporarily taken over Doctor Wagner's position and was hoping you'd stay, at least until Doctor Wagner is back in charge.'

Erika liked Doctor Pletscher. He always had a kind word for patients and staff alike.

Somehow, she couldn't imagine him being involved in the cover-up between Doctor Wagner and Hamburg Pharma AG.

'Today is my day off,' she said. 'But tomorrow I'll be there.'

TWENTY-FIVE

At the police station, after the mountain rescue, Lenau followed Brückner into the interview room where Christa Sachs was seated at a table. The men took seats opposite her.

'I want to be there when you interview the Social Services Director,' Lenau had told his friend beforehand.

'Go home, Klaus. You shouldn't even be here. Or have you forgotten you're retired now?'

'You got me involved when you asked me to interview Bodo Freitag. I know more than you do about this case. I've interviewed Mrs Sachs before. Come on, Stefan, you owe me one.'

'I do the questioning. You keep quiet.'

Lenau had agreed.

The woman who now faced them acted the innocent victim of a misunderstanding, without convincing Lenau or Brückner.

She received Brückner's opening question: what was she doing at the mountain cave, early on a Sunday morning, with a widening of her eyes and a charming smile. 'Simply my job, Chief Inspector. Taking care of a group of lost children desperately in need of adult help.'

'How did you know these children would be there?'

'I was told by the mayor and Doctor Wagner.'

'How did they know?'

Christa Sachs shrugged and made a grimace, as if to express that she didn't know.

'You see, what I don't understand is why you were the only person from social services present,' Brückner went on. 'As far as I'm aware, there were no other social workers. But there were a lot of nurses from the Koppenberg Klinik, a psychiatric hospital. I would have thought a group of lost children is a matter for social services, not psychiatric medical staff. Can you explain that to me?'

'For some reason the Wagners knew the children would be there. I presume they asked as many adults as they could gather to help them find and look after the children. That the adults happened to work at a psychiatric hospital had nothing to do with it.'

Her reply came haltingly. Making it up as she goes along, Lenau thought.

Brückner tried again. 'Normally, in cases like these, when children are lost, the police are the first to be notified. They then contact social services. Sometimes it's the other way round, but either way, social services work closely with the police. Why did neither you nor the Wagners contact us? It seems to me that you wanted to keep it quiet.'

'Not at all. It happened so suddenly. There was no time to contact the police. I'm sure we would have done, afterwards.'

Lenau thought Sachs' lies had gone far enough. He had been furiously scribbling on a notepad and now slid the pad towards Brückner.

Brückner glanced at it before continuing the interview. 'Thirty-three years ago, in 1978, you were involved in a similar event, as was Chief Inspector Lenau here – and me. It involved a group of unknown children, roughly the same age as those who were discovered on the mountain early this morning, who were found wandering the streets. They too claimed to have emerged from a mountain cave, having woken up in there. It's a similar story. Do you believe there is a connection?'

Christa Sachs' reply almost sounded sincere. 'Possibly. I wouldn't know.'

Brückner took another look at Lenau's prompts on the paper in front of him. 'What exactly happened to that first group, the ones who were children in 1978?'

Sachs looked from Lenau to Brückner. 'He asked me that same question. You already know the answer. The first year or two they were looked after by the Sisters of Mercy at the old orphanage. Then they were transferred to the Koppenberg Klinik.' Here, she stopped abruptly.

'And then?' Brückner prompted.

Christa Sachs expelled a sigh of irritation. 'Look, I've already been over this with your colleague. Then nothing. They're still there, is what I was told. I didn't know, but I do know why they went there. They were dangerous.'

'Because of the whistling?'

Brückner was one of Lenau's men who, in 1978, had worn ear defenders to prevent him from hearing the children whistle and to stop them leaving Hamelin.

'Of course.'

'But you could have separated them by finding families for the children during the two years in the orphanage. They're only dangerous when they're together, aren't they?'

'It wasn't that easy in those days. Besides, they weren't just dangerous. They were also different from other children, peculiar. It would have been hard to find families who wanted them. Do you have any more questions, inspector? I've told you everything I know. Either you let me go or I want a lawyer present.'

Brückner got up. 'No, thank you. That's all, for now.'

Mrs Sachs stood up too.

'Just answer me this,' said Lenau. 'Why would you leave your nice warm bed before dawn on a freezing Sunday morning to help out the Wagners? I don't believe a word of what you just told us.'

For a moment, the woman looked stunned, before she recovered and snapped at him. 'How dare you! I've been very compliant in answering your questions, but I'm not going to listen to your insults. I will only answer further questions in the presence of my lawyer.'

Lenau did not intend to let her off that easily. 'You could have stopped those children from being incarcerated in a mental institution for thirty-three years. But you didn't. I'd like to know why. What hold do the Wagners have over you?'

'We're just friends, that's all.' Christa Sachs put her gloves on and picked up her bag. 'If you find that hard to believe, ask them.'

'Don't worry,' said Lenau, 'we will.'

Brückner waited until she was gone, before he turned to Lenau. 'Really, Klaus, I asked you not to intervene.'

'I tried, but she lied through her teeth. In the end, I couldn't keep my mouth shut any longer. Sorry.'

'Apology accepted. Now go home. I'll let you know how my interview with the Wagners goes.'

'Can't I join you?'

'Certainly not. They know you're retired. They'll know you shouldn't be there.'

By late afternoon Lenau still hadn't heard from Brückner. After lunch he had tried to distract himself by watching a football match on television: Karlsruher FC versus Fortuna Köln. The match was anything but exciting, and he kept listening for the phone to ring, while his thoughts returned again and again to what had happened that morning. He hoped Brückner would ask Claudia Wagner what she had intended to do with the new children.

A thought struck him. Perhaps he should pay a visit to the youth hostel, where the new arrivals were being temporarily placed. He couldn't sit here any longer. There must be something useful he could do, or could find out.

The youth hostel, the largest in Hamelin, had no other guests at present due to planned redecorating. Not being one to get on with Google Maps or GPS, Lenau opted for the old-fashioned way and studied his trusted printed map in the car, before taking to the road. Ten minutes later he arrived at the hostel and went in search of Bodo, Alana and Katrin, who had offered to translate between the children and the authorities.

'Everything in order?' He greeted the two police officers at the gate who, recognising him, let him pass and enter the premises. In a large common room downstairs Bodo was doing a jigsaw puzzle with a small group of children.

'Alana and Katrin are upstairs,' he told Lenau, after exchanging slightly awkward greetings, soured by their first encounter at the police station. 'Most of the children are exhausted and lying down for an afternoon rest. They've had all kinds of checks – medical and others – then showers and warmer clothes.'

Just then, Katrin joined them. She said Alana was staying with the children upstairs, who were lying down and listening to music, from a stack of CDs she had found along with a CD player. 'They think it's magic.'

Lenau told Bodo and Katrin about the interview with the Director of Social Services, Christa Sachs.

'And what did she say?'

'That they were just good friends.'

'Oh, but she was more than that,' Katrin reacted thoughtfully. 'At least with Thomas Wagner.'

Bemused, Bodo and Lenau stared at her.

'What do you mean?' Lenau asked.

'All these years, I hadn't thought of it. But today, at the cave, when I saw her looking at him, it all came back to me. It was only a brief glance, but it reminded me of something when we lived at the orphanage. Mr Wagner and Miss Sachs, our social worker, were in a relationship.'

'Did Thomas Wagner visit the orphanage?' Lenau asked.

'I only saw him that one time.'

'Right. But I interrupted you. You were telling us about their affair.'

'I don't know if it was an affair. But I saw them kissing each other passionately. Trude and I made fun of it at the time, pretending to be her, playing out what I had seen and heard. "Oh, Thomas, I love you so much. I will always be there for you." Then we'd collapse in fits of giggles.'

'What if that explains her actions? As simply as: she was in love with him, possibly still is, and therefore would do anything he asked her to do?' Lenau wondered aloud.

'They were both married though, weren't they?' Bodo asked.

'They were,' confirmed Lenau.

There was still no news from Brückner. Lenau waited until after dinner and around eight, he picked up the phone and tapped in Brückner's number.

'I was just about to ring you,' the voice at the other end said.

'Liar. Tell me what you learned from the Wagner interview.'

'Nothing. There *was* no interview. As I was getting ready, I received a phone call from Commissioner Kruse, who ordered me to let the Wagners go at once or a complaint would be made against my department.'

'What kind of complaint?'

'Harassment while carrying out their civic duty. The Wagners told the commissioner that during a dawn walk with colleagues and friends they found a group of children, lost and half-frozen. To prevent hypothermia in the children they went to get blankets and were in the middle of organising transport back to Hamelin, when police helicopters arrived and they were arrested.'

'Damn it, Stefan. The commissioner has obviously been bought by the Wagners. It's a well-known fact that they sponsor the Police Association.'

'You're right. Unfortunately, there's very little I can do about it for now.'

Lenau thought for a moment. 'On the contrary, there's one important thing you can do without anyone objecting.'

'What is it?'

'Keep an eye on the children, those that were found this morning. Make sure you know what happens to them next.'

'Why?'

'Long story. Humour me, will you?'

Katrin and Alana were the first to arrive at Schwab's bakery and coffeeshop, where they had arranged to meet their friends at 11am. It was the first Sunday in January, two weeks after their attempt to rescue the third wave of children from the hands of the Wagners and their helpmates.

As they walked through the door, a drizzly rain fell.

'I hoped for snow during my first winter of freedom,' Katrin said. 'Do you remember the masses of snow in winter when we were children?'

Alana nodded and they entered the bakery. The place was busy and the delicious fragrance of freshly-baked breads and pastries invaded Katrin's nostrils. Behind the bakery counter, loaves and buns in all shapes and sizes were stacked high. There were plaits and cobs, round rye breads with crunchy crusts, spelt wholegrain loaves, sunflower and pumpkin breads, breads covered in poppyseeds, rolls with sesame seeds or salty crusts, milk rolls, soft and sweet. Katrin had never seen or smelt anything like it during her years in the klinik.

They were lucky. In the corner, people were leaving while a waitress cleared the blue and white checked table. Alana and Katrin were about to order coffee and pastries, when Peter, Erika, Bodo and Lenau trooped in together.

Bodo had spent Christmas Day with Alana and Katrin. Other than that, they hadn't seen each other over the Christmas period. Katrin, who had become ever more restrained in her emotions over the years at the Koppenberg Klinik, was surprised to experience waves of warmth and happiness at seeing the others again. Her feelings were reflected in the general mood. Cheerful new years' wishes bounced back and forth across the table.

The reason they were here was to find out from Lenau how things stood with the investigation into the Wagners and the Koppenberg Klinik.

'It's not good news,' Lenau began. 'There might not even be an investigation.'

At that, everyone started to talk at the same time.

'What about the use of unlicensed medication?' Erika wanted to know.

'How do they explain capturing the children from the cave and spiriting them away?' Alana asked.

'And the unexplained deaths that occurred at the klinik?' Peter butted in.

'The secrecy with which the secure unit is treated and everything that got hushed up over the years?' Erika asked again.

'The Wagners have an explanation for what happened on Midwinter's day, making it sound as if they came across the children on an organised dawn walk and took care of them,' Lenau said.

The others were gobsmacked.

'And the police believed them?' Peter finally asked.

'My friend, Chief Inspector Brückner, never got a chance to question the Wagners. His superior prevented him from doing so.'

'Meaning, his superior is a friend of the Wagners,' Peter said.

'Afraid so.'

'And the new children? Are they going to disappear into the Koppenberg Klinik for the rest of their lives, being used for drug trials and slowly changing into vegetables?' Katrin heard herself asking the question that was foremost in her mind.

'No,' Lenau said with emphasis. 'I won't let that happen. And neither will Brückner.'

Alana turned towards Katrin and spoke quietly. 'Why don't you tell them what we discussed earlier?'

Katrin nodded. 'I've decided to sue Claudia Wagner for incarcerating me and the others on the grounds of a false diagnosis.'

With everyone staring at her, Katrin went on nervously. 'I

came to that decision realising how wonderful my life is now, compared to my life at the klinik or even before that, at the orphanage. I can make my own decisions, discover the world for the first time, travel, meet new people and make new friends. I no longer live in isolation. I can try new things and have new experiences. Those are all freedoms Claudia Wagner took from me. I've been drawing and painting more than ever and Alana helped me frame those pictures.'

The waitress arrived with everyone's order and conversation paused while coffees and pastries were placed on the table.

It was at that moment that, sitting near the window, Katrin's attention was drawn towards a passer-by, who had halted on the other side of the glass. She recognised the figure and stopped breathing. Tall and slightly stooping, a mocking smile on the lips, his eyes caught hers. One was pale blue, the other black. She couldn't tear herself away from the blackness of that ever-expanding pupil. Katrin felt herself sucked into that black hole, even as she perceived the emptiness that awaited her there. She trembled.

'Katrin? What's wrong?' Erika, beside her, touched her arm.

Katrin tore her eyes away and turned towards her friends, who stared at her with worried faces.

'Did you see him?' Katrin didn't recognise her own voice.

'Who?' Erika's reply got lost in the hubbub of everyone talking at the same time after the waitress had left.

'I think Katrin should exhibit her work,' Alana was saying. 'We just don't know how to go about organising that.'

'I might know someone. He has a small gallery. I think I mentioned him to you before, Katrin. He might be interested,' Erika said.

Katrin smiled, but her thoughts were still with the image of the piper. Real, or hallucination?

'You were telling us what made you decide to sue Doctor Wagner,' Peter reminded her.

Katrin forced herself to focus on the here and now. 'Over Christmas, I was thinking, why should I be the only one given the opportunity of a normal life? What about the others? Don't they deserve a full life? What they have is no life. That's just an existence. So that's why I decided to fight Doctor Wagner in court.'

Peter looked thoughtful. 'You need a good lawyer. The best. And they don't come cheap.'

'I might be able to overcome that problem,' Bodo said. 'All my adult life I put my earnings in the bank, invested and was lucky. I could probably afford to pay for a lawyer.'

Katrin smiled broadly at him and her cheeks flushed with warmth.

'Even obtaining the best lawyer to argue your case might not be enough for a conviction and a review of the klinik's patients,' Lenau said carefully.

Peter agreed. 'What we need is evidence of Hamburg Pharma AG paying huge sums of money to the Koppenberg Klinik for testing drugs on patients whose legal guardian is Doctor Wagner, plus the real autopsy results of those patients who died in her care. Such evidence as might be found on Claudia Wagner's computer.'

'You're not suggesting we steal her computer, are you?' Erika sounded uneasy.

'We don't need to. A good hacker can get into her computer without physically going into her office or home. Only, I don't know anyone. You?'

Peter looked at Lenau, who thoughtfully rubbed his chin.

'I might.'

TWENTY-SIX

'This is Jan Mazur,' Erika said. 'He's come to look at your paintings and sketches.'

Katrin saw a slim young man of medium height, with a stubble beard, warm, hazel-brown eyes and fashionable clothes, standing with Erika on the doorstep of Alana's house.

After Katrin, who had expected them, introduced herself to Jan, she invited them into the living room where her artworks were displayed. When Erika had suggested she bring her art-connoisseur friend round for a viewing, Katrin spent a lot of time completing and framing her sketches and paintings.

The gallery owner took a long time to study the pictures. The longer his silence lasted, the more insecure Katrin felt.

She braced herself for a polite but humiliating verdict.

He turned towards her. 'They're exquisite. Erika was right. People need to see these. Where did you find these models? Who are they? They're unlike any models I've seen portrayed.'

'They're family and people I knew from a long time ago.' Katrin exhaled slowly and her shoulders relaxed. 'I drew and painted them from memory.'

'Who's this?' Jan pointed at a delicate water colour of a

young girl with vivacious blue eyes, a wicked smile and arms spread wide in an all-embracing gesture.

'That's my sister, Trude. She's no longer with us.'

'I'm sorry,' Jan said. 'This one is probably my favourite.'

'Mine too. It's not for sale.'

They sat down and discussed the practicalities of an exhibition. Jan explained he needed time to contact customers who might be interested and to organise the viewing at his gallery.

He took out his phone to look at dates. 'How does Easter Day sound? That's 8 April this year.'

When Peter had asked him if he knew someone who could hack into Claudia Wagner's computer, Lenau was reminded of Gert Keller, a hacker the police occasionally used. Keller was the best in the business. The day after his meeting with Peter and friends at Schwab's coffee shop, Lenau phoned Keller and invited him for a beer in Adler's Bar that evening.

Lenau arrived just before the appointed time, ordered two bottles of Kölsch and went to sit in a quiet corner, out of earshot from other patrons. Minutes later, a baby-faced lad in an expensive overcoat and a fedora on his floppy fair hair, joined him there.

The hacker, who was twenty-six-years old but looked ten years younger, greeted Lenau. 'You wanted to see me, Chief Inspector? What's this about? We'll have to make it brief. Bertha doesn't like being tied up outside.'

Lenau was familiar with Keller's constant companion, a mastiff as big as a calf. Dogs were not allowed inside Adler's.

Keller might not have realised the man seated opposite him

was no longer a chief inspector of police, but Lenau did not enlighten him.

'We suspect something unethical and unlawful is going on at a private establishment, but we have no evidence. Getting into their computer system might help.'

'Which private establishment are we talking about?'

'It's a psychiatric hospital: the Koppenberg Klinik.'

The hacker let out a long low whistle. 'Hamelin's pet project. A monument to experimental psychiatry.'

'Do you know it?' Lenau was surprised that the klinik, located on the outskirts of Hamelin, was that well-known.

'I know a girl who spent some time there. Her parents are filthy rich. She told me it didn't look like a hospital inside. More like a spa, very fancy. She was almost sorry to leave, she had such a good time.'

'Different patients have different experiences. What I'm talking about is a secretive, secure wing. We need information on payments between the Koppenberg Klinik and a company called Hamburg Pharma AG, as well as details on the medication taken by patients who died at the klinik, what the possible side effects might be and the results of post-mortems. Anything like that.'

Keller rubbed his chin, where some light-coloured fluff indicated the beginnings of a beard. 'That's a big ask.'

'I know. Can you do it?'

'The question is not: can I do it, Chief Inspector. Of course, I can. The question is: can the police afford me? It's going to cost you. Big asks cost big money.'

Lenau had forgotten how pedantic the young man was – and how expensive. After some back-and-forth haggling, they settled on the payment, finished their beers and left.

A couple of days later, Lenau received a phone call from Keller, who had obtained the requested information and was about to send him the files. It didn't take the retired chief inspector long, once he started to study the files, to realise the contents of the documents would provide plenty of damning evidence against Doctor Wagner in a court case.

He finished reading at 2 am and rubbed his tired eyes, sore from staring at the screen. Then he switched off the desktop computer and quietly tiptoed up the stairs, not wanting to wake his wife. Too excited about what he'd read to sleep, he stayed wide awake during the remaining hours of the night.

The following morning, he went to the police station to see the chief, Stefan Brückner. After Lenau handed him the USB stick, Brückner took a cursory glance at its content.

Lenau's old friend looked up, his usual jovial face grave. 'How did you get hold of this?'

'I didn't. It was Gert Keller. Remember him?'

'The hacker?'

Lenau nodded. 'This clearly shows Doctor Wagner getting paid handsomely for drug trials and there's no evidence the patients had been asked for or had given their consent. It also shows how the side effects of those same medicines might have killed some of those patients. It's enough to start proceedings for a court case.'

The chief shook his head. 'No. What the hacker did is illegal and can't be used in court.'

Silence stretched between them as Brückner looked keen to get rid of his former boss and Lenau, stubborn, stood deep in thought.

'Remember the Krasnapolsky case?' Lenau said, finally. 'We searched those premises in the hope our suspicion of fraud and embezzlement was correct and we were right. North Hamburg Chief of Police, Falke, is a friend of yours. You could organise simultaneous raids on Hamburg Pharma AG and the Koppenberg Klinik on suspicion of unethical and immoral dealings between them. We have more than a suspicion here and, after the success of the operation, you could say it was your idea.'

'I want the killing to stop,' Lenau pressed, when his friend still hesitated. 'Those patients are being used as lab rats. And I want to be there during the raid at the Koppenberg. You could temporarily reinstate me, just for this operation.'

Ten o'clock on a Thursday morning in February, three days after Lenau had shown Brückner the incriminating evidence on his USB stick, Lenau swiftly entered the Koppenberg Klinik's main entrance and marched towards the startled receptionist, followed by six uniformed police officers carrying cardboard boxes.

Following Lenau's request to be taken to Doctor Wagner's office and that of her secretary, the receptionist led them through a passage with doors on both sides, where tranquil harp music could be heard.

She halted and indicated one of the doors. 'That's the secretary's office. You have to go through there to get to Doctor Wagner's office.'

The receptionist was about to knock, but Lenau nudged her out of the way and opened the door with no such courtesies. He stepped inside and glanced at the secretary, who looked up from her desktop computer.

'Please stop what you're doing and step away from your desk. I take it that is Doctor Wagner's office?' Lenau indicated with his head.

Before the dumbfounded secretary could answer, the door

behind her was opened by an irritated Claudia Wagner. 'Astrid? What is...?' She stopped when she saw Lenau and his officers.

Lenau waved a sheet of paper at her. 'This is a warrant signed by a judge. We have permission to search these premises and confiscate your computers and those of your secretary.'

'On what grounds?' Bright red spots started to appear on Claudia Wagner's high cheekbones and her voice sounded tight from withheld fury.

'On suspicion of unlicensed drug trials on certain patients.'

'That's nonsense. As I told you before, we don't put our patients through drug trials and we only use licensed medication. We also have regular accreditation audits.'

'Then you won't have any objection to us taking your computers and checking if what you say is true.' Lenau knew precisely what they would find and where to look.

A lifetime of policing had taught him to remain rational and professional under any circumstances. However, the thought of vulnerable children being locked up in a closed unit, enduring drug experiments and unnecessary deaths – for profit! – galled him. He had to restrain himself in order to remain calm, not to handcuff her and march her to the police station.

'I'll have a word with Commissioner Berghaus.' Claudia Wagner reached for her phone.

'Be my guest. But with a legal warrant signed by a judge there's very little even a commissioner can do for you.'

She tried a different tack. 'Those computers contain confidential and valuable information about patient treatments. Without them, we can't do our jobs.'

'I expect you'll have them back in a few days,' Lenau told her, curtly.

He concentrated on overseeing the search and collection and packing up of the hardware. It didn't take long. They left having barely spent twenty minutes at the klinik.

In the days that followed, Gert Keller's hacking results were backed up by legitimate evidence from the computers confiscated by Lenau and his officers. This led to the arrest of Claudia Wagner, Senior Staff nurse Bauer, the Koppenberg's pathologist in Hamelin, as well as Doctor Jens Hagedorn and his colleagues in Hamburg. They were all now officially awaiting trial.

Katrin hadn't expected so many visitors to turn up. After months of preparation, she felt exhilarated but exhausted, even more so from the attention she had received during today's exhibition. It seemed everyone wanted to talk to her, ask questions, take photos, arrange magazine interviews and take her contact details. If it hadn't been for Alana, Erika, Peter and Bodo, Katrin felt she would not have been able to handle it all. Now it was over, and all the visitors were gone, she felt empty.

'Here you are. Drink up and don't move,' Erika ordered, leading Katrin towards one of the sofas and handing her a glass of champagne.

Sipping obediently from the tall, pink glass, Katrin watched her friends take down her art works, separating and putting stickers on those that had sold and would be picked up from the gallery or delivered to their buyers.

In a corner of the long, narrow room, Jan was deep in conversation with another man. When he turned, Katrin recognised retired Chief Inspector Lenau.

He strode towards her. 'Congratulations, I hear it's been a great success.'

'Thank you for coming. I haven't seen you for a while. Do you have any news about...'

'The Koppenberg Klinik?'

Katrin nodded.

'I have, as it happens.'

Peter, within earshot, suggested packing the unsold paintings into the car before finishing the champagne and listening to Lenau's news.

By the time they assembled in a small circle, with Peter and Erika sitting on the floor, and the others on sofas and Jan disappeared into his office, the sky was darkening and the streetlamps lit.

Peter looked at Lenau. 'Go on. Don't leave us in suspense any longer.'

Lenau told them about the hacker, then the subsequent raids on the Koppenberg Klinik and Hamburg Pharma AG. 'There will be a court case. We have concrete evidence for justice to be done.'

'That's fantastic news.' Peter smiled broadly.

'Thank you,' Katrin said. 'Not just from me, but also from those still locked up at the klinik.'

'What happens next?' Bodo took a wad of tobacco from its pouch and calmly rolled a cigarette.

'Well, there will be a trial at court, attended by those arrested, including Doctor Wagner and co. The same applies to her counterpart in Hamburg.'

'Doctor Jens Hagedorn,' said Peter.

'Does that mean I don't need to sue Doctor Wagner and Bodo doesn't need to pay for my lawyer?' Katrin asked.

'That's exactly what it means. The state will do that for you. I suspect you will be an important witness though, and will have to give evidence in court.'

'I'm looking forward to that day.'

'You wouldn't be if you knew what it involves. Claudia Wagner's lawyer will tear you to pieces. He or she will do anything to demonstrate to the judge that you are unfit, mentally ill and belong in the Koppenberg Klinik.'

'Then I will have to convince the judge that I am not. How do I do that?'

Erika answered promptly. 'There are tests. You could make an appointment with an independent psychiatrist for an assessment and diagnosis. Best not to use one in Hamelin, but somewhere out of Doctor Wagner's sphere of influence. Someone in Hanover, perhaps. I'll help you find someone. Then take that statement with you to court.'

'Erika is right,' Lenau added. 'When you get to court you can give that document to the public prosecutor as evidence of your fitness to testify. Also, if you're going to be a key witness, the police and prosecution barrister will interview you and coach you on how to deliver your evidence. They will help you prepare.'

TWENTY-SEVEN

Hamelin possessed many attractive, half-timbered buildings but the court house was a rectangular eyesore, built in the sixties, mundane and practical rather than charming, as were so many other office buildings.

On that breezy April morning, Katrin waited to be called as a witness for the prosecution in the trial of Claudia Wagner, taking place in the adjoining courtroom. While waiting, Alana kept her company. Not much was said between them. They sat stiffly on straight, uncomfortable chairs in the empty room. Katrin tried to concentrate on the advice drummed into her by the prosecutor. Anxiously fingering the piece of paper on which she had written everything down, she was aware of her sweaty hands and rapid heartbeat.

'Nervous?' Alana whispered.

Katrin nodded.

'Drink some water.' Alana rose to go to the water cooler.

'I'd rather not. It'll only make me go to the toilet and they might come and fetch me just then.'

'A peppermint?'

Katrin took one and sucked on it as she listened out for

snatches of conversation from the courtroom. What went on in there was inaudible.

'What if I get confused or don't understand their questions and mess it all up? What if they don't believe me?'

'What did the prosecutor tell you?'

'To tell the truth and if I'm asked where I'm from originally, say I don't remember. I was only eight years old.'

'And if they ask you why you told Doctor Wagner that you are one of Hamelin's children who followed a brightly dressed stranger into the mountains in 1284?'

'I'll say that's what we were told by the people we lived with before 1978: a group of adults and children all living together on a farm, in the country, I don't know where.'

'Excellent. We must keep the truth about your past a secret. And you have a copy of the letter to hand from that psychiatrist you saw?'

'It's in my pocket.' Katrin's hand touched the envelope tucked inside.

Alana took her other hand and gave it a little squeeze. 'You'll be fine. Stay calm, take deep breaths when you feel panicky, and concentrate on what you want to say. You were sectioned for no valid reason and kept isolated even from your sister. Your sister, who was healthy and strong, who suddenly died in mysterious circumstances. You were afraid the same would happen to you. That's why you escaped.'

Alana's last words still hovered in the air, when a clerk appeared and asked Katrin to follow her. When she did, Katrin found her legs had turned into jelly instead of muscle and bone.

Heads turned to stare at Katrin when she entered the courtroom. Her mouth was dry. She swallowed with great difficulty as the clerk led her to the witness box. Katrin sat down, but was almost immediately asked to stand and swear to tell the truth.

In the pause before the questioning started, Katrin became acutely aware of voices whispering, bodies shifting in seats and throats coughing. She forced herself to look up and in the sea of faces she recognised Lenau, Erika, Peter and Bodo.

Claudia Wagner, the accused, sat with her defence team on a front bench and behind them, Thomas Wagner and several employees of the Koppenberg Klinik, Nurse Bauer amongst them.

The prosecutor turned to Katrin and commenced. 'Those present here in this room might think that there was a good reason you were at the klinik, that you are mentally ill and not fit for living life independently. What would you say to that?'

Katrin remembered to speak up as she had been told to, and speak slowly and clearly. 'Very recently I have visited a psychiatrist in Hanover, Doctor Wernsz. His assessment and diagnosis is on this piece of paper.'

Despite all parties having already seen the document, the prosecutor handed the sheet of paper to the judge, who took one look at it and declared that Doctor Wernsz had found no evidence of mental illness in Katrin.

The prosecutor continued. 'Can you tell us why you escaped from the Koppenberg Klinik?'

These questions, as well as her answers, had been rehearsed beforehand.

'Many of us in the secure unit had died over these last few years, for reasons unknown and unexplained. My sister had been amongst those. I was afraid if I stayed, I would die too.'

The prosecutor had no further questions for Katrin and now it was the defence's turn to cross-examine her.

He too started off in a friendly tone. 'How would you say you were treated at the klinik? Were you ever treated badly, cruelly or inhumanely?'

Katrin had been prepared for this kind of question. 'I was

never treated badly. I had a beautiful room, food was plentiful and staff were kind and caring. Nevertheless, I was lonely and isolated. My door was always locked and I wasn't allowed to socialise with my fellow patients, not even with my sister. I wasn't free or allowed to decide over my own destiny. I was restrained and forced to take medication against my will.'

'You have told us *why* you escaped the klinik,' the defence lawyer continued. 'But I am more interested to learn *how* you managed to escape the Koppenberg Klinik. Surely you must have had some help?'

The question was unexpected and Katrin, unprepared, froze.

Instantly, the prosecutor rose. 'Objection! That has nothing to do with this case.'

The judge agreed.

Defence continued his examination. 'Why did you tell Doctor Wagner you belonged to the original Hamelin children abducted in 1284? That would mean that you are either more than 700 years old, or able to travel through time. Which is it?'

He paused to allow a certain amount of sniggering from the public benches.

Katrin responded with the answer she had prepared, namely that's what she'd been told by the people she lived with before 1978: a group of people living communally on a farm, somewhere in the country, and that at the time she'd only been eight and didn't know any better.

He looked at her long and hard before proceeding. 'So you were lying. You know what they say about liars, don't you? Once a liar, always a liar. Your story doesn't sound very convincing to me.'

The words hit Katrin as if she'd been punched in the stomach. How did he know? Could he read her mind? Was the truth written on her forehead? She shook her head, afraid to speak.

Again, the prosecutor stood up and addressed the judge. 'The defence is trying to intimidate my witness.'

Again, the judge agreed.

And so it went on, for an interminable time. Just when Katrin hoped the cross examination had come to an end, Claudia Wagner leant towards her defence lawyer and whispered something in his ear.

He renewed his interrogation. 'What can you tell us about the whistling?'

'The... whistling?' Katrin echoed slowly, to gain time.

'The whistling, yes. You know what I mean.'

Before the prosecution could object, the judge addressed the defence. 'Explain the relevance of your question to the case.'

'Certainly. The question has everything to do with explaining why Doctor Wagner was convinced that these particular patients were dangerous and needed not just social care, but psychiatric treatment as well.'

'Proceed,' said the judge.

'Eyewitness statements from that time suggest that when these children whistled in chorus, every person who heard it became hypnotised, as it were. Everyone and everything halted: people going about their business, car drivers, cyclists. Imagine what would have happened if these children had run free. The damage, the chaos, the terror that would have ensued. Instead of being criminalised, Doctor Wagner deserves our gratitude, for having saved Hamelin from such danger.'

The judge frowned and addressed Katrin. 'Can you tell us what exactly happened in 1978? What about the whistling? Why do you think Doctor Wagner deemed it necessary to section you and your companions?'

Katrin briefly glanced across at her friends as if to draw

strength from their support, before responding. 'I can't remember much of it, of what happened in 1978. I was eight years old. I remember the whistling only vaguely. It happened when we were scared, terrified. Something came over us, something we had no control over. We had no evil in mind. We just wanted to escape, to be free.'

At that, Katrin saw Claudia Wagner again whisper fervently in her lawyer's ear. Would she tell him about what had happened at the mountain cave recently, when Katrin clearly had had control over her whistling, initiated it even? But before the defence lawyer could continue his cross examination, the judge, with an eye on the clock, discharged the witness and rose. The case would proceed in the afternoon. Katrin might be called to return on another day.

Five minutes later Katrin, accompanied by Alana, breathed fresh air outside the court building, relieved to be going home. They decided to walk rather than taking the bus.

At a busy zebra crossing, waiting for the traffic lights to turn green, Katrin got a nasty shock. On the other side of the road, amidst a group of pedestrians clustered together, Katrin spotted the same figure she had recently seen through a coffee shop window. The figure had haunted her dreams ever since. For a split second he looked straight at her, smiled, and winked conspiratorially. Then he was gone. She didn't notice that the traffic light had changed and people around her started to cross the road. She stood and stared at the spot where a moment ago she had seen the embodiment of her fear. In disbelief, in shock, she thought: it's an illusion, a trick of the mind. Or it could have been someone else, someone who vaguely looked like him. She was tired; her court appearance had been stressful. She shivered though it wasn't cold.

Alana, who had walked on when the light changed, turned back. 'Are you all right? You look as if you've seen a ghost.'

'I'm fine. Just a little tired.' Katrin couldn't bring herself to tell Alana what she'd seen.

'Wasn't Katrin impressive in court?' Erika, in front of the full-length mirror in the bedroom, critically checked her outfit: smart black trousers, black top and a sparkly, colourful blazer. It was not long after the Wagner trial, which had taken a few weeks. She and Peter had watched some of it from the public benches.

'Spectacular,' Peter agreed absent-mindedly, searching for a suitable tie.

'Without her testimony, I doubt the trial would have ended the way we hoped it would.'

'Do you think these shoes need polishing?'

Erika nodded and Peter went off to smarten up his shoes in the kitchen.

Erika added the finishing touches to her hair, picked up the invitation from Peter's desk and went to get her coat. The doorbell rang.

'That's our taxi,' she called out, 'are you ready?'

Minutes later, in the back of the taxi, Peter reflected. 'Who would have thought, of all people, that it would be Bodo who invited us to a posh dinner at the Wolrath Hotel with a printed invitation. Can you even imagine he has the kind of clothes to wear in a place like that?'

For Erika too, it seemed inconceivable. Bodo, the night cleaner who lived in a run-down mobile home. On the other hand, he had mentioned he owned 'a tidy sum' from speculating on the stock market.

Contrary to Peter's expectations, Bodo looked magnificent in a well-tailored dark green velvet dinner jacket and bow tie, as he stood in the hotel reception to welcome them, with his long white mane smoothed back. Behind Erika and Peter, the Lenaus arrived and, when Alana and Katrin soon afterwards entered the lobby, Bodo invited everyone to move through to the next room where a table had been set for them.

Drinks appeared and orders for food were taken, after which conversation quickly turned to discussing the trial they had recently attended.

'Are you happy with the verdict?' Erika asked Katrin across the table.

'Happy isn't the right word. I'm more... relieved that it's finally over. Perhaps now I can stop worrying about being taken back to the klinik. And I'm satisfied I got justice for Trude and the others who died unnecessarily. Claudia Wagner received what she deserved. Once she leaves prison, she will never be able to practise psychiatry again.'

Doctor Wagner had been sentenced to fifteen years' imprisonment for multiple manslaughter. Her accomplices, Doctor Polat, who had been responsible for yearly quality control visits, and Doctor Wieland, the pathologist, received shorter prison sentences while Doctor Jens Hagedorn, the chief executive at Hamburg Pharma AG, was still under investigation.

Erika informed everyone that Peter had been offered a fulltime job at the *taz* based on the article he sent them.

Everyone congratulated a beaming Peter.

Dinner arrived and conversation dwindled while everyone enjoyed their food. After desserts, coffee and liqueurs, Bodo tapped a teaspoon against his glass to get everyone's attention.

'It's not only to celebrate the results of the trial that I have invited you all here. I would like you to look at this.' He opened a briefcase and took out a stack of papers.

'These are an architect's plans for a new housing estate at the edge of Hamelin, showing yet-to-be-built, sheltered-living accommodation for Katrin's fellow patients who are still at the Koppenberg Klinik, waiting to be released.'

They cleared the empty plates and dishes on the table out of the way and spread the papers out for everyone to study the drawings.

'It looks very impressive,' Lenau said after a while.

'Wonderful, it looks wonderful,' Erika agreed.

'The question is: who will pay for this? Because it'll cost a fortune to build.' Peter looked at Bodo.

'I will,' Bodo said. 'I will pay for it.'

Peter raised his eyebrows. 'How? Will you be able to afford it on your salary?'

'I only became a cleaner to be near those in the klinik. I didn't need the money or the job. My adopted parents left me a substantial inheritance. In the late nineties I invested in some small and unknown software companies. When they hit the big-time, I made a fortune.'

'So, the mobile home was all part of your disguise?' Erika asked.

Bodo nodded. 'I didn't know how long I would stay in Hamelin. I needed something temporary, a hiding place. I came across the caravan in the small ads of the *DeWeZet* and decided to rent it.'

'Where will you live in future?' Lenau asked.

Bodo gestured towards the architect's drawings on the table. 'In the sheltered-living accommodation, with the others. They need looking after and I can help with that. Alana and Katrin have already said they want to move there too. There'll also be staff to help ex-patients adjust to a more normal, twenty-first century life.'

'How long will it take to build?' Peter asked.

'The architects expect it to take about a year,' replied Bodo. 'I've spoken with the current director of the Koppenberg Klinik, Doctor Pletscher. He has agreed to keep Katrin's fellow patients at the Koppenberg for the year, gradually rehabilitating them.'

'Some changes have already been implemented,' Erika elaborated. 'Starting with gradually reducing their medication. We now keep doors unlocked during the daytime and we are in the process of reintroducing patients to one another.'

'What's that like for them?' Katrin wanted to know.

'They don't recognise each other at all. It's been too long.'

'Hopefully, once they're off the medicines their memories will return,' said Katrin.

'Some will be all right. Others, I don't know. Years of taking these drugs may have caused irrevocable damage.' There was sadness in Erika's voice.

Everyone agreed that the assisted living accommodation was a wonderful solution, and they continued to discuss the future of not only the incarcerated patients in the Koppenberg Klinik, but of the newer children to have emerged from the cave as well.

TWENTY-EIGHT

Claudia Wagner, alone in her cell, sat on the bed with her knees drawn up against her chest and her fingers in her ears. She didn't know how long she had been sitting like that, or what time it was, but the small space was cloaked in darkness. Every so often, she called out to the children eerily whistling beyond her door. 'Enough! Stop it, d'you hear? I know what you're trying to do and I won't have it. Did your parents never teach you to respect your elders? I'll come and get you if you don't stop this.'

For a while she was silent as she lay on her side with her hands over her ears to block out the tune that, like an earworm, continued to play until she sat up and exploded once more. 'Didn't you hear me? Be quiet! You have no right to come here and disrupt my sleep. Not many rights are left in this place, but I have the right to sleep. You little bastards, if you're trying to drive me mad with your sodding whistling, you're succeeding. And I should know. I'm the psychiatrist, here.' She laughed and the joyless sound of it echoed in the dark. When this had no effect, she jumped up from the bed, crossed the cell and banged on the door. 'SHUT UP! SHUT UP! SHUT UP!'

Heavy footsteps approached and stopped outside Claudia's door. A face appeared through the porthole in the cell door.

'What's the problem? You're being too noisy. Others are trying to get some sleep.'

'It's not me making the noise,' Claudia fired back. 'It's those wretched children. Tell them to stop whistling.'

'Not this again,' the guard sighed. 'Look, you must stop this nonsense. There are no children here.'

'But you can hear the whistling, can't you?' Claudia urged.

For a moment, the guard cocked his head to show her he was listening, then shook his head. 'No.'

Sometime afterwards Claudia, exhausted, drifted off towards the edge of sleep.

When she woke up, daylight was only just creeping in. The chorus of whistlers had ceased for now. In the half-light dim shapes were making an appearance in the tiny cell. Claudia recognised them as Thomas Wagner and Christa Sachs.

'What is *she* doing here?' Wagner snapped at her phantom husband.

'She's been a great support,' Thomas said. 'Have you any idea what you have done to me? I can't stay in Hamelin. I've lost everything: my job as mayor of Hamelin, my money after I paid off that law firm you employed, my reputation. All gone because of your shady dealings.'

'You need to contact those lawyers again and tell them I want to appeal.'

'Didn't you hear me? There's no more money. You spent it all.'

'Sell the house. It should be worth at least a million euros.'

'Yes, and that's precisely what we need to leave Hamelin behind, go someplace where the name Wagner doesn't ring a bell, and build a new life.'

'We?'

'That's right. We.' The corners of Christa Sachs' lips turned upwards into a triumphant little smile. 'That's the one good thing that's come out of this: we don't have to hide what we feel for each other any longer. All those years of pretending he still loved you, they're over.'

Claudia considered her manicured, almond shaped nails and wondered about their effect when used on Christa's eyes, but dropped the idea. 'You're welcome to him. But you'd be naive to think you were the only one. There've been plenty of others. Ultimately, he's always come back to me.'

'Not anymore. Not while you rot in here for the next fifteen years. You'll be a sad old bag when they let you out.'

'Come,' Thomas Wagner touched Christa Sachs' shoulder to nudge her away, 'we need to go.'

'Where to?' Claudia asked.

'Somewhere in the south, perhaps, where the weather and the people are less depressing.'

By now, the ghostly visitors were fading fast.

'Wait!' Claudia called out. 'Phone Mayer & Partners. Talk to them before you leave, is all I'm asking. They must appeal. I have to get out of here. These damned children, they won't stop whistling. They're torturing me to breaking point.'

'Goodbye, Claudia.'

She was alone.

In the passage beyond her cell door, a dawn chorus of whistlers was taking up that tune again, quietly at first but soon it would be growing in strength and volume.

2012

MIDSUMMER'S DAY

The 21st of June fell on a Sunday that year. During the late morning, Erika's sister Ulrike had taken her children, Jonas and Suzi, to Hamelin's main shopping area. It was busy. Sunny weather had tempted people outdoors. Throngs of parents and children filled the high street, eating ice cream and going in and out of shops and coffee shops.

And then it happened. The moment Jonas had told his mother about. The moment the children had been waiting for: the arrival of the leader. It started with a single sound. A flute or a recorder. Nothing loud or bombastic. An unobtrusive, modest sound, only just audible in that noisy crowd. And yet, it was a signal of sorts, because of what happened afterwards. Ulrike felt Suzi's hand slipping out of hers and saw eager smiles appear on her children's faces. As Jonas and Suzi walked away from her, all around her, children's voices recited: 'Follow the Leader.'

Through the crowd, she caught a brief flash of a tall figure in gaudy attire parading in the high street while holding a flute of sorts to his lips. Ulrike moved to catch up with her son and daughter, but was prevented by a feeling of extreme lethargy surging through her limbs, which grew heavier by the second.

As her body turned to stone, all around her adults stopped dead while their children walked away, smiling and chanting 'Follow the Leader'.

Towards Bungelosen Street they walked, where an inscription attached to a wall, read:

> *'Through this street, in 1284, a piper led Hamelin's lost children out of the town towards the Koppenberg mountain.'*

Katrin, at that hour, was on her way to the youth hostel to be with the children whom she and her friends had saved from a fate like hers, the children of the third wave. Some had already been taken in by foster families, the others still remained at the hostel.

Her step was quick and light. She couldn't wait to tell the children her plan for this morning.

They were to take the number eleven bus to a nature park outside the city walls and spend this sunny morning exploring its grounds. She looked forward to seeing their delight at their first ever bus ride, then showing them everything the park had to offer: a variety of trees to climb, rare plants and flowers specially cultivated, the rock garden, the duck pond and the children's play area with its swings, slides and climbing frames. She knew the park well, having frequently spent time there sketching, but for the children it would be a fresh adventure.

The streets seemed unusually quiet, but she didn't think anything of it. Her mind was pleasantly occupied with activities she could do with the children now that the weather was so fine.

In the distance, a wind instrument struck up a tune. Only when Katrin recognised the melody did she halt on the pavement and listen intently as her body stiffened and the hairs on her neck stood on end.

Now, the strangeness of the silence struck her – along with how a change had come over that part of the city.

It's happening again.

She stood and her breath caught in her throat as long-buried memories resurfaced. Memories of another Midsummer's day, the festival of St John in the year 1284, the year when she had been eight and Trude just six. There were celebrations that day, as there always had been, every year. She remembered a large, outdoor grassy space with wooden benches and tables piled high with food and drink. Bonfires were stacked and prepared for the evening. She'd been chasing and catching the other children in spite of her bad leg, her summer dress swishing around her, laughing and screaming with excitement. Later, they'd played hide-and-seek and she had discovered a hiding place where no one had found her. Bored with waiting, she'd left the barn in search of the others. Then, as now, an eerie silence had descended on the town, a quiet pierced by the tune of a single musical instrument.

Katrin let out the breath she'd held for far too long and made a decision. If it was happening again, she had to stop it. She hastened through the streets as fast as her leg allowed, towards the music, and her thoughts raced on ahead. She needed to find out what was going on.

Katrin turned a corner and was confronted with the very sight she had dreaded: a line of children marching through the high street with eager faces and a bouncy tread, while adult shoppers or people going to work stood and watched, still as statues, their frozen faces expressing horror. Katrin pushed a nauseating wave of anxiety away and tried to think. What could she do to stop it? Should she contact someone? The police, perhaps? Or Lenau? No, that would take time. This was for her to act upon, for her alone.

She stepped from the pavement and joined the parade. She

didn't know where they were going, or where it would end. Possibly in some other cave, in some other mountain. She turned towards the children and searched for a face showing a sign of consciousness, of being aware of what was going on. She saw none. They all looked as if they were sleepwalking or had been hypnotised. Whatever she did to stop this, she would have to do it by herself.

By now, the procession had reached the city's gate. No one tried to stop them as they trooped through the gate and beyond. She didn't know how many children followed the music but she wouldn't be surprised if it was 130. He was taking back what had escaped his grasp. The ancient debt had to be paid to restore the balance.

Katrin's forebodings were confirmed once they headed towards the mountains. Should she move to the front of the parade and try to talk to the music maker? What would she say to him?

Katrin accelerated her steps, but the children beside her remained the same and the tall figure in front still seemed the same distance away. It was no use. Dismayed, she ran out of breath and out of energy. Exhausted, she slowed down. In a moment of clarity, she whistled the tune that had always worked in the past. Not one person in the procession halted or turned. She tried to pull at the children closest to her, but they were as strong as oxen.

Minutes passed and the children marched on, with the mountains looming closer. Her thoughts turned defeatist. She'd been wrong to think she could save these children. She should return to the city, before it was too late. She turned and limped slowly in the opposite direction until she passed the rear of the procession.

Katrin stopped and turned to take a last look at the long column of innocents marching steadily onwards. Earlier this morning, they had been full of joy, hope and dreams as they carried the future within them.

A sob escaped her. Something sinister had taken hold of them and would not let them go. A bitter taste of hatred towards the luridly dressed figure at the head of the parade burned on her tongue.

In 1284, Katrin had followed the music maker for one reason only: to stay with Trude, her little sister, and protect her. Not because she was under his spell. The tune had had no effect on her. In 1978, when they left the cave, she was the only one to remember the tune and the other children had followed her and adults had turned to stone while their whistling was going on. It was the same power the music man possessed. As far as she knew, she was the only one he had no hold over. She might even figure out how to defeat him and save the children, but that would take time. And time was what she didn't have right now.

She knew then what she had to do. Once, she had accompanied Trude in order to protect her. Now, she must do the same for these children.

For a moment she considered what she would leave behind and miss most. Her friends. The young children at the hostel she'd helped to support. Her passion for painting. A life worth living.

Painfully, with regret, she let go.

There was nowhere else to be but here. To be here was the only thing that mattered.

She hastened to catch up.

ACKNOWLEDGMENTS

I had lots of help on the long road between the idea for this book and its publication.

I am most grateful to my tutor at the Open University's M.A in Creative Writing programme, Dr Louise Tondeur, for her encouragement and support.

I would also like to thank Dr Stephen Carver at The Literary Consultancy for his positive assessment of the manuscript. Without it, I doubt I would have had the courage to submit it to literary agents and publishers.

I am much obliged to The Pied Piper Museum in Hamelin, Germany, especially to Wibke Reimer and Michael Boyer who invited me for a visit and a private tour, when I was doing my research there.

Thanks also to my friend Robert Hell for reading and commenting on the manuscript from a German perspective. Thank you for your kindness, suggestions and support.

I am profoundly grateful to the team at Bloodhound Books for believing in me and this story, with a special thanks to my brilliant editor Rachel Tyrer.

A huge thank you to all those who were willing to read and review the book before publication.

I would also like to thank my family in The Netherlands, my sister and brother, for their support and belief in me.

And finally, a huge thank you to my 'writing buddies', Toni Barrett and Sue Manning, for straightening out all the language mistakes I made as a non-native speaker. For their ideas and contributions to this story, for being there and walking that long road beside me from the start to the finish. Without them, this book wouldn't exist.

A NOTE FROM THE PUBLISHER

Thank you for reading this book. If you enjoyed it please do consider leaving a review on Amazon to help others find it too.

We hate typos. All of our books have been rigorously edited and proofread, but sometimes mistakes do slip through. If you have spotted a typo, please do let us know and we can get it amended within hours.

info@bloodhoundbooks.com

Printed in Great Britain
by Amazon